THE BARTER

S.G. BOUDREAUX

S.G. BOUDREAUX

Shawna Boudreaux
The Barter

ISBN: 978-1-7361117-9-6 (Paperback)

ISBN: 978-1-960091-02-4 (Digital)

Zanchier Publications

Printed in the USA

Sgboodro2@yahoo.com

www.SGBoudreaux.com

Chapter 1

"Good morning Aurie!"

"Good morning Mr. Kim," Aurelie Haydel yelled back to the older man whose booth was next to hers each week at the small beach-side market.

Kim Yamada came to a stop beside her booth. "Well now, looks like you got a good yield this season." He admired the display of vegetables and fruits from Aurelie's farmstead.

"Yes, we've been very fortunate. The farm has been doing well with all the extra rain this year. I've canned and stored all I can keep and have a lot more to barter with than usual."

"That's wonderful, Aurie. Me and the misses will be by later to trade up with you."

"Great! I'll put your usual order aside. Anything else you need?"

She motioned to the large harvest of mid-summer fruits and vegetables.

"I'll ask the misses. She can come check things out in a bit." Mr. Kim smiled and winked, turning to head back to his own produce stand.

Mr. Kim and Mrs. Kei Yamada were a Japanese-American couple who had lived in this area for as long as Aurelie could remember. They were the kindest of people and had taken to watching over her when her mother died twenty years back, and then again after her father had passed away four years ago.

Aurelie hefted another of the large crates of freshly picked turnips onto the table. Their garden and orchard this year was having a banner harvest, and her trades for the barter market offered many varied types of fruits and vegetables.

The small coastal town of Holly Beach, Louisiana enjoyed a cool summer breeze off the ocean which was tinged with the salty ocean spray. Aurelie was watching the market fill with people there to barter goods. Since the world collapsed into disarray several decades back, people tended to keep to themselves. Everyone was just trying to survive in this new world of every man, woman, and child, for themselves. She and the three orphaned kids her father had happened upon six years back kept to the homestead most days. Things were, however, beginning to change as people began to interact more. Like on market days where everyone from the surrounding area got together to trade goods, barter services, or help one another with needed repairs to small necessary farm equipment. Their small, tightly-knit community fared better than most other areas around the world; if radio reports were to be believed. The great thing was that now with the serious decline of the government and civilization as it was, the threat to their quiet, little, forgotten, community was all but non-existent. Not many people knew there were still people inhabiting the coast of Louisiana in the small beach community way out past the marshlands. There wasn't much to bring people this far out unless they just wanted a view of the ocean. Gasoline operated vehicles were no longer an option with the oil and gas industry bombings which destroyed most industrial areas during the wars. Much of the population of the world was decimated due to nuclear weapons being used at all the plants, and now there was no need for automobiles since those that were left went nowhere.

People kept to their homes, towns, and cities, and simply tried to stay alive. Money was also of no use anymore, unless of course you had precious gems or metals to trade, and the average person didn't have such things. People only had that for which they worked -things such as food, non-fuel type equipment such as bicycles, or old radios that still transmitted on radio waves that ran on rechargeable, solar-powered, batteries.

Aurelie had been one of the lucky ones since her father had taught her from an early age to live off the land. Her father, Privat Haydel, was born and raised on the Louisiana coastline. He had been a fisherman all of his life, following in the footsteps of his father, and his before him. They had lived a simple life already, void of many of the modern-day conveniences. So when things of the world went south, their small community was nearly untouched, not counting of course things like electricity and automobiles. There were, however, those whose family members went to serve in the wars. Because of the wars over property and territories after the world collapse, everyone, everywhere, suffered some sort of personal loss or tragedy.

Electricity had been a nice commodity to have, especially with the Louisiana heat and humidity where summer temperatures could often reach a high one-hundred and ten degrees. But with the shutdown of the power grids along with everything else, their small outlying community was all but forgotten. And those of them who lived here were glad for it. They didn't like to see strangers come into town. That only meant trouble. Anyone who came through was usually looking for some-thing. Meaning, those strangers would beg, borrow, or steal from anyone they could; not caring for anyone else. Who they affected or what chaos and problems they would cause was not their concern. But here, their small community stuck together and protected one another as much as possible.

Aurelie busied herself stacking and off-loading her farm's harvest from the small solar powered side-by-side. It had once been fuel-powered but had since been converted by Foesy Divins. Foesy was an older man who lost his son in the land wars fifteen years back. He and his wife Reesa raised their only granddaughter Reine who was fifteen.

Aurelie looked over at the couple's electronic stand. The Divins property was small and located directly on the beach where produce was nearly impossible to grow. So, he traded for new inven-tions that ran on solar power and bartered his services to fix broken electronics or carts for much needed food supplies. His wife Reesa mended clothing, tents, tarps, and anything really that needed sewing.

Everyone in their community of eighty-four people had different skills or talents with which to barter; most discovered out of pure necessity. Even those that were gifted musically contrib-uted. When there were events or birthdays, the musically talented were hired by bartering to sing or perform for such events. No talent, ability, or gift was too small.

Aurie smiled as Marie Louviere, a young woman who was mentally challenged that lived with her mother, played in the shadows produced by the bright sun overhead. Marie loved all things that flew and often pretended she could fly herself. She was a bright spot amongst them and made everyone smile with her upbeat personality and near constant, happy, countenance. She and her mother raised chickens, ducks, and quail, and they bartered the birds and eggs, but Marie could do little else. So, on market days, she would come and tend to the animals that were brought to market for bartering, helping to keep track of trades, and making sure the animals were all fed and watered. It was in this way she was of service, and the kind folks of the Beach Village bartered with her for whatever her heart desired. Michael Guittreaux, who was one of the wood-workers often carved her toys, most of which had wings.

"Hello," Marie said, smiling as she stopped by Aurelie.

"Hello, Marie. Are you enjoying the warm sun-light this morning?"

"Yeah, I'm playing with my shadow. We're going flying."

"That sounds fun. Where are you flying off to today?"

"Here silly." Marie laughed.

Aurelie smiled, knowing Marie's imagination to be a great one, but her experience with travel to be non-existent, so of course she wouldn't fly anywhere but here.

"Well, Marie, you be careful not to fly into any birds, okay?"

Marie giggled. "Okay." Away she flew to visit with someone else.

Aurelie's bright mood began to turn to a shade of gray as Arjit Chiasson approached. He was a pushy man twelve years her senior, who had taken it upon himself to court her, unencouraged and completely unwanted, for the last six years.

"Morning, Aurelie."

"Arjit."

"Do you need some help off-loading today?"

"No thanks, I've got it, just like every other market day." She stiffly grinned at the man who stopped just a foot in front of her, causing her to pause in her movements, a crate of carrots in hand.

"I don't know why you won't let me help you, Aurie." He smiled down at her.

"I don't need it. I'm perfectly capable of taking care of myself."

"But what about the kids? It has to be tough handling three younger kids that aren't even yours. I can help with that burden, you know."

"Oh, well Arjit, the kids aren't a burden at all. As a matter of fact, they're a great help. So you see, I have all the help I need." She moved around him to set the crate in position, tiring of the same old conversation nearly every week.

When she turned to grab another crate, Arjit was nearly touching nose to nose with her.

"I just don't understand why you are so standoffish with me. We'd make a great team, Aurie, and you know it. Besides, I can offer more than just help or companionship."

"I already have enough companionship Arjit. And I don't need any more team players."

"Maybe, but you don't have anyone on your team that can make you feel the way I could."

The Barter

"Well, Arjit, you're definitely right about that." She stood with her hands on her hips staring him down, trying to keep a snarl of distaste from curling her lips.

Arjit simply smiled and stepped back.

"I'll make you mine sooner or later Aurelie Haydel. Just you wait and see." He turned to walk away, back toward his own booth, which thankfully was on the other side of the market.

"Ugh…" She rolled her eyes in disgust as a shiver ran up her spine. She couldn't even entertain the thought of that man's hands anywhere on or near her. Sure Arjit was an attractive man. He was fit, strong, had a good working farm with strong live-stock, but his overbearing personality and suggestive remarks often made her skin crawl. Arjit Chiasson might be a catch for someone here, but it definitely was not her. He could likely have his pick too, she just wished he would move his attentions onto anyone else but her.

Aurelie was shaken from her thoughts by the murmur of whispering that was forming all around her. She stood from her bent position to look around and see what was causing all the excitement. Walking toward their quaint little market and oceanside village was the first stranger they had seen in over eight years. It was hard to make out what he looked like under the cap and thick beard and mustache. But he was tall, lean, and strong looking, and appeared to be close to her age. And it seemed like he was making a bee-line straight for her booth.

Arjit noticed the stranger who suddenly appeared out of nowhere. He watched the man carefully, as did everyone else in the community. But what Arjit didn't like about the stranger already, was the fact that the man was headed straight for Aurelie.

"Morning, Ma'am. I noticed you had some of the best-looking fresh fruit that I've seen in a while. I'd like to purchase a few apples, pears, and some fresh vegetables."

"I'm sorry, Sir…"

"Rennet. The name's Rennet McCabe."

"Mr. McCabe, we don't take money. It's no good here. Unless you have something to barter with then I'm afraid that I can't help you."

"Some forms of money are starting to take on again in other places."

"Well, that may be so, but not here." She motioned around their small community. "No one comes out this way selling anything anyone here needs, and we only barter here. So, unless you have something to trade you're out of luck."

Rennet thought for a moment and searched his pockets for anything that he could spare.

"Can I help you?" The gruff sound of a man's voice echoed behind him.

Rennet turned to see a man, arms crossed, staring him down.

"No, just trying to get something to eat."

"Arjit," Aurelie groaned, "I can handle my own transactions if it's all the same to you. Besides, you best mind your own booth. Old man Eloi is over there in your absence and is helping himself to your stuff."

Arjit turned to yell at the old man and hurried back to his stand.

Eloi was the ferryman from the east toward Rutherford beach, and he often showed up at market days to pilfer things for himself whenever he could. He made his own moon-shine, but not many here at market could stomach the stuff, so his trades were slim and few unless the crabs were running.

Aurelie smiled at the scene and then she sobered, her attention turned back to the man before her. His steel blue eyes seemed to see through to her soul. She cleared her throat and waited as his hectic search continued. His mind seemed to latch on to something as he removed his backpack to pull out a long, tunic-style, half-cable-knit sweater in a beautiful ocean-colored blue. Not the muddy brown water of the Louisiana ocean either. It was the blues of the Florida beaches she remembered from childhood trips, or somewhere far off on a tropical island. It looked to be fairly new as well. She hadn't had new clothing in ten years.

"Will this do?"

"Doesn't the woman this belongs too want it back?"

"Nope. We parted ways many months back. I just kept it for some odd reason."

"Well, it does get cold here in the winter, so I can always use another sweater. I guess this trade is worth about a dozen pieces of whatever fruits and vegetables you want to choose."

"Great!" Rennet smiled and began his selections. He then asked, "Is there a place to barter for some fresh drinking water? It seems you have all the water you could ever need, yet nothing suitable for drinking." He nodded to the ocean behind her and smiled revealing a row of straight white teeth. At least she thought so; it was hard to tell under his thick mustache and beard.

"You can talk to Emilie Comeaux at the booth over there."

Rennet turned to look where she was instructing him to go and noticed a young girl smiling from ear to ear in his direction.

"Yes. I see the booth."

"Yep. You can't miss Emilie, and I'm certain she won't allow you to." Aurelie smiled to herself at the obvious attention Emilie was oozing to give this stranger.

"Thank you… um… can I have your name?" Rennet stood looking at her, waiting for a reply.

"Whatever for?"

"So that I may address you by it the next time I see you." He grinned ever so slightly.

"So I guess that means you'll be staying around, not just passing through?"

"I haven't decided yet."

"Well Mr. McCabe, my name's not important since I doubt you'll be staying long. And, let me just warn you; don't make waves here. We don't like troublemakers. We have a nice, friendly, working, community here where nearly everyone gets along."

Rennet noticed her eyes cut toward the man she called Arjit when she said 'nearly'.

"No worries, ma'am. I'm no troublemaker. Just a man out exploring the new world." He gave her a side-ways smile, nodded his thanks for the food, and walked toward Emilie Comeaux's booth and the water source.

Aurelie's pulse quickened just a tad at the lingering smile and look the stranger gave her as he departed. She stated to herself, nearly inaudible, "Well, Aurelie, that was your excitement for the next several years."

The Barter

Arjit stood at his booth, his arms crossed against his chest as he watched the interaction between Aurelie and this stranger. He didn't like the way Aurelie continued to glance at the man as he made his way around to other market booths. If he dared to come to his, he'd have to have a little chat with him and make sure he knew that he wasn't welcome here. And that if he chose to hang around, Aurelie Haydel was off limits.

Rennet stepped up to Emilie's booth and smiled.

Emily smiled brightly in return. "Well, hello there." The twenty-two-year-old beamed at the handsome stranger whose attention seemed to be taken by the glares that Arjit threw his way. *Wouldn't she just love to go out traveling with him? To go anywhere and get away from this nearly non-existent place would be a dream come true.* "Can I help you with something? Anything?" She smiled broadly once again, leaning forward flirtatiously.

Rennet smiled cautiously at the young woman. "I hear you have water to barter here."

"Sure do." She continued to smile.

"What will you take for a few bottles?"

"Well, how about you take me with you when you leave, and you can have all the water you want." She giggled at the broad smile that leapt to his lips.

Rennet didn't reply, only grinned. "How about I give you this?" He pulled a magazine out of his pack and handed it to her. The look of amazement on her face brought another smile to his lips.

"Are you serious?" Emilie questioned, stunned. "I haven't seen a magazine from anywhere but here, ever. The ones here are so old and have the same old boring information. This is simply amazing!"

"Great. Emilie is it?"

She nodded her head, the fact that he already knew her name made her look up briefly. Her attention returned to the brightly colored women's magazine as she smoothed her hand over the cover. She absentmindedly handed him several large bottles of water.

"Well, Emilie, can you give me the name of that woman over there?" He nodded slightly with his head in Aurelie's direction.

Emilie looked at him again, her smile returning. "Aurelie Haydel. And if you're interested in her, you're gonna' have to take that up with Arjit Chiasson."

"So, they're an item then?"

"No. But Arjit thinks they are, and he'll have words with any man who says otherwise." She smiled broadly as Rennet turned to take a quick look at the man whose eyes he could feel boring through his back.

Chapter 2

Aurelie could feel the sweat beginning to bead on her brow beneath her large, brimmed hat as the hot noon-day sun blared down on her. Fortunately, market day was coming to a close, and trading had been good for everyone this week. Before perishables became wilted and ruined, the booths shut down and packed up, and everyone returned to their own homes.

She finished packing and slid onto the side-by-side's seat. She had quite a night to prepare for so she needed to get back quickly. Her mind wandered through her list for the day. Today was Birdie's twelfth birthday. Birdie was aptly named for she could sing prettier than any songbird Aurelie had ever heard. Tonight, the town was gathering in the large beach-side, open-air pavilion for the event. Many of the ladies were coming early to help Aurelie get ready for the party, each one bringing a snack or decoration. Their gifts to Birdie for the beautiful songs everyone knew she would share with them tonight. Turning twelve was a big step in a young girls life, preteen status was something Birdie talked of often; so ready to grow up. Aurie smiled as she remembered the day her Father, Privat, had taken in the three orphaned kids.

Birdie had stepped up and told him, "Sir, I can't do much else, but I can sing for our supper."

Privat had laughed and said in his thick Cajun accent, "Aldough I love a good tune, an' you and me, we'll sing dem togeder, but you don' have to do anythin' fer your supper; jus' sit an' eat Sha'."

Birdie's smile was so big that the borders of her face could barely contain it. It was then that the eight-year-old-boy, Baxter, softened some to the man who seemed to simply want to help them.

Baxter was now fourteen, and still small for his age. However, his size didn't deter him from protecting what was his. He could be meaner than a cotton mouth snake when riled and sweet as a sun-ripened strawberry at other times. He was high-energy and never stopped. Her father had said once that his personality had to be ranked high on the Attention Deficit Hyperactivity Disorder charts; ADHD for short; for the intense energy and lack of concentration he displayed at all times. Not that any diagnosis mattered these days, it was merely an observation.

The youngest of the three, little Katie, short for Katherine, was barely a toddler when Privat had found the three of them living in one of the abandoned houses furthest from the beach. He had watched Baxter sneakily snatch a few pieces of fruit, some dried meat, and a few bottles of water from the market stands. So stealthy had he been, that no one had ever even seen the boy or knew he was there; no one except Privat. Her father had followed him back to the house where he discovered they had lived alone for nearly a month. Baxter reluctantly told him that their parents had been traveling together and stopped at the abandoned house for the night. In the morning, they were gone and the kids were left alone. Privat promptly took them to live with him and Aurelie. Baxter was an only child while Birdie and Katie were sisters.

Aurelie shivered, the thought of children being left alone to shoulder the weight of such responsibility; not only for themselves but for a toddler as well. The cruelty of people never ceased to shock her, especially the children's own parents. Her father had respected Baxter and Birdie for being so grown up and handling themselves. Privat had never treated them as children, but as little adults. Able to handle things on their own and learn to do just about anything needed for survival in this new world. He had told her once that it was not his place to tell them they couldn't do things when they had already done more than many adults could even handle. He had the utmost respect for them and treated them accordingly. Aurelie's respect and love for her father blossomed even more as she watched him interact with the children over the next several years, until the day her father had been taken from them.

Privat had a bad heart but hadn't told Aurelie or the others about it. Mr. Yamada knew, as he was Privat's oldest and dearest friend, and after his death Mr. Kim had taken up the role as Aurelie's surrogate father should they need anything.

Yes, their little community was a very special one. So much so that if the world hadn't turned so cruel, and the life changing events of the world crash and fuel crisis followed by the wars hadn't happened, you would have never known any-thing had changed. The people here tended to stick together, helped one another, and still had compassion for others. God was still God, and as a community, they respected the Bible and what it taught. They even still had services on Sunday mornings beneath the beach-side pavilion when weather allowed; which was coming up in just a few days. Today was a Wednesday, and she needed to go over the music with Birdie to sing for Sunday services. Fortunately there were other more experienced musicians in their community, so she didn't have to play guitar on Sunday's. Her nerves seemed to give her fits when she had to play in public.

Privat had been an avid music lover, teaching himself to play the French accordion and Aurelie the piano and guitar. She wasn't much of a singer, but music was in her blood and she and Birdie often sang together while doing chores. She would harmonize with Birdie's melodic voice while Baxter would beat on anything that made a sound, and little Katie would clap and twirl.

She smiled at the memories. She was grateful for the three of them; especially since her father's passing. It would be a very lonely existence without her three foundlings.

Her side-by-side pulled into the completely hidden property. Privat had made certain to fence everything in and grow any kind of wild-vining plants that would quickly overtake the fences and hide their property from prying eyes. He knew he had limited time to protect his kids and did whatever was needed to set them up for the future. Looking at the mass of jumbled trees and vines, one would never think there was a house or anything else alive inside the canopy.

She entered the small access on the side of the property, pulling the small vehicle to a stop beneath the coolness of the massive oak's tree canopy. Dappled light filtered through, illuminating small areas of the yard in bright sunlight. The only trouble with having this much greenery was the dampness at times, which tended to breed mosquitoes. They battled them frequently with a homemade spray made from the lemon grass and spearmint leaves that surrounded their property. The plants helped keep the pests at bay, but did not completely deter them from lingering near, or in, the house.

The house was old, nothing too large, but had been their ancestral home for a hundred years or more. It had started as a small dwelling, then over the years with each new generation came a new addition. It had survived a few hurricanes, and had taken a beating from others, but the old, hardwood home had been built solidly and was still standing today. Sure it had its share of spots on the aging roof, which seemed to rot faster beneath the low hanging branches of the large, moss-covered oaks with their sweeping branches that touched the ground in some spots in the yard. A few of those branches even ended up coming through the roof during two previous hurricanes. The floors dipped and sagged in a few other spots, and creaky stairs led up to a half second story where four small bedrooms were located.

Aurelie swung open the squeaky screen door and yelled into the house.

"I'm back! Come help with the off-loading."

She turned back toward the side-by-side when a jumble of thumping began vibrating through the house's outer walls and all three kids came bursting through the screen door into the yard.

Baxter smiled, anxious for news. "Aurie, did anything interesting happen at market today?"

Birdie snickered. "Bax, nothing ever happens at market, or anywhere else."

Aurelie smiled at them. "As a matter of fact," she turned to look at them, "a stranger came to town."

All three kids stopped and looked at her, their eyes growing wide.

"Who?" they all pleaded at once, bounding up and down with excitement.

"Just a man passing through is all. He tried to use money to pay for his purchases, which likely means he's a trickster or a thief. We'll have to keep a close eye on things for a while."

Baxter grabbed a crate from the wagon. "Is he staying around?"

"I don't know. I hope not. We don't need any trouble." Aurelie's mind drifted back to their conversation where she had told Rennet McCabe the same thing, and he assured her he was no trouble. She shook her head to clear her thoughts realizing she was once again thinking of Rennet.

Birdie grinned. "How old was he? Like, really old or just old like you?"

Aurelie turned to her, pretending to be wounded, giving her a crooked grin. "Old like me."

Baxter replied as they all walked into the house and through the door being held open by Katie. "So he's fairly healthy."

"Yeah, I'd say so. He didn't appear to be too worn or sick from his travels. I just wonder what in the world he would be doing way down here. I mean, it isn't like there is anything to bring someone all the way out here to the coast."

Katie's young brows knit together in thought. "But Aurie, we're here."

Aurelie smiled down at her and stroked her hair with her hand, turning her face up to look at her. "Yes, we are sweetie, but we were born here; we live here."

Baxter corrected her. "We weren't."

Aurelie stopped and turned to look at him. "True, and I often wonder what would have brought your parents here, but I sure am glad they did come, or otherwise I wouldn't have you three." She smiled brightly at them.

They all smiled back, Katie wrapping her arms around Aurelie's waist.

"Now, let's get the rest of the wagon unloaded and everything put away. We have a party to get ready for."

Birdie smiled broadly, bouncing up and down and clapping her hands. "I'm so excited."

Baxter teased, "You're always excited."

"Am not!"

"Yes you are. You see a butterfly in the yard, or a shooting star run across the sky and you get all giddy."

"So. Can I help it if I enjoy God's creation. He made me this way."

"Yeah, yeah, yeah, I know." Baxter rolled his eyes and gave a pained grin.

They spent the next thirty minutes unloading the wagon, storing the food items that were canned on the pantry shelves, fresh vegetables that they planned to use that week into the Zeer Pots located on the screened porch just off the kitchen, and the rest that needed to be kept cool was stored into the in-ground cellars made from old freezers that Privat had buried after the world power-grid shut down.

Privat had been a smart man. Always prepared for whatever life might throw at him. He was also a junk collector, and the back outer section of their two-acre property was strewn with all manner of things. When Aurelie was little, her father's junk collecting used to drive her mother crazy, but now that collection came in handy more times than not. They had used many of the things from the old cars, engines, freezers, and other things to make everything they currently used for survival. Her father even figured out how to make use of some old solar panels to give them some light, and to run a few of the outlets in the house for short periods of time. He also made a water catch basin so that they would have fresh drinking water and be able to bathe. Their property was blessed with a smoke house that they used to dry and smoke meat to help preserve it. Aurelie had a ham hanging in there at the moment that was nearly done and would soon be ready to eat or put into cold storage, however, the smoke-house was not a survival addition. It had been there for as long as she could remember; making sausage every year was part of their heritage.

The Barter

When cold weather threatened, it would be time to make pork and deer sausage, the only problem with that was that deer populations had been scarce with the world hunger issue. Although they didn't see many of them anymore, they were still able to hunt them occasionally since their little corner of Sportsman's Paradise was mostly unpopulated. During the fall months Aurelie and the other three kids would trek out through the swamplands checking gator snares and spend their days hunting from the duck blind and watching for deer. Privat had fashioned a type of silencer for her pistol to help keep their hunts quiet, but that was only if she were close enough to hit her prey. Too far, and the rifle had to be used, but everyone could hear the shot that way; which could cause people to scavenge someone else's hunt. But now a days, things were beginning to improve as some of the animal population was slowly returning, and if anyone shot anything worth sharing it was prepared and brought to market for trade, allowing everyone to partake. That was one of the many things she loved about their little hidden community.

Aurelie yelled out through the screened porch. "Baxter, did you check the crawfish traps for tonight?"

"Yeah, we got a load too. At least a hundred pounds worth I think. I still have three more to check but I think we'll have plenty; especially with Mr. Kim, Sophanes, and Anytos bringing crawfish as well."

"Great, thanks."

"Is Arjit doing the boiling?"

"Yes, some of it. Foesy, Adam, Sophanes, and Procne will also be boiling, so it should go quickly."

"Awesome. I'm so ready for tonight!" Baxter hardly ever got excited, but a party with everyone else in the community was something they were all ready for.

Aurelie smiled at his reply as her thoughts returned to the sweater she had acquired earlier today. If only it were cold enough to wear. It was beautiful and she could just imagine the soft, thick, fabric against her skin. She would wash it and hang it to dry on the screened porch before stowing it protectively in her closet.

She busied herself with making the cake for Birdie's birthday, while the girls gathered all the seasonings to use in the crawfish. They also went out to the freezer cellar to gather about ten pounds of potatoes and a few sausage links to add to the crawfish pots. Several other people were bringing cob corn, whole yellow onions, some hot sauces, and dips. Aurelie needed to remember to bring her catchup and mayonnaise dip to cool her tongue and lips. Some of the men liked to spice the crawfish up a bit too much to her liking.

She hummed a little Cajun tune as she set the cake in the fire warmed oven, offering up a small prayer that it would come out just right. She liked to bake, but it was a privilege she seldom got to enjoy.

Chapter 3

The sun was beginning its slow descent toward the water's horizon line as party goers began filing into the large, covered pavilion just at the beach edge near the water.

Rennet McCabe, who had taken to lying on the beach and enjoying the cool ocean breeze and the sound of the waves while he ate some of his earlier trades from the market, sat up as people began to move about. He noticed several men setting up large pots filled with water and seasonings. The pots sat on iron clad stands over-top holes dug into the sand just a little ways from the edge of a large pavilion. He stood up, dusted the sand from his clothing, and decided to go see what was taking place, hoping they wouldn't run him off.

"Evening," Rennet said, approaching a tall, strong-looking, man who was dark complected and had black hair and a thick square chin.

"Evening," the man replied stiffly, unsure as to Rennet's intentions.

"I'm Rennet McCabe." He smiled and offered his hand as a friendly gesture.

"I remember you from this morning." The man sized him up for a second, then gave a small grin and took his hand. "Sophanes Leos."

"Sophanes, eh. Sounds Greek."

"It is." His deep baritone voice rang out.

"I detect a hint of an accent as well. You obviously weren't born in these parts."

Sophanes smiled at Rennet. "No. Me and a friend," he pointed to another man who was hauling large sacks toward them, "Anytos Ariti, moved here many years back to work the oil rigs in these parts." He motioned to the large oil platforms that still sat off the coast many miles out, abandoned, and useless. "Now we just fish out there. The rigs make for excellent fishing and shrimping."

Rennet nodded his head in understanding. "I photograph nature myself. Trying to find ways to support myself and just live. I'm not really old enough to have had a job before the collapse and wars."

"I'd think you're old enough to have served in the wars for a bit though, eh?"

"Nope. Just missed it by five years or so. I'm twenty-nine."

"Oh, well, it's kind of hard to tell underneath all that facial hair," Sophanes stated factly.

Rennet rubbed at the thick beard and mustache. "Yeah, I guess I do look a sight. Haven't had a reason to shave in a while. I guess I could go clean up a bit." Rennet changed the subject, deciding to do just that later. "So, do you mind if I ask what's going on?"

Sophanes straightened from stirring the large pot. "We're about to have a crawfish boil to celebrate the twelfth birthday of young miss Birdie Haydel."

Rennet smiled and nodded. "Sounds fun. I take it that Birdie is the daughter of Aurelie, was it?"

"Not her daughter, sort of like her adopted sister. Her pa found some kids years ago living in one of the old houses on the edge of the road back that way." Sophanes pointed. "Took them in as his own. Their parents just up and left them here."

Rennet was surprised to hear the story. "Sounds like a good man. I'd like to meet him."

"You can't. He's dead. Died six years back. Aurelie's been raising them kids on her own since. Of course, everyone here helps each other out when we can. Like this party here for Birdie. We all like getting together and dancing and eating." He smiled broadly at Rennet.

"Sounds like you have a great community here. I haven't been to too many places where people still celebrate together like this."

"So, where do you hail from?" Sophanes eyed him curiously.

"Nowhere really, and everywhere I suppose. I've traveled all over the U.S. for the past ten years. Walking or riding a bike."

"Well, I noticed you walked here. No bike?"

"No. I warped one of the rims in the last city. And since there wasn't a bike repair shop, I went back to walking."

"What brought you way out here? There isn't a thing for miles between here and the closest cities in either direction."

"Maybe that was why I came; to explore. I like to photograph nature in its purest form. Out here, there is nearly nothing but nature. I have to say, though, I am glad I found your community when I did. I was starting to worry that I would die from dehydration this far out. Like you said, there isn't anything between here and the last city." Rennet grinned a little sheepishly.

Sophanes smiled. "Yes, good thing. So, when will you be moving on?"

"I'm not sure. This place out here is peaceful, and as far as nature goes, it seems like the animals are starting to come back here faster than in the cities. I may stay here for a while."

"Well, as far as nature goes, there is a lot to draw birds and things here with all the marshes, swamps, and the ocean of course. So I guess that makes sense," Sophanes stated, changing the subject as Anytos approached with a large sack of crawfish. "You ever had boiled crawfish, Rennet?"

"No sir, I can't say that I have."

"Do you like spicy food?" Sophanes asked.

"Sure. I've had Texas food recently. Some of it was quite hot, but I handled it all right."

Sophanes smiled oddly at him. "Texas eh. Well, Rennet, if you want to help with the boiling here and party set up, I don't think folks will mind you partaking of the party foods and pleasures. That is, if you want to join us?"

"Sure, thanks for the offer."

Rennet sat his pack down on the ground and watched as the men dumped the still kicking, sack of crawfish into a large pot filled with holes. He watched the crawfish twitch their tails, flicking about the pot. He turned to the other pot sitting over the fire and leaned forward, breathing deeply of the pleasing scent wafting from the seasoned pot of nearly boiling water. His nose instantly felt as though hot pokers were shoved up his nostrils. His eyes began to water and his breath stilled for a moment. He quickly stood up, turning away from the pot, and coughing and sputtering from the intensely hot scent wafting up from the steaming water.

Sophanes and Anytos laughed heartily at his reaction. Sophanes slapped him on the shoulder, and said, "Texas heat eh. We'll see if you can handle our Louisiana heat, Rennet McCabe."

Rennet smiled, swiped at his watering eyes, and cleared his throat over and over, trying to clear the burning sensation that still lingered.

He finally managed to choke out, "What do I do to help?"

Anytos answered him. "You can help me haul the other sacks of crawfish off the cart."

"Lead the way." Rennet smiled, following the man to a side-by-side which held another twelve large sacks of the small creatures. "So, where do these crawfish come from?"

Anytos replied as they each carried two sacks over and laid them on the ground in a shady spot. "We farm them. They live underground in wet areas and surface when that area floods. They are a seasonal catch, so this will likely be some of the last we get until next year."

"So this isn't a year-round thing you eat?"

"No. Crawfish are a treat we only get to enjoy for a while from January through July. But with all the extra rain this year, the season has been extended a bit."

"I've never had crawfish before. I'm sure it'll be a treat."

Anytos looked at him with an amused expression.

"Just make sure you have plenty to drink next to you."

Rennet nodded, a bit apprehensive because of his expression and the still slight burning sensation in his sinuses from his mistake earlier.

"Will do. Thanks for the warning."

Anytos nodded and smiled broadly.

Others began to arrive at the pavilion, some setting up like Sophanes and Anytos. Large pots filled with boiling water rimmed the outside edge of the pavilion on two sides. Others began cleaning tables and setting up chairs and party decorations. Rennet had never witnessed a community that worked and lived together like this one.

His attention turned back to the men and the crawfish. He watched Anytos wet the crawfish in the sacks with water as they waited to fill the large, perforated, pot with their catch. They dumped the sack into the pot and dropped it into the larger, boiling, pot of seasoned water. Then they took some potatoes, onions, corn, and mushrooms tied in smaller sacks; which were brought to them by others who were arriving; and dropped them into the top of the boiling water. They did this over and over, dumping the cooked crawfish and sides into very large coolers.

The tables under and around the pavilion were covered with small tarps or pieces of plastic. Large, clean, garbage cans were placed at the end of each table. Strings of lights were hung from the edge of the pavilions eaves and draped in big loops from one nail to the next, the dangling solar-powered lights swung gently in the breeze. Another man and woman were setting up a couple of chairs on one end, and set a guitar on a stand, then placed a French-accordion on one of the stools.

Rennet smiled at the charge in the air. He could feel the excitement of the evening building as more and more people appeared, many giving him a wary look. He nodded and smiled at them, letting them know he was a friendly fellow and not to be feared. He continued helping Sophanes and Anytos boil and dump the food into the quickly filling coolers.

Aurelie and the kids piled out of the cart and began hauling food to the tables. Baxter and Birdie hauled sacks of crawfish to the men boiling, while she and Katie carried the other food items to the tables. Birdies birthday cake took center stage. It wasn't a large cake, so other people in the community also brought baked goods and desserts for everyone to partake. After placing the cake on the table, Aurelie walked toward Sophanes to thank him for doing some of the boiling. She stopped short, shocked to see Rennet McCabe still here and helping the two Greeks.

Rennet stood up and smiled at her, making her take a deep breath and release it. She acknowledged him with a nod and continued forward to speak to the two men.

"Sophanes, Anytos, thank you both for helping tonight, Birdie is beyond excited."

"No problem Aurelie. That little girl brings joy to everyone. Besides, we like a good boil." Sophanes smiled and winked at her.

"Don't we all," she laughed.

Rennet approached her and grinned.

"Miss Haydel."

"Mr. McCabe."

"You can call me Rennet. I don't think anyone has ever addressed me as Mr. McCabe before."

"Well, Rennet, I guess you decided to hang around here for the day."

"Yes. The beach and ocean is quite a refreshing change from the city views. Especially since most of what you still see up that way is destruction. Your community here has really done a great job of rebuilding after the wars."

"Yes, we have, but we weren't hit as hard as most areas were. So, when will you be leaving us?" she asked pointedly.

Rennet smiled and thought a moment. "I'm not sure that I will. I may decide to stay here, for a while at least. It feels like the way the world should have been before the wars, minus a few of the conveniences of course."

"Well, just where will you be staying then, Rennet?" She said his name a little too forcefully, her words laced with aggravation.

His smile waned a bit. "I'm sure I'll figure that out."

Sophanes offered, "There are several abandoned cottages down the beach in that direction. You could take up one of those. Anytos and I will show you where they are later."

Aurelie gave Sophanes a strained look, to which he shrugged and grinned.

Rennet smiled at him. "Thanks, Sophanes, that would be great."

Aurelie turned to get back to party organizing while the men finished their task, trying to put as much space between her and Rennet McCabe as she could. She didn't know why, but she felt his presence in their community would stir the pot so to speak, and cause unrest between some of the residents here, and she wasn't much one for change, or problems.

Rennet watched Aurelie's back stiffen when Sophanes offered to show him a place he could squat at for a while. He got the feeling she didn't care much for him. He didn't understand why, except for the fact that he was a stranger to their quaint little community. However, everyone else made him feel quite at home so far, except for her and Arjit Chiasson. Perhaps, if he stayed here long enough, he could change her mind. Why it mattered to him he wasn't sure about, he just knew that for some reason, he wanted Aurelie Haydel to like him.

After the boiling was done, another man, maybe in his sixties, told everyone to bow their heads to pray. After the prayer they took the coolers over to the tables and scooped the large, juicy, boiled, crawfish and sides onto and down the entire center of every table. Everyone gathered around the tables to sit and eat, making sure to have plenty of towels for their hands, and water for drinking. There were even some different types of sauces, which he assumed were for dip-ping things into. Sophanes and Anytos grabbed

Rennet by the arms and led him to a table directly across from Aurelie Haydel. He could tell she wasn't too thrilled.

"Aurelie, I see that I vex you for some reason. If you like, I can trade seats with your friend Arjit?" Rennet grinned inside but kept his face stoic as though he didn't know she really disliked the man. At least he thought she did by her reaction this morning during the market.

She held up her hands to stay his assent from the table. "You're just fine where you are Mr. McCabe…"

"Rennet."

"Okay, Rennet. I'm just not good at change or surprises." She glanced over her shoulder at Arjit whose jaw was clenched and his expression was grim as he stared at Rennet McCabe. She rolled her eyes as she turned back to face the stranger directly in front of her.

Rennet looked at her with a questioning gaze. "So, how do you eat crawfish?"

"Well, you pick one up," she did so as she talked, "grab the head here where the tail starts, twist the head off, suck the juice and discard it. Then you pinch the tail at the base where it fans out, grab the meat with the fingers of your other hand, pull it out, and eat."

"That doesn't look too hard."

Rennet picked up a crawfish and did as she instructed.

She watched him do exactly what she showed him, and after completing each step a few times, he began drinking a lot of water and fanning his lips. Then he started coughing a little when the juice in one of the heads was much too hot. He cleared his throat, downing more water. After a few seconds of guzzling more water he said, "How do you people eat this stuff. It has a good flavor, but my mouth, throat, and lips are seriously on fire." Aurelie smiled and slid over her homemade dip. "If you can't handle the heat, dip the meat in this. It helps to cut it back. A lot of the guys add a bit too much seasoning for my taste."

Rennet pealed another crawfish and used the dip. It made all the difference and tasted good. "You could have told me about this dip first."

"What would have been the fun in that?" She grinned cockily at him.

Rennet nodded at her. "Okay, I see how it's gonna' be. You're a prankster are you?"

"Not really, just occasionally lucky enough to catch someone off guard."

Aurelie grinned at him as they ate dinner. She helped Katie peel a few, her smaller hands having a bit more trouble. Rennet watched her interact with the kids, watching how well they got along. They sat for the next thirty minutes eating crawfish, corn, potatoes, onions, mushrooms, and even some sausage; all of which had been boiled in the same water as the crawfish. He found he really liked the potatoes dipped in the mayo and ketchup sauce blend.

As dinner finished up, and the tables were cleaned, everyone stood up as the musicians announced Birdie's birthday, making her stand in the center of the pavilion. Everyone began to sing the birthday song as Birdie smiled from ear to ear. Then, after, the cakes and desserts were cut and people got what they wanted from the long dessert tables and went to sit back down while birdie serenaded everyone with more songs. After her singing the musicians picked up the pace and the French-accordion squeezed out many Cajun tunes to the thrill of those who loved to dance.

Rennet sat and watched everyone at the party interacting with one another. In all his travels across the United States over the last ten years, he had never experienced a community like this one. And he had a mind to stay and see if this was the place he had been searching for; a place to call home.

Chapter 4

Rennet watched everyone dancing and smiling and was soon whisked off to the floor by Emilie Comeaux, who was delighted that Rennet was a willing and very capable dancer. He wasn't used to the Cajun style of music and dance but caught on quickly. Emilie giggled and fawned over him; her flirtations obvious to anyone watching.

Two young men, both separated in age by six years and vastly different personalities, watched with angst; which caught Rennet's attention.

Rennet yelled over the music as they twirled around the floor. "Can you do me a favor, Emilie, and tell me who some of these people are?"

"Sure. Who do you want to know about?"

"Let's start with those two fellas staring at us." Rennet nodded to opposite ends of the floor. "One can't take his eyes off of you, and the other looks like he wants to throttle me." Rennet grinned nervously. "Boyfriends?"

Emilie threw her head back and laughed out loud. "Nope, but they both want to be. That one over by the dessert table is young Kester Bourgeois. He's nineteen and still way to immature for my tastes. I like my men older." Her eyes fluttered at him a bit as she smiled brightly. "Then, the other one standing beside Aurelie is Adam Boudreaux. He's a little older than I am, and really nice. Just too dull for me. I want excitement and adventure, and to get out of this stuffy little community and see what's still left out in the wide world."

"Well, let me tell you what's out there, Emilie. There isn't another place like this one anywhere that I've found. It's a hard existence. I've traveled for years through many towns and cities. Some places are being rebuilt but slowly. And I've never found another place like this one. Your community here is very special."

"Yeah, yeah, I know. There's no place like home, right?" She giggled. "So, where is your home?"

"Well, I was born far from here in the top left corner of Washington State."

"I don't know too much about geography. Survival is mostly what we learned growing up. Stuff like fishing, hunting, trapping, water distillation; you know, the typical survival stuff."

"It was the same with me, but with my mom being a schoolteacher before the collapse I was educated on many things. Especially since we had so much time on our hands."

The music changed to a slower tune and Emilie happily sidled up closer to him. Rennet tried to keep a safe distance.

"She didn't balk at you taking off on a walking tour of the battered and dangerous countryside?"

"Nope. She died right before I left."

"Oh, I'm so sorry." Emilie's bright countenance fell a bit.

"Thanks, but it's okay. She was the one to encourage me to take off and find something better. To find my own way in life."

"Wow. My parents would never do that. They would flip if I left."

"Well, it would be much more dangerous for a young, attractive, woman to travel alone. I've even had my share of mishaps and troubles; especially near the inner cities."

"So, you think I'm attractive?" she asked, and smiled as he twirled her to a stop facing Adam Boudreaux.

Rennet said, "Thanks for the dance Emilie." Rennet then grabbed Aurelie's hand, who happened to be standing nearby, and pulled her to the dance floor.

Emilie's smile soon turned to one of defeat. But before she could protest, Adam smiled broadly, grabbed her around the waist and twirled her skillfully around the floor. The young man nodded his thanks to Rennet, who nodded back. Kester, who watched Emelie from across the room, grumbled and stomped.

Aurelie was taken by surprise by the man pulling her onto the floor, but when she noticed what he had done for Adam, she had to smile. She also smiled at him when his eyes grew large and he audibly sighed as he grinned at her.

"That was pretty smooth on your part. Adam has been pining over Emilie for years, but never had the courage to ask her to dance before now." Aurelie smiled at him.

"Well, he sure looked forlorn enough so I fig-ured he needed the help. Besides, conversation was starting to get a little too personal. She sure doesn't hold back on letting people know what she wants does she?" He grinned.

"No, she doesn't."

"Well, she was instructing me on who people are, so if you wouldn't mind finishing that task, I'd appreciate it."

"I can do that." Aurelie started naming the people on the dance floor first, then went around the room. "Dancing over there, the Asian couple, that's Mr. And Mrs. Kim and Kei Yamada. They happily became my surrogate parents after my parents died."

"Who's Kim? Both sound feminine to me."

She smiled at him. "Kim is the Mr."

"Got it, thanks."

"The tall man dancing over there, the one who led prayer, is Procne Crusenberry. He's sort of our Mayor. The lady he is dancing with is Sandra Louviere. Her daughter Marie is the young woman who is twisting and turning all around the floor and beach by herself."

"Yeah, I noticed her at the market this morning. She sure seems to have a happy little spirit."

"Yes, not much ruffles Marie's feathers." Aurelie giggled at her own pun. Marie always pretended she was some sort of bird.

Rennet noticed her giggling and looked at her questioningly.

"Sorry," she apologized, "inside joke."

"With yourself?"

"Yeah, you get used to loneliness, you know?"

"I do."

Rennet's gaze and honesty made her weak in the knees which caused her to stumble. Rennet caught her and looked at her questioningly.

She grinned at him, cleared her throat, and straightened her back; the feel of his hands in hers suddenly making her nervous. She continued her introductions.

"Those three over there are the Divins. Reine is their granddaughter. Foesy and Reesa have raised her since their son was killed in the after-wars. Foesy is the town electrician and Reesa can sew very well."

"And who is the woman lingering next to Sophanes and Anytos?"

"That is Jess Evanko. She has had a thing for Sophanes for years now. I'm not sure if he is simply clueless to it or is just being kind so as not to hurt her feelings by leading her on."

"She's quite attractive. Why wouldn't he be interested?"

"I'm not sure. Maybe he likes a different sort of woman. Although, pickings have always been sort of slim around these parts."

"I wouldn't say slim." Rennet's gaze and meaning was not lost on her. She glanced around trying to change the subject when her eyes fell upon a couple of men off at a back table, pouring moonshine into their cups and toasting each other. Her broadly growing smile drew his attention to where she was looking.

"Those two gentlemen are definitely the ones who keep things very interesting around here. The smaller one with all the crazy hair and shorter beard is Eloi Theriot. The other larger man dressed mainly in leather is Archimedes Bourgeois."

"Archimedes eh. Not really a Cajun name is it?"

"Not at all. I heard, through the grapevine of course, that his mother was a scientist and named him after Archimedes himself, much to the chagrin of his father."

"He looks like he bears the name well. I certainly won't be the one to tease him about it."

"No one does." She smiled. "Most everyone calls him Archie, which is usually at his insistence. I don't remember the last time anyone called him Archimedes."

The song ended, and Aurelie dropped her hands and stepped back. "Thank you for the dance. You dance quite well for someone who isn't from around here."

"Your welcome. It's really just simple rhythm. And uh, thanks for the introductions to some of the people. I really think I'm going to like it here."

He grinned at her again. His smile reaching all the way into his kind looking eyes.

She glanced at the ground to find her footing before addressing his statement. "There isn't much to keep a body here, Rennet. I'm afraid you would get rather bored of us and the coast after a while."

"There's much more here than you think. Take it from someone who has been all over the United States and back again." He nodded to her and then turned to go speak to someone else.

She was about to walk off the floor when someone else stepped up beside her. Arjit was standing there staring after Rennet McCabe.

"I don't like that fella' one bit."

Aurelie heard the irritation in his voice and couldn't help herself. "Oh, I don't know, he seems like a very decent sort of *fella'* to me. And, very nice to chat with."

The Barter

Arjit fumed as he watched Rennet make his rounds, chatting amiably with everyone. When he managed to get his temper under control, he turned to speak to Aurelie but was surprised to find she had disappeared.

Aurelie took the opportunity to slink away from Arjit before he could claim her for a dance and went to walk the dark shoreline of the beach.

Rennet watched as Aurelie headed toward the water, deciding to follow her out. He'd sure like to get to know her better, and a quiet walk on the beach might just be the ticket. Although, he'd have to make it look accidental. If she knew he had followed her, it might make her nervous or leery of him.

Just then a shouting match started at that very same table where Eloi and Archimedes sat drinking, and from the looks of the near empty bottle, they had drank a lot.

"You old coot! You're crazy, you know that?"

Rennet watched as the two men now stood facing each other, nearly nose to nose.

"I ain't a lying!"

"You always lie, Eloi. Over-exaggeration is your middle name!"

"At least I don't have a sissy name like Archimedes!" Eloi jabbed a pointing finger at the man who now towered over him by several feet. To rectify the situation, the little man stepped up on the seat of the pick-nick table and stared at Archie, eye to eye.

Rennet noticed no one made a move to stop the altercation. So, he decided to step in and try to still the brewing tempers.

"Gentlemen, please, let's not let alcohol turn our heads here."

They both looked at Rennet with confusion and irritation as he slowly approached the table with hands raised in the air.

"Surely, whatever has both of you upset can be settled amicably."

They both turned their attentions to Rennet. Eloi jumped down from the seat and came to stand closely in front of him.

"And just who are you young fella' to tell us what we should be doin'?"

"Just new in town. We're all just trying to let a young lady enjoy her birthday celebration."

"Well, Mr. *New in town*," Eloi said, "you just go on and mind yer own business. Me an' my friend," Eloi turned to look at the large man and said loudly, "Archimedes, is having an argument, and we'd like to get back to it."

He noticed the big man stare down the little man in agitation again. His shoulders bowed up in tension.

"Okay." Rennet coughed a little from the smell of the alcohol emanating from the shorter man's breath. "Just trying to quell any issues before they start."

Archimedes stepped over toward them.

Rennet looked up at the man who towered over him. Nothing but muscle, beard, and tattoos. He swallowed hard.

Archimedes bent down and said, "We don't need no one *quelling* anything. You best just get back to the party before we have issues with you."

Rennet noticed that no one came to his rescue. They all just watched him, some with amused looks on their faces, others looked terrified for him.

"Okay, sorry for the intrusion. I can see you gentlemen can handle your disagreements yourselves. Mr. Eloi, Mr. Archimedes."

"What did you call me?" Archimedes' voice seethed.

Everyone behind him began yelling, "No Archie, don't do it!"

This made Rennet turn to look around the room, curious as to what they meant. When he turned back around and looked up at Archimedes, a fist flew at his face knocking him to the floor. He laid there, his nose feeling as though it were going to swell shut, and his eyes feeling as though they were welded closed and ready to pop out of his head, and they began to water incessantly.

The room erupted in a mix of moans of agony for poor Rennet, or laughter. Eloi Theriot jumped up and down awkwardly, bounding from foot to foot, laughing and clapping at Rennet's expense.

Aurelie had heard the usual altercation between the two men start from down by the water, and she also heard Rennet trying to calm the situation.

"Oh No!"

She turned to rush back to the pavilion, reaching it just in time to hear Rennet use Archie's given birth name. She yelled along with everyone else, just before Rennet McCabe hit the floor. Arjit Chiasson nearly fell forward in laughter, slapping his knee in enjoyment, while most everyone else either did the same or winced at the pain inflicted on their newcomer. She ran over toward Archie with a reprimand on her lips, but Sandra had beaten her to it. The tiny woman stood toe to toe with him, her finger pointed in the air.

"Archimedes Galileo Bourgeois, have you lost your ever-lovin' mind?" She gave Eloi the evil eye, and he too stopped his jumping and clapping, cleared his throat, and stood still, averting his eyes to anywhere but in Sandra's direction.

Archie clamped his jaw shut at the use of his full given name. Sandra was the only woman who ever had the courage to say it other than his own mother, God rest her soul. She and his mother had been friends years back when he was just a kid, and she had taken care of him like a mother when his own had passed on.

"But Ms. Sandy, you know how I feel about my name."

"Yes. But that poor boy doesn't. He's new here."

"Then he should mind his own business. Me and Eloi were doing just fine."

She continued her onslaught. "We all know that Archie, but again, poor Rennet doesn't understand things around here yet. He was just trying to help. Shame on you. You and Eloi have had enough fun for the night. You two git on down the beach with your drinking and arguing or head home, you hear?"

"Yes ma'am."

The large man slunk his shoulders, grabbed the nearly empty bottle of moonshine, threw his arm around Eloi's shoulders and the two of them stumbled out into the dark night. Everyone, including Rennet from his place on the floor, watched as Eloi yelled up at him, *"Archimedes Galileo Bourgeois,"* he said, cackling wildly.

The Barter

Archie pushed the man away from him toppling him over onto the sand and left him there. Eloi rolled onto his back, still laughing, and soon passed smooth out from intoxication.

Everyone went back to partying and chatting like nothing happened. Except those that bent over Rennet, who sat on the floor holding his bleeding nose with his hand.

Sophanes grinned and handed him a rag he had pulled from one of the tables, and Rennet pressed it to his nose.

Sandra, a nurse before the collapse, instructed Aurelie and Emilie who were on either side of him, where to deposit Rennet so she could have a look. He stumbled slightly as they pulled him up from the floor, still a bit dizzy from the hit and trying to keep his head back to stop the bleeding. They sat him down at one of the tables, facing out. Sandra removed the rag to study the damage.

Emilie immediately squeaked her distaste and shuddered. She patted him on the shoulder and hurriedly got up and walked away.

His paranoid eyes cut to Aurelie who saw the question there.

"It isn't that bad. Emilie just can't handle blood," she reassured him.

He sighed, relieved.

Sophanes smiled in appreciation. "You've got a nice wound there."

Sandra agreed. "Nice is right. The bleeding is stopping a little, probably from the swelling inside the nasal cavity. You might have two black eyes for a while too. The damage doesn't look too bad, but it did split the skin across the bridge of your nose. Sit tight for a bit, I have some butterfly bandages at my place." Sandra left him to Aurelie, Sophanes, and Anytos.

Sophanes said, "You're either really brave, or really stupid."

"How about just ignorant?" The muffled answer came from behind the rag now placed back on his still dripping nose.

Aurelie grinned slightly at his pitiful state. "I told you Archie was sensitive to his name."

"This is a might more than sensitive. Volatile would have been the correct term to use." He cut his eyes sideways at her; unwilling to turn his pounding head.

"Yes. I guess I should have been more descriptive." She grimaced apologetically.

Anytos said, "Looks like he's going to have to bunk with us tonight. We can't leave him to himself in this state."

Sophanes shook his head in agreement. "As soon as Sandra gets back and patches you up, we'll take you to our place and let you get some rest."

"Thanks," Rennet stated.

Aurelie watched him ease back against the side of the table, resting his back on the edge.

Rennet closed his eyes to the dimly lit but now irritating brightness of the pavilion.

Sandra soon returned with an ice pack, cleaning solution, butterfly bandages, and pain medication. She patched Rennet up, gave him the pain meds, and Sophanes and Anytos led him out of the pavilion and out across the sand toward their house high up in the air on piers.

Aurelie watched them lead Rennet away. Her opinion of him increased slightly because of his brave stance against the largest and the most unruly men in their community, Archie, and Eloi; all because he wanted to salvage Birdie's birthday party. The poor guy obviously had no way of knowing that Archie and Eloi, who argued incessantly, especially when liquored up, were the very best of friends. She smirked and shook her head at the pitiful man who stumbled slightly across the sand, pulled along by the other two. Her thoughts ran through her head as she tried to figure out if he was truly that brave or just really unobservant; or just plain stupid as Sophanes suggested.

Chapter 5

Rennet woke with a headache, and his nose was a little sore and stuffed up from some swelling that was still present. He lay there in the quiet of the room until he heard whispered giggles.

His eyes fluttered open and he lifted his head from the pillow to see two young children staring at him and smiling.

"Hello." Rennet looked at them as they watched him curiously.

"Hello," they answered in unison, smiling and giggling even more.

Anytos walked into the room. "All right you two, get along and let Mr. Rennet alone."

The two children giggled again and ran off.

"Sorry, my children are curious to see the new man to our town." Anytos sat a coffee cup on the stand beside his bed.

Rennet sat up with a strained grunt, taking the offered cup in hand. "Thank you for this." He held the cup up. "And thank you for the comfortable bed last night. I slept pretty well, except for obvious reasons." He pointed at his nose.

"You are welcome. And your nose should heal in time."

"I just hope it doesn't take too long."

"At least both of your eyes are not black this morning." Anytos grinned appreciatively.

"That is a good thing." Rennet nodded. "So where is Sophanes this morning?"

"Making breakfast." Anytos turned to leave the room.

"Since you have children, where is your wife?" Rennet asked.

"Oh, she is sleeping late. She's pregnant and nearing the last trimester. She is tired most days. We help when we can when we are home. Now, you must come out to the kitchen to eat some protein to help your body heal."

Rennet smiled and nodded. "Breakfast sounds great, thanks."

The two men walked from the room into the kitchen. Sophanes noticed Rennet walking behind Anytos, who stopped to play with his children in the living room area.

"Good morning, Rennet. You don't look too worse for wear."

"I may not look it, but I feel it." Rennet tried to smile but the motion caused some pain and pulling in his face.

"It will heal. Just try not to smile today."

Rennet gave him a small lopsided grin, nodded his understanding, and pulled a tall stool out from the bar to sit upon.

Sophanes placed a plate of eggs, bacon, sausage, and grits in front of him. Rennet had not seen that much food at one time in a while.

"Sophanes, this is too much. I don't need all of this."

"Eat, Rennet, you will need your strength today. You will fish with Anytos and me."

Rennet shook his head no between bites of the wonderful tasting food. "I appreciate your offer, and your kindness, but boats and I do not get along, mainly on the ocean because of the waves. I get horrible sea-sickness. I've tried many times over the years. It's not something that will just go away either. I'll just have to figure out something else I can do here on land to make a living."

"Well, I understand. I am sure that you will figure something out."

Rennet nodded in reply. "Thanks. So, Sophanes, where were those abandoned houses you were telling me about?"

"Just walk west along the shoreline. You will see the camps in question."

"Camps?"

"Yes. Many of these dwellings here along the beach were temporary vacation homes. Many called them camps. People owned them and would come to enjoy the beach whenever they could but lived elsewhere. We can eat, then I will show you where I am building."

"You're moving from here?"

"Yes. Anytos' family is growing quickly. They need the extra room. Besides, this was supposed to be a temporary arrangement. I have overstayed my welcome by many years." Sophanes smiled. "But Thalia and Anytos have been kind, and she appreciates having the extra help in her pregnancy, but it is time I get back to work on my own place."

"Perhaps we can help each other out with construction on both our places?"

"That sounds like a good idea. I assume since you are wanting to build a home, it means that you are staying on here?"

"Yes, even with all the trouble I got into last night. I'll just try to remember to keep my nose out of other people's business from now on." Rennet smiled a little.

"That would be wise." Sophanes smiled back at him and finished cooking breakfast. He dished up plates for everyone else and then sat with Rennet at the bar. Anytos took a plate into a bedroom, Rennet guessed to Thalia, and the children climbed up into the stools at the bar with the two of them; smiling and giggling at Rennet as they all chatted. Anytos soon joined them in eating and talking about what they were all going to get into that day.

After breakfast and kitchen clean-up was complete, Sophanes took Rennet to show him the abandoned places.

Rennet stood looking up at small buildings on tall piers; many at least twelve to fifteen feet in the air.

"Why are the buildings placed so high up?"

"We have had many hurricanes hit this area over the years. These were all regulated to building specifications years ago. This one here," Sophanes pointed and smiled broadly, "is the one I have started to rebuild. I will finish it soon."

Rennet looked up at the home that Sophanes so proudly spoke of. "You've been here for a long time haven't you?"

"Yes," Sophanes answered.

"I just thought you would have already had a home somewhere."

"I did. It was not here near to the beach. It was further inland. When the collapse happened, I tried to work from and live in my home, but it was just too far out from the market here. So

The Barter

Anytos and I, with his wife, moved down here to the coast where survival was easier. We took up an abandoned camp and rebuilt it. That is where we all live now. Anytos' family has grown over the years, and I need to find my own space. He and I work on this place in our free time. Most days, we take my boat and go out fishing and shrimping to trade at market. Today, however, since market was just yesterday, we will take the day and work on our homes, yes?"

Rennet stiffly grinned. "Yes. That sounds like a good idea. I only have one question. Where do we get lumber to rebuild?"

Sophanes smiled again. "We go see Archie."

"I'm assuming there aren't two Archies that live down here." Rennet sighed.

"No. It is Archimedes Bourgeois. He has some lumber he trades for services and goods."

"Wonderful. Let's hope he'll trade with me." Rennet was skeptical that the man would do so after last night.

"I am sure he will, as long as you have something to barter in return."

"Well, first I suppose I need to find one of these in decent enough condition that doesn't need too much work to fix up." Rennet looked around at some camps that looked too far gone to repair. "Why couldn't we use some of the materials from the camps that are still standing? Perhaps most of them still hold some decent wood?"

"Yes, I suppose we could scavenge from some of the other ones." Sophanes shook his head appreciatively.

Rennet climbed up many sets of steps that appeared to still be safe and peered into the buildings, also inspecting their structural integrity. He finally settled on one in particular that sat just behind a few others on one of the back road beach accesses. As he and Sophanes, soon joined by Anytos, worked, and chatted throughout the day, Sophanes filled him in on the towns people.

Many of the residents of Holly Beach lived very near and around these camps. Even though there were several unoccupied, there were many which were full. Most everyone lived close by, helping one another. Sophanes told him that there were only a handful of people, those who had been born and raised here for generations, that lived off the beach area in other places. Arjit Chiasson and Aurelie Haydel were two of them. They both owned bigger spreads and farmland in and around the marshlands.

It was just at that time that Aurelie, Baxter, Birdie, and Katie appeared riding toward them on her side-by-side. She stopped just in front of them and all four climbed out and came to stand with them, looking up at the dwellings.

Sophanes boomed, "Good morning, all."

They all replied in kind. Aurelie stopped walking when she reached Rennet, grimacing at his appearance.

"So, Rennet, how are you feeling today?"

"Okay, all things considered."

"It looks better than it did last night."

"It feels a bit better as well, though now with all the activity today, I do feel a headache coming on."

The Barter

"I'm sure you can get some more pain medication from Sandra if you need it. She lives twelve houses down that way closer to the main access road. Her place has all the chickens."

"Thanks, I may head over there in just a bit. Working on this place has caused my head to pound. "

She looked up, surprise on her features. "What, you're going to stay and fix up this old place?"

"Yeah, I think so. Sophanes and I are going to work together when we can to get both of our places livable."

"I really thought you would be moving on after last night." Aurelie wasn't so sure she liked the fact that Rennet McCabe was staying here.

"Call me crazy, and I might just be, but I like it here."

"I can't believe that after ten years of walking and seeing different places, that this is the place you choose to remain."

"Well, it is. You all have a sense of community here that I haven't experienced anywhere else. And not to mention, some very colorful characters."

Aurelie grinned. "Yes, we certainly do."

"Any particular reason you came looking for me?" Despite the discomfort it caused, Rennet grinned at the uncomfortable look his question caused her.

"Birdie wanted to thank you for trying to salvage her party last night, even though it really wasn't necessary."

Just then Birdie walked toward them. "Hello, Mr. Rennet, I just wanted to thank you and say sorry that you got punched in the face."

Rennet smiled, wincing. "Thank you, Birdie. I appreciate that."

"So you're going to live here?" she asked curiously.

"Yes, that is the plan."

"Good. I like you. Maybe Bax and I can come help you with fixing things?"

Aurelie looked a bit nervous. "I don't know if that is a good idea."

Rennet cut her off. "I'd like that very much, Birdie. Though it will be very hard work, and I have no way of paying you."

"You don't have to pay us. We help each other out, it's what we do here. Besides, if you wish to give us something, we can barter for things."

"Well, until I can figure out what I have to offer the community, I'm afraid I have nothing to barter either."

Birdie just shrugged. "Like I said, we help each other." She smiled and walked away to look at something Sophanes and Anytos were hunched over.

Baxter asked, "Can I stay and help, Aurie?"

Aurelie looked at Rennet, unsure. "I don't know, Bax…"

Rennet said, "It is fine with me, if it is all right with you, of course."

She sighed, looking at Baxter. "Fine, but just for a few hours."

"Me too?" Birdie asked hurriedly, turning back to them.

"Yes; you too. But like I said, only for a few hours. We have our own lives to tend to and you both have chores to complete today."

"Yes ma'am," they both agreed, a bright smile upon their faces.

"One question," Rennet asked. "Where do I find Archie?"

Aurelie smirked. "Are you sure you want to find him?"

"Well, apparently he has wood that I may need to rebuild."

"Yeah, but do you have anything to barter with?"

"Not yet, but I want to find out what I'm dealing with."

"I'm sure Sophanes and Anytos will go with you to visit Archie. You probably shouldn't go alone anyway, especially after last night's altercation," Aurelie warned.

"Well, how about you? You can be my buffer. I figure the man has some manners, especially toward the female gender if Sandra chewing him out was any indication?"

"Well, you see, not just anyone can speak to Archie that way. Sandra basically raised the man after his mother passed, so she is like a mother to him. I can't say that I will have any kind of pull with Archie."

"Maybe not, but you know him better than I do."

Aurelie sighed again, not really wanting to get much involved with this stranger but feeling a little responsible for not warning him better last night. "I guess I can take you over. Do you want to go now?"

"No, how about when you come back to get the kids? I should have a better idea of what I need by then."

"Fine. I'll bring some dinner for the three of you when I come back. Nothing much though. I also carry a few extra bottles of water in the side-by-side that I will leave with them."

"That sounds fine, thank you, Aurelie."

"Don't thank me yet. Baxter is super hyper, and Birdie will talk your ear off." She grinned sideways at him.

Rennet smiled broadly and winced, grabbing his nose from the pain it caused.

Aurelie decided it was time to leave and hopped back into the cart as Katie waved to everyone. They took off down the cracked, pitted, and mostly sand-covered asphalt road, waving to their friends who were outside working under their camps or around in the sparse, grassy, areas.

Aurelie turned to Katie. "What do you say we stop at Sandra and Marie's for a little while? If they aren't too busy maybe I can help Sandra with the chores while you and Marie play."

"Yes, please," Katie said excitedly. "I like playing with Marie. She's funny."

Aurelie smiled. "Yes, she is fun to watch."

They pulled up to the Louviere's place and stopped. Marie saw them coming and excitedly waved and flapped her arms as she sailed toward them.

"Hey, have you come to play with me?" she asked.

Katie squealed excitedly, "I have, Marie." She jumped out of the cart and the two of them took off down the road flapping and giggling.

Sandra had stopped her morning rituals of animal feeding and watched the two girls run and play. She yelled to Aurelie, "Good afternoon."

Aurelie waved back and walked to where Sandra was bent over a feed bucket. "Hey Sandra. I hope you don't mind my stopping by like this."

"Not at all. What brings you by this way today?"

Aurelie grabbed a feed bucket to help Sandra in Marie's place.

"Birdie had wanted to thank Rennet for his bravery last night. She and Baxter are over at a camp he is trying to rebuild. They offered to help him, so I figured Katie could do with some playtime as well."

"Anytime. She is a welcome respite from our drudgery, and Marie gets so lonely at times. I don't have the energy or time to keep up with her." Sandra laughed. "Now, as for the other thing you mentioned. Rennet McCabe is going to brave staying here after last night?"

"I suppose so. I just can't understand why he would want to stay here?"

"Why not here?"

"Well, I'm certain he has been everywhere. There must be places that offer much more than what we have."

"Perhaps. But maybe it's not about what the community can offer, rather than what a single person can?" Sandra grinned at her with raised eyebrows.

"Surely you're joking." Aurie shook her head. "The man has been here for one day, Sandra."

"Yeah, and I saw how he watched and looked at you."

"I'm not the only person he spoke to or danced with."

"No. But you are the one *he* chose to dance with. Emilie grabbed him first remember."

"Yes, and he spun her off to Adam who was standing there pining like a puppy. I just happened to be nearby and a safe alternative. Besides, we all know how pushy Emilie can be when she wants something."

"Yes. And it appears her sights are set on young Rennet McCabe. Besides, what's more exciting than a stranger who walks into town, has wandered the wide world on foot for ten years, has a good personality, and looks like he does?"

"I don't think I'm ready for that kind of excitement, Sandra." Aurelie smiled.

"Honey, we are *all* ready for *any kind* of excitement." Sandra smiled broadly and the two of them laughed as they continued their chores.

Chapter 6

The next few hours flew by quickly as Aurelie and Sandra finished outside, and Sandra poured all four of them a glass of sun tea she had brewed that day from a new variety of tea leaves she had bartered from Kei Yamada. They all sat at the wrought iron metal table that Sandra had tucked beneath the corner of her home, enjoying the cool, refreshing beverage. Marie and Katie took their glasses and sat on the swing that hung from the underside of Sandra's home near the center.

"Thanks for your help today, Aurie," Sandra said appreciatively. "Marie tries, but I usually end up redoing whatever she does." She grinned.

"You're welcome. And anytime you need extra help just say the word and we can come back. As a matter of fact, why don't you let Katie come once or twice a week to help Marie, and the two can keep each other company?"

"That would be wonderful." Sandra smiled. "Marie would love that, and Katie is such a blessing."

"Good. Just remember that she is coming to help do chores." Aurelie smiled. "They can play when things are done."

"And what can I offer you in trade for this luxury?"

"Your friendship is enough, Sandra."

Aurelie smiled and raised her glass to the woman.

Sandra smiled and toasted back, the two of them clinking their glasses together. They finished their beverage and Aurelie yelled, "Time to go, Katie."

"Awe…" came the reply in unison. Aurelie and Sandra smiled broadly at one another.

"You can come back. As a matter of fact, Mrs. Sandra and I just had a discussion about that very subject. I'll tell you about it on the way home. We need to go grab dinner. I promised Mr. Rennet I would feed him tonight when I picked up Bax and Birdie.

Katie sighed.

"Okay. Bye Marie, see you later."

"By Katie. I had fun playing with you."

"Me too." Katie smiled brightly, placed the now empty glass on the iron table, and looked at Sandra. "Bye Mrs. Sandra, see you later."

Sandra smiled brightly. "We sure will. And Katie, thank you for being such a good friend to Marie."

Katie beamed at the woman.

She and Aurelie climbed into their cart and made the two-mile trip home in just a few minutes, discussing Aurelie and Sandra's plans for the two girls twice weekly.

"That would be so great, Aurie. And I promise to help Marie with her chores and do whatever Mrs. Sandra asks."

Katie's excited answer warmed Aurelie's heart. Why had she never thought of doing this before? Perhaps they were all just settled into their own lives. Everyone was just trying to make do within their own little worlds. Birdie's words replayed in her mind as she prepped dinner.

The Barter

"Like I said, we help each other."

Her words weren't unusual; their community did help and support one another, but usually at a price of some kind, a trade or promise of future help when needed. She didn't know the last time anyone offered their services freely, just because they wanted to be kind. Birdie's offer to Rennet had been just that, an offer of free services with no strings attached. She smiled at the thought of the kids becoming kind people.

Over the last twenty years her father Privat had driven caution into her head, and rightly so. Humanity had turned inhuman after the collapse and then civil wars. The reports from larger cities were horrible as people fought just to survive. You couldn't trust anyone it seemed. And even though their little community here had suffered, it wasn't quite as bad as other places seemed to have had it. Still for a while, even here, it was every man for himself. People scrambled and scrounged to get by. Some of the older people who lived alone or too far out suffered and died with too little resources. Her father would go check on those who he could get to, sometimes getting there too late. She had helped her father bury a few people; him explaining that it wasn't right just to leave them in their houses. Soon, as more people died off, her father went to the older men in the community and formed a health watch-force. He reasoned that if the death toll continued to rise unchecked, then disease would soon overtake everyone. This seemed to get people involved with one another again, which led to bartering and eventually the market. Now, lives meshed more here because of the human connections made early on with dealing with the unpleasantness of war, destruction, and death.

"Aurie, it's getting late. Are you ready to go?"

Aurelie was shaken from her musings as Katie's voice broke through her thoughts.

"Yes, just finishing dinner." She smiled at Katie and the two of them loaded up to travel the two-mile trip back toward the beach. The night air was warm and balmy as the breeze off the ocean ruffled their hair and clothing adding to the force of the thirty-mile-an-hour cart ride. When they reached Rennet's camp, Sophanes and Anytos had already left for home, and Aurelie could see they had made quite a bit of progress already. There were still a few holes in the walls, but they had cleaned up all of the rotten wood and made a bonfire with it. Aurelie pulled the cart to a stop just at the edge of the over-head building. Baxter and Birdie were feeding the fire as Rennet tossed a few remaining pieces of wood to them from above.

"Hey you three, dinner's here." She and Katie climbed out of the vehicle and walked over to the roaring fire, handing off cloth-wrapped packages and bottled water to both kids.

Rennet came down the steps and stopped beside Aurelie. "Thank you for dinner. I am quite hungry this evening. All this physical labor sure does stir up a hunger in a body."

"I figured walking for the last ten years would be an equal physical challenge." Aurelie offered.

"Yes, it did require a little more nourishment, but today I have used up a lot more calories."

The Barter

Rennet smiled before taking a bite of the tortilla wrapped meat and vegetable meal. He grinned again, and nodded his appreciation of the taste as well, taking a long drink of the offered bottle of water.

Aurelie looked up at the camp in progress as she ate. "Looks like you all did quite a bit today."

Birdie groaned. "I had no idea that helping people could be so hard."

Aurelie grinned and Rennet nearly choked at the torturous tone of her voice. Aurelie said, "It's not like you aren't used to hard labor. You work at home."

Birdie nodded. "Yes, but this is much harder. All the walking up and down the stairs has worn my poor little legs completely wobbly."

"Well, just think how well you will sleep tonight." Aurelie grinned at the tiny girl. "And I'm sure Mr. Rennet much appreciated the help."

Rennet added his reply here. "Greatly. I wouldn't have gotten nearly as far without you two." He pointed to Baxter and Birdie.

Baxter, who had been quiet due to the intense hunger he felt had finished his meal and spoke up. "I really like the tearing apart and rebuilding process. You can really get out a lot of frustration. I'm tired, but I feel really good."

Aurelie could tell that Baxter's words were heartfelt. He had been growing a little anxious as of late, probably due to his teenage hormones and ADHD afflicted body and mind. This added physical labor would likely do him good.

"Well, Baxter, you and Birdie can come help Mr. Rennet and Mr. Sophanes everyday they work on their places if you like. As long as your chores at home won't be affected."

Baxter grinned. "Really? Thanks Aurie. I'd like that."

Birdie sighed. "Well, if I'm needed. I'm not quite as stout as Baxter, but I'll do what I can since I offered."

Aurelie and Rennet exchanged hidden grins at her pained answer.

Rennet replied, "Well, Birdie, you do what you can. I think your offer and the work you put in today can be considered complete."

"No sir, Mr. Privat or Aurie, would never let me squelch on a deal. I offered to help and I will. I just might not be able to do as much as everyone else."

Aurelie's heart filled with pride at Birdie's resilient answer. The values her father had instilled in all of them shone through at that moment as tears filled her eyes. She blinked quickly and swiped to dry them before anyone noticed, but the motion was not lost on Rennet.

Rennet answered, "Well, Birdie, that is a very grown-up attitude to have. I'd say Mr. Haydel taught you all very well. And I promise to give you an easier job next time. Besides, I think the hardest part is done. Now I just have to start the rebuilding process."

As everyone quietly finished their meal, Aurelie and Rennet exchanged looks of appreciation. Not only for the upstanding attitude of Birdie, but the emotions behind what the evening evoked. Aurelie cleared her throat before speaking.

"All right you three. Time to head home before dark settles in."

Rennet spoke up. "I thought you were going to take me to Archie's?"

"Not tonight. Once the night settles in, we try to keep close to home unless we are at a large gathering. Especially since the headlights on my side-by-side are failing."

"Oh, well I can probably fix that for you."

"Oh, no, you don't have to do that. I just need to take it over to Foesy Divins. I just haven't had the time. Besides, it just started happening."

"Well, If you can come back in the morning and take me over to Archie's then I can look at the wiring then when we have plenty of daylight."

Aurelie really did not want to take the man to Archie's, but she did agree to it. "Fine. We have some chores to take care of first thing, but we can be here by ten a.m."

"That'll be great, thanks."

"So where will you sleep tonight?" Aurelie's question surprised herself. Why did she ask that?

"Here probably. Anytos offered for me to stay with them again, but they are already bursting at the seams." He grinned crookedly at her.

"Well, good luck with the mosquitoes."

"I have ways of dealing with such things. I learned a lot of survival tricks over the last ten years of traveling through every state in America."

Aurelie grinned and then breathed deeply. "Well then, we'll see you in the morning."

Baxter asked, "Can I stay and help Rennet tomorrow after we see Archie?"

"If you get all your home chores finished before we have to come here," Aurelie stated plainly.

"Yes ma'am, I'll get up extra early and take care of everything." Baxter excitedly sat in the side-by-side smiling from ear to ear. "I think I have a few ideas on how to strengthen some of the support poles too."

"Great, we'll talk about them tomorrow," Rennet replied to the boy who nodded happily in return.

As the side-by-side drove away the children all yelled and waved to Rennet who responded in kind. Aurelie looked over at Baxter who had relaxed in the seat but still wore a satisfied look on his face. She realized that Baxter had been missing the camaraderie of another male being around. He did live with three females and was never around any other men except at market days, if they went along with her, and community gatherings which happened only about once a month. Even if Rennet McCabe decided to finally move on, she would make certain that Baxter got more time with the men in the community. Perhaps letting them all go out a few days a week to help others would be good for the kids. Maybe having a few days to herself would even be beneficial for her? What would she do with that time if she had it? It was something she would have to think about.

Rennet watched them leave for home, his thoughts returning to the sadness in Aurelie's eyes when Birdie had spoken of Privat Haydel, and then the change to pride for the girl's attitude and resilience. Their little family unit seemed perfect, except there seemed to be something wanting in all of them. Perhaps it was just the loneliness of the world now that he sensed, and the excitement of someone and something new being here in their out of the way community. Baxter and Birdie both had chatted about everything and everyone all day long. He felt as though there wasn't much left to learn about anyone in the community.

Rennet rubbed his tired eyes and face, being careful around his still sore and sensitive nose, and realized he still had a thick beard. He decided to get cleaned up and shave tonight; especially with the heat of the summer months here in Louisiana. It was hotter here than anywhere else he had traveled to, and the humidity was high; so much so that it felt like he was breathing underwater at times. If it weren't for the near constant breeze from the ocean, it would be unmanageable outdoors during the hottest part of the day, which here was late afternoon. He climbed the stairs to his new home, mosquito proofed the area where he was to sleep by hanging netting from the ceiling in Tee-pee style over his sleeping bag, then took his razor, small mirror, and some soap, and went to work on his face. It had been months since he had shaved and his thick shaggy beard was proof of that. He rinsed his now clean, shaved, face and then washed the sweat and grime of the past several days away. He grabbed a book from his pack and settled onto his bedroll until it was too dark to see. He lay in his bed covered by the thin netting gazing up at the stars through the missing part of the roof. He prayed to God, thanking him for bringing him to a place where he could call home.

Chapter 7

Aurelie hummed as she prepared breakfast. She had let everyone sleep a little later this morning since they all had a day of extra physical labor yesterday. The kids were quiet last night from the exertion of helping Rennet; their tired bodies were worn, but their spirits soared. The satisfied look on Baxter's face was enough to convince her that he needed more male company.

It was nearing eight o'clock when everyone made an appearance in the kitchen.

"Good morning y'all."

"Morning Aurie," came the scattered replies. Baxter and Katie looked refreshed and excited. Birdie still looked tired and not quite as exuberant at beginning her day.

"Aurie, can I go to Marie's today?" Katie bounced up and down as Aurelie finished cooking their breakfast.

"How about we wait until Monday morning, Katie? You were just there last evening."

"I know, but I'm sure Mrs. Sandra won't mind."

"Okay, we'll do this, while I take Mr. Rennet to Archie's to see about some lumber, you can visit and help, but I still need to talk to Sandra about which days would work best for her."

"Okay." Katie smiled happily.

Baxter asked his question as they all piled around the kitchen table. "What about Birdie and me? Are we staying to help Mr. Rennet today?"

"Well first, there isn't room for all of us on the cart with the addition of Rennet. So, you and Birdie stay here for now and finish your morning chores. If Rennet manages to procure some wood to work with, when I come back I can take you over there."

Baxter grinned; his mouth full of food.

Birdie did not smile today, but she was true to her word and would do whatever was required of her.

Aurelie smiled at Katie and Baxter's excitement for the day, and at the woeful look on Birdie's face.

They all finished breakfast and Aurie and Katie cleaned up the kitchen and finished a few necessary morning chores before heading off toward the beach area.

As they neared Sandra's place, Marie saw them coming and bounced up and down excitedly.

"Mama, Katie has come to play again."

Sandra answered, "Yes, but chores first, Marie."

"Yes Ma'am." Marie's excitement could not be crushed by a few morning chores.

Aurelie's cart came to a stop. "Good morning Sandra, I hope you don't mind, but Katie was so excited to get started today, and I have to take Rennet to Archie's anyway."

"Sure. I don't mind at all. Katie, you, and Marie take the crushed shells and scatter them in all the bird pens. They like to eat them, and it hardens their eggs and keeps them from breaking so easily."

"I didn't know that chickens and quail ate seashells." Katie smiled and giggled as the two girls jogged away, carrying their buckets.

"Thanks Sandra, all this getting out and doing things for others really seems to have lifted the kids spirits."

"Katie sure has lifted mine. It gets tiresome with just me and Marie all the time."

"Anytime you need some time to yourself, Sandra, Marie is welcome at the house."

"Thank you Aurie, I'll likely take you up on that."

"Do you think she'll come over without you?"

"Definitely, especially with Katie around."

"What time would you like me to pick Katie up?"

"She can stay the day. She's such a blessing and help with Marie."

"Are you certain?"

"Absolutely."

"All right, I'll see you around dinnertime then." Aurelie sighed heavily. "I need to take Rennet to Archie's. I'm not sure how this is going to go over." She climbed back into the seat of the cart.

"It'll be just fine. Archie has cooled off, plus most of that was the moonshine talking. But, if he does give you any trouble, just tell him I said he best behave and not make me come down there."

Aurelie laughed at the threat. She knew Sandra could handle the man, she just thought it funny since Archie was head and shoulders above Sandra's small frame.

"Thanks Sandra. I'll use whatever leverage I can get." Aurelie waved goodbye and headed off toward Rennet's place about twelve houses down on the left.

Aurelie parked, climbed out, and walked the steps leading up to the cabin level. As she stepped onto the porch landing, she could see through the main wall of the house. Rennet's back was facing her and he was bent over, hammering on something.

"Good morning, are you ready to go?" Aurelie yelled.

Rennet jumped and the hammer went flying out of his hand toward Aurelie, landing a few feet in front of her on the floor.

"Good grief, Rennet, why are you so jumpy?" Aurelie's eyes left the hammer lying in front of her and landed on a freshly shaven Rennet McCabe. Her astonished look was not lost on him.

"Sorry, when I'm homed in on a project I get lost in it. Sudden disturbances can jolt me back to reality." Rennet walked toward her and picked up the hammer; his eyes locked on the shocked look on Aurelie's face.

"Aurelie, are you okay?"

Aurelie noticed the slight crooked grin that played at his lips depressing small dimples on either side. That grin unnerved her. He was quite striking to look at without all the facial hair. She had known he was good looking beneath it all, but good grief, this was sinful!

"Uh, yeah. I'm fine." She cleared her throat. "I just didn't expect to see someone else here this morning. You look quite different without all that facial hair."

"Sorry, I didn't mean to startle you. I just figured with the heat here it was time for a shave." Rennet laid the hammer down where he had been working, then returned to where Aurelie stood watching him. "So, are we ready to go?" He smiled again.

"Oh, yes." Aurelie quickly turned to walk back down the steps, taking deep steadying breaths to try and clear her mind. *Snap out of it Aurelie. So he's gorgeous, so what. You do not need any complications in your life. It's perfect just the way it is.*

"Aurelie?"

"Hmm…"

"I asked where the kids were?"

"Oh, sorry. Katie is at Sandra's and the others are at home doing chores."

"Are they coming by today?"

"If you need them. I wasn't sure what the plan was until you spoke with Archie. Plus the cart only seats four."

They climbed into the cart and started off toward Archie's place. Aurelie tried her hardest to avert her eyes from the handsome, chiseled, dimpled, face of Rennet McCabe.

"That sounds like a plan. I am curious as to whether Archie will deal with me at all. I can only hope."

They set out on the ride in relative silence which felt strange to Aurelie so she asked, "How's your nose?"

Rennet touched his face. "It's healing quite well. Hardly stuffy at all anymore. I guess it looks all right?"

Aurelie turned to look at him. "It looks fine. You probably won't even have a scar."

"Thanks to Sandra. I'll have to stop by later and thank her. Which is her place?"

"We passed it a minute ago. Her place is on the corner of the main access road. Her backyard is fenced pretty high to keep the chickens from escaping."

"Yeah, I saw that house. It had a large, cushioned, swing hanging from the under-rafters."

"Most of the places here do. It's nice to sit outside and enjoy the cool breeze and the sound of the ocean waves."

"Yeah, I have to admit, the holes in the roof and walls does make for a beautiful sound to go to sleep too. I might install a few screened windows so I can open them at night. I don't want to lose that sound." Rennet smiled broadly.

"I know what you mean. The sound, smell, and feel of the ocean breeze is something I wouldn't want to live without." Aurelie returned his smile with one of her own.

They turned the corner back toward the shoreline and a large building on the left side of the road came into view. It was somewhat battered, but sturdy looking. As Aurelie parked, Rennet looked over the building's exterior. It was part cinder-block from the ground about halfway up, then was board and bat style wood to the partially rusted metal roof. They stepped from the cart and walked toward the building as Rennet continued his inspection. He figured that years of storms, and constant salt spray from the ocean had taken its toll on the metal. But he hadn't seen anything using cinder-blocks in all his travels. This building must have withstood decades of massive storms and survived.

The Barter

As they entered the dark building, Rennet waited for his eyes to adjust while Aurelie yelled, "Archie?"

It was just a few seconds before they heard his reply. "Comin'."

There was a slight ruckus, something fell over with a loud bang, and Archie could be heard fussing.

Aurelie looked at Rennet with a slight giggle. Rennet smiled nervously, unsure what to make of the large man after their last encounter.

Archie stepped out from behind some tall wood and doors leaning against a wall. He was still fussing under his breath when he looked up at them.

"Morning, Aurie." He looked at Rennet, a little confused and nodded at him.

"Good morning, Archie. Rennet here needs some lumber for a place he is fixing up down the beach." Aurelie looked to Rennet, an amused look on her face.

Rennet looked at the large man looming over them, his hands on his hips waiting for Rennet's tongue to untie.

"Well?" Archie asked.

Rennet cleared his throat. "Sorry, I uh, need some lumber. I wanted to know what you would take in trade?"

"Well, what do you got?" Archie stared down at him.

"Not much I'm afraid. I can see what I have in my pack."

Rennet picked up the large backpack he carried with him. He sized up the man in front of him as he dug through his bag. He pulled out a cased set of Hohner harmonicas.

"Do you like music?"

Archie's eyebrows lifted in interest.

"Well, I do like to play. I haven't had a set of harmonicas since I was a kid."

Aurelie was amazed at how Rennet always seemed to know what a person would like. Either that or they were all just desperate for anything new or different.

"They're yours if you'll take them in trade for lumber?"

"Well, how much lumber are we talking about here?"

"I'm not sure really. I can work off the rest if what I need is more than the harmonica's will cover."

"Well, I guess that'll work."

Aurelie asked, "Archie, can you ride over to Rennet's with us to see what you think it will take to fix up his place?"

"Sure, I can do that. Let me go get my shades. I'll be right back."

Rennet exhaled loudly and Aurelie smiled. He turned to her and said, "That wasn't so bad."

"No. I'm not sure he even remembers you."

Rennet turned to look at her with surprise. "Really?"

"Archie's behavior the other night wasn't so unusual. If you noticed, the entire town yelled before he hit you. Everyone knew how he would react. Many of the men here has had to deal with him at one point or another."

The Barter

Rennet noticed her smile spread across her face and was about to reply when Archie reappeared.

"All right let's get this show on the road. I've got work to do." Archie passed them and climbed into Aurelie's cart in the front seat.

Rennet sat in the rear and the three headed back to his house.

Archie leaned over to Aurie and as quietly as possible asked, "Who's the new fella'?"

Aurelie about choked on her short burst of laughter. "I knew you didn't remember him."

"Should I?" Archie asked confused.

"Um, yeah, Archie, you should. Of course he does look a little different after shaving; but how many newcomers do we actually get here?"

"You got a point." Archie looked over his shoulder, curious to the stranger. "What happened to his nose?"

Aurelie burst out laughing this time. "Good grief, Archie, how much moonshine did you consume at Birdie's party the other night?"

"I don't know. You know how Eloi and I get when he brings his moonshine into town. Why?"

"Archie, *you* did that to his nose. He called you by your given name and you punched him."

"Oh. Well, he should know better."

"No, he shouldn't. He had only been in town for that day when you hit him. And he was just trying to save Birdie's party by stopping you and Eloi from quarreling."

Just then they pulled up to Rennet's and they all stepped out to inspect his place.

Archie turned to Rennet. "Sorry about the nose." Archie made a fist and looked at it then at Rennet. He shrugged and turned to inspect Rennet's house.

Rennet stood there for a second then replied, "Sure, no problem. I've learned my lesson."

Aurelie stopped beside Rennet giggling under her breath.

"Did he just recognize me or something?" Rennet asked confused.

"Nope. He doesn't even remember hitting you."

Rennet looked at her, surprised. "Are you kidding me? If the man is that lucid and precise with his aim while being that drunk, I'd hate to cross him sober."

Aurelie continued to giggle while Rennet rubbed his nose, confused about the giant of a man walking around his house. They followed Archie up the steps and inside.

Archie turned and said, "Looks like you'll need a good bit of wood. You've got a few framing boards that are starting to rot. I'd go ahead and change those if I were you, but all in all the rest isn't in too bad of shape. I'd say the harmonica set will be good for at least half of what you'll need. You can come by my place after noon each day and work off the rest."

"For how long?" Rennet asked.

"It depends on how hard you work." Archie stood sizing him up.

Rennet thought for a second and agreed. "Okay. How about I start tomorrow?"

"That'll be fine. Of course, we don't work on Sunday's so tomorrow and then again on Monday. Now, let's go get your lumber so you can get started."

The Barter

They all returned to Archie's, loaded a small trailer that Archie had with what Rennet would need, attached it to the hitch on Aurelie's side-by-side and Rennet and Aurelie returned to his place, parking the trailer beneath the elevated home to protect it from rain.

"Thanks for your help today Aurelie. I'm sure I've taken more of your time than was expected."

"Yes, you have. But I wouldn't have missed seeing Archie's confusion for anything." She smiled, shaking her head at the man.

"Yeah, that was a little odd." Rennet smiled with her.

Aurelie said, "I'll go get Baxter and Birdie and have them here as soon as they have had lunch."

"Sounds good, thanks."

Aurelie looked at him. "Rennet, do you have food?"

"Yeah, I have some dried meats and a few canned goods I can heat up."

Aurelie sighed. "How about I bring you a ham sandwich and some fresh fruits and vegetables when I bring the kids?"

Rennet smiled brightly.

"That would be amazing. I haven't had ham in years."

Aurelie grinned, climbed into the cart, and rushed back to her place a few miles away. Birdie was already making lunch for her and Baxter so Aurelie added a sandwich for herself, Rennet, and Katie; which she would drop off at Sandra's on the way.

"How about we all eat at Rennet's with him instead of making him wait. That way, you can all get to work after lunch instead of waiting on him to eat?"

"I'll go for that." Baxter smiled. "Besides, I'm ready to get started."

"All right then, grab the basket, add the drinks, and let's get going."

They all made the short ride back to Rennet's, dropping Katie's lunch in the process. As they pulled up to Rennet's, they were surprised to find Archie there helping Rennet haul the wood up the stairs.

"What's going on here?" she asked Rennet who stopped for a minute to welcome the kids back.

"I'm not sure. Archie just showed back up and said he knew I couldn't haul the wood by myself." Rennet shrugged.

"I think his conscience has gotten the better of him. I believe he feels bad about punching you, although he'll never say that."

"I'll take whatever I can get." Rennet grinned.

Aurelie handed him a sandwich and they all sat and ate. When Archie reappeared a few minutes later Aurelie apologized for not having a sandwich for him.

"No problem, Aurie. I ate before I came. I promise you I don't go hungry." Archie grinned, patted his stomach, and flexed his muscles.

Everyone smiled at his antics.

Rennet added, "I'll be done in a minute, Archie."

"Take your time. A little fella' like you needs your nutrition."

Rennet blanched at that. "Little fella'?"

Aurelie grinned. "Next to Archie, everyone is a little fella'. He didn't mean anything by it, it was just an observation."

"I know that, but I'm not sure I like the observation." Rennet's face scrunched up in distaste.

They all smiled at his discomfort, finishing up their lunch. Everyone stood and Rennet stretched his frame as tall as he could, realizing he was taller than Aurelie, and she was an average height for a woman.

"Thanks for the lunch Aurelie, it was delicious. I haven't had fresh bread and smoked meat in a while."

"You're welcome. I'll also bring you some provisions back later when I pick up the kids."

"That would be most appreciated. And in exchange I'll look at those failing headlights when you come back. Just give me enough daylight to see what I'm doing."

"You got a deal."

Aurelie packed up the basket and got ready to leave while the three got to work helping Archie.

Aurelie watched the scene before her. What a strange spirit that had come over their community since Rennet had arrived. They had always had a good community where they helped one another, but now people were beginning to help each other without any form of payback required. Perhaps it was just a coincidence, a sign of things getting better; one that had nothing to do with Rennet McCabe.

S.G. Boudreaux

Chapter 8

Aurelie looked around her quiet home. She had never had a day to herself without someone around. What would she do with herself? Granted she truly only had about five hours, but that was plenty to tackle something that needed doing without interruption. Or perhaps she would do something that she wanted to do. But what? She had spent so many years taking care of everyone else, she didn't really know who she was; in the sense that she didn't know what she liked or aspired to.

"All right Aurelie, it looks like you need to figure out who you are and what you like to do for yourself; especially if you're to have so much time on your hands."

She looked around the house. There were many repairs that needed doing before the winter months set in, but the kids could help with those. She went to her room and looked around at the things she had collected over the years. She lovingly ran her hand along the cool surface of the large shells that adorned her dresser top. She looked up and gazed out of the large, double, picture-window at the sunlight streaking through the tree canopy in the yard. Her eyes landed on the two, fern-type, potted plants which sat upon her desk; the desk she had forgotten all about. Sure she recognized it as a piece of furniture that sat in her room and held her plants up to the light, but she never sat at it anymore.

Aurelie walked over to it and ran her hand along the smooth pecan wood top; the light color of the wood dotted with dark swirls in the grain. The writing desk had been in her family for as long as she could remember. She slid the chair out and sat down smoothing her hands over the surface. She lifted the small, hinged door that sat at the back and peered inside at the notebooks, pens, and pencils that lay within. She lifted one of her old notebooks out and flipped through it, smiling at memories created by the pictures and words that lay on the pages before her.

She used to like to write and draw when she was a girl. Since the collapse and life change, she hadn't done much of either. Learning to survive had been what was important for so many years, then the kids came along and things changed again. She peered down at the notebook. Perhaps she might pick it back up. But what would her subjects be? What was there to draw and write about?

She sat for the next few hours looking over all her old memorabilia, then decided to tend to some chores that needed doing outside before getting dinner ready. After her chores, she packed a small care basket for Rennet while dinner simmered on the stove. She really couldn't give him anything perishable because he had no cooler of any sort.

Thinking about this, she walked outside on the screened porch, deciding to make Rennet a couple of Zeer pots from some leftover materials she had. Besides, she had plenty of clay pots and sand with which to make them.

The Barter

Dinner had finished, the Zeer pots were done, and the basket for Rennet was packed. She took a couple of large, empty, plastic soda crates and set all the items snuggly inside. She placed the crates on the back seat of the cart and strapped them in place, then set out for Sandra's to collect Katie before heading to Rennet's.

All the driving around lately was a nice break, but if it were to be a daily thing, she would have to make some changes or else their own home and chores would suffer. Not to mention, they would have to begin hunting soon to prepare for winter. The meat cooler was getting a little low for Aurelie's comfort.

Winter in Louisiana was unpredictable. It hardly ever snowed, but the wind off the water joined with the extremely high humidity made the cold cut right to the bone. It was downright miserable most of the time. Thankfully the cold, icy, days were short lived, but hunting the swamps and marshes was harder in Winter.

She collected Katie, making plans with Sandra to bring Marie over to her place for a play-date the day after tomorrow, giving Sandra a much-needed day to herself as well. They soon reached Rennet's place where the three of them were still working on his home. The walls were all dried in from what she could see, and it appeared that Archie had left. She and Katie each grabbed a crate of goods and walked up the steps. As they stepped inside, Aurelie could see that the roof had been finished as well, and Rennet had marked the walls where he wanted to cut out to install those large windows he had talked about.

"Well, you three have really been hard at it."

The appreciation in Aurelie's voice made them all turn to her with a smile.

Rennet lay down his tools and walked over to take the crate from her, placing it on a make-shift table.

"The kids have really been a lot of help."

Baxter, and even Birdie, beamed at the praise.

Aurelie smiled brightly. "Glad to hear it."

Katie spun in circles around the empty room. "Mr. Rennet, this is going to be so pretty to live in. I would love to be able to see the water this closely all the time."

"Well, Katie, you can come visit whenever you like." Rennet grinned at her and Katie clapped her hands happily, spinning even faster.

He turned to Aurelie. "Thanks for the provisions; I really appreciate them, more than you know."

"Well, we have plenty right now. Our garden did very well with all the extra rain this year."

Rennet's faced took on a look of confusion when he gazed down at the pots. He lifted the lids off and examined the large clay pots lined with smaller ones; each filled with food. He was also curious about the sand which lay packed tightly between the two sides.

"What's this?"

Aurelie smiled. "They are called Zeer pots. It's a way to preserve food, sort of like a small refrigerator."

Rennet's surprised look told her he had never heard of them.

"How does that work?"

"You just keep the sand wet between them and it acts as an insulator."

The Barter

"That is really good to know. Let me find somewhere to put the food so you can take these home."

"No, Rennet, these are yours."

He turned to look at her, gratefulness written in his expression. "Thank you Aurelie. This is very thoughtful. What can I give you for them?" Rennet turned to grab his backpack.

"I don't need payment, Rennet. We had plenty of extra supplies to make them. I just figured you would need somewhere to keep the provisions I brought."

He stopped, looked at her thoughtfully, and grinned.

Aurelie's heart felt as though it skipped a beat. Those stinking dimples were going to do her in. She turned her attention to the house and the work they had done. "Looks like you can sleep mostly mosquito free tonight."

"Yeah, I hope so. I still plan on using my netting though. They seem to find the smallest space to get in, and one mosquito can buzz around your head all night driving you crazy."

Baxter cleared his throat. "Aurelie, can we eat now? I'm starving."

Aurelie suddenly realized the kids were there, just waiting to be fed. "Oh, I'm sorry Baxter. Yes, help yourselves. I brought some plates and silverware also."

Baxter and Birdie unpacked the dinner, while Katie took out plates, cloth napkins, and silverware. Rennet turned the crates that Aurelie had used to bring in the supplies on their sides to use as stools, while the kids sat cross-legged on the floor, their plates in their laps. The five of them enjoyed a nice meal together, discussing the work they had accomplished that day, and what tomorrow would look like.

Aurelie said, "Unfortunately, tomorrow, the kids have chores that need looking after. Their work at home is starting to pile up already."

Rennet said, "I'm sorry Aurelie, I didn't mean to take the kids from their regular work."

"No, it's fine. Their routine is just a bit off is all."

Baxter pleaded, "But Aurie, I really like helping Rennet with the building. Besides, he is teaching me good life skills."

Aurelie grinned ever so slightly at the sly twisting of Baxter's words. "I understand that Bax, but I said when you started this that you had to keep up with your work at home. I'm afraid that you are so tired and it is so late when you get back that your chores are suffering."

The wheels of Baxter's mind turned as she spoke. "How about I just come in the mornings then? And I can ride my bike over, you won't have to bring me."

Aurelie thought a moment. "What about Birdie?"

"She can ride her own bike," he stated, confused.

"I meant, what if that doesn't work for her." Aurelie grinned at him.

"I don't have to come *every* time Aurie. Besides, most of what they do only requires the two of them. I'm basically in the way."

Aurelie grinned at her attempt to get out of the work which she promised to do.

Rennet replied, "That is true, Aurelie. There is very little time where we need her. She does help, don't get me wrong. She runs and gets things for us. She runs up and down most of the time."

"Well, won't you still need her to do that?" Aurelie argued, watching Birdie out of the corner of her eye. Birdie fidgeted in her seat, looking woefully uncomfortable with each word Aurelie said.

"Not really," Rennet replied. "We can do things smarter, by bringing what we need up-stairs. We've just taken it for granted that she is here. She can come if she likes, but it isn't really necessary." Rennet grinned slightly, and he and Aurelie exchanged amused looks at the look of relief that flew across Birdie's features.

Birdie put in her two cents. "Besides, Aurie, I can take over a few of Baxter's chores at home. Not all of them mind you, but I could check the crawfish traps, and tend to the garden weeding."

Katie excitedly said, "I'll help her Aurie. I am getting older and can handle more of the chores too."

Aurelie sat for a minute, looking into the expectant faces of the three kids before her. She sighed heavily and said, "All right then. Baxter, you can help Rennet in the mornings until noon, then home and on with your regular chores."

"Yes!" Baxter said excitedly.

"Birdie, you can come help Rennet on days that he sends for you. He can let Baxter know the day before if he will need you. Other than that, you and Katie can help fill in when Baxter isn't there. But, Birdie, I need you to be extra cautious with Katie. You have to pay close attention to where she is at all times. Checking the traps can be dangerous."

"Yes, Aurie, I understand."

Aurelie looked at Katie. "Katie, are you going to listen to Birdie?"

"Yes ma'am. I promise."

"Then it's a deal. But, if it becomes too much trouble and things start lacking, then we will have to revisit the terms. Do you all understand?"

"Yes ma'am," came the unison reply.

Rennet put in, "It really shouldn't take but a few more weeks, a month at the most, to finish things up here."

"Let's hope so."

Aurelie grinned at all of them and as they finished eating their meal they talked about the plans that Rennet had made and the contribution to those plans that Baxter supplied.

Darkness began to trickle across the beach as the sun descended below the water's surface.

Rennet jumped to his feet, looking at Aurelie.

"I just remembered my promise to fix those headlights of yours."

He extended his hand to her to help her to her feet. She reluctantly took it, feeling like his hand was a hot poker beneath her own. She quickly dislodged her hand from his.

Baxter asked, "Can I come too? That way, if it ever happens again, I'll know how to fix it."

Aurelie smiled. "Sure. Girls, you two pack up the dishes and food; except for what we brought to Rennet; and bring the crates downstairs to the cart."

The Barter

"Yes ma'am," they replied.

The three of them walked down to the cart and Rennet and Baxter leaned over the motor, tracing the wires from the lights back to where they attached to the cables that led to the wiring harness. Rennet scooted beneath the cart to further inspect the wires, followed closely by Baxter. Aurelie smiled at the mimicking nature that Baxter had taken on where it concerned Rennet. She hadn't realized how much Baxter had needed this male companionship until now. He had never taken to any of the other men in the community like he had Rennet. This realization also made her a little nervous. She wasn't entirely sure that Rennet McCabe was that trustworthy of a man. She surprised herself with her thoughts, especially since she had left the children alone with him. She knew nothing about the stranger who just appeared one day and decided to call Holly Beach his home. His actions and deeds appeared to be those of an honorable man, but people pretended all the time, especially when survival was key.

Perhaps Aurelie would have a chat with the kids when they returned home, just to make certain they closely watched Rennet, just to protect themselves when she wasn't around.

"Found it!" Rennet called from under the machine. "It's a small cut in the main wire. I think this is what is causing them to flicker like they do. Baxter, run upstairs and look in my backpack. I have a roll of electrical tape in there."

"Yes Sir." Baxter quickly slid from beneath the cart and ran up the steps.

Aurelie smiled at his words. "Mr. McCabe, you seem to have everything anyone could possibly ever need in that backpack of yours."

Rennet slid out from under the cart and looked at her.

"Well, when you live on the road like I do, or did, you tend to collect anything of use. I've learned to fix nearly anything with whatever I have on hand."

"So did you help out other people in your travels like you are us?"

"Yes, many times."

"And there was never another place you ever thought of settling in over the last ten years?"

An unrecognizable emotion flashed in Rennet's eyes at her question but was quickly gone.

"There was one other place where I almost settled, but that changed after a few months." He quickly changed the subject. "I mostly aided people with work they needed doing for a place to stay for a few days, or a meal or two. Bartering is still the preferred currency across the states, but people are trying to trade paper again. Except up near the mountains and streams where mining has taken on a new life. People are trading precious minerals."

"Really. That sounds interesting." Aurelie was curious what had caused him to cut his last home-steading short.

"Here it is!" Baxter yelled from the stairs as he joined them at the cart once more.

"Thanks, Baxter."

Rennet took the roll of tape, and Baxter climbed back under the cart to watch what Rennet did. A few minutes later, the two of them were sliding out from under the cart, dusting the sand from their clothing.

"Well, you should be good to go. But if it gives you anymore problems, we can trace down any other cuts in the line." Rennet looked at Aurelie, a small grin gracing his now hairless lips.

"Thank you, Rennet. Having working lights will greatly benefit us."

"No thanks necessary. You've done far more for me than I could possibly ever repay."

The two of them looked at one another, no words to exchange. Strange emotions began to stir in Aurelie. She shook them off and turned to look at the kids that now busily encircled the cart. Baxter proceeded to strap the crates in place, making sure to leave enough room for him to sit.

Aurelie broke the silence between them. "Well, I think we should be going now."

"Bye Rennet, I'll see you tomorrow morning." Baxter excitedly stated as he settled into the seat.

"Great, Baxter. I'll provide lunch for us tomorrow." Rennet said, shaking the boy's hand. He then turned to Aurelie. "Thanks again for everything, and for letting the kids come to help. I really appreciate that. A lot of what I have to do would be very hard if I had to do it alone."

"Not a problem." She smiled. "Besides, I think it does Baxter as much good as it does you."

Rennet nodded. "Goodnight Aurelie Haydel."

She offered him a crooked grin. "Goodnight Rennet McCabe."

As she drove away, the kids all yelled their goodbyes, waving to Rennet as they disappeared down the street.

Rennet wasn't sure why he was so drawn to Aurelie Haydel, except for the obvious reasons of course. She was physically beautiful for one, and he greatly admired someone of her age taking care of three strangers and treating them as her own. Plus, she had a sweet spirit, what he had witnessed so far that is. Everything that he had asked of her, she had done, even though he could often sense some hesitation, but that was to be expected. She didn't know much about him either and yet still trusted him with the kids. He would have to make sure not to harm that growing trust in any way.

God had brought him all the way out here to explore. He had passed many a back-road in his travels, inquiring of the locals where those roads led. Like all the other times, the people closer to the larger towns had told them there was nothing to see this far out. Nothing but the muddy ocean water of the Louisiana coastline. But something still stirred him to travel that long, lonely, desolate, highway to this small community where he thought he found what he was searching for the last five years. A place to call home, and maybe even someone with whom to build a future.

Rennet stood gazing out at the breaking water on the beach. He pondered the darkness of the ocean before him. He had seen blue water elsewhere and was curious as to why it was so muddy looking here; another question to ask Aurelie later. He grinned to himself. Hopefully Aurelie wouldn't grow tired of his questions because he was growing to like her quite a lot, and he hoped that one day she would return those feelings.

Chapter 9

Aurelie awoke to the sound of the screen door slamming. She sat up in her bed and peered out the picture window just as Baxter flew out of the yard on his bike, headed toward Rennet's. She smiled at his exuberance and swung her legs over the edge of the bed. She stood up, slipped on her house-shoes, and stretched. She padded into the kitchen, which was just a few rooms away and noticed that Baxter; in his haste to help Rennet; had left behind a small mess from his quick breakfast of boiled eggs and toast. But Aurelie didn't mind cleaning up after him.

After she tended to the small mess, she put on some coffee and went back to her room to change. She then stepped out the back door off the screened porch and went to check on Baxter's morning chores. She realized that he had already completed some of them before he even left. One of which was feeding the dogs. They had two hounds, one was the mother and was ancient, and the pup, another female was nearly six years old. They used them when tracking prey during hunting season.

Aurelie smiled and squatted as she petted the dogs. "Good morning girls. Baxter must really want to continue to help Rennet." The animals returned her affection, nearly bowling her over in the process.

"All right, that's enough. I don't have time to romp with you this morning." She stood and walked over to the garden, grabbing a basket off the porch steps, and harvesting whatever was ripe and ready to be picked. While tending to that, she also picked off any bugs and dropped them into the bucket of water that sat at the garden's edge for just this purpose. She was bending over plucking a rather large horned wormed from one of the tomato plants when someone startled her.

"Good morning, Aurie."

She nearly jumped out of her skin, dropping most of her collected produce on the ground. No one ever visited unannounced. Plus, she couldn't mistake that voice for anything.

She didn't even bother looking up as she bent to pick up the spilled basket. "Arjit, what on earth brings you out here this time of the morning?" She finished picking things up and walked to the edge of the garden to set the basket on the ground.

"Can't a friend come to visit?" He smiled at her, hoping to ease the intrusion.

"You don't normally." She looked at him point blank, shoving her hands into her back pockets.

"Oh, well, I had a cow get loose and I came over to see if she was here."

"I haven't seen any of your cows. They don't normally escape do they?" Arjit prided himself on keeping his livestock inside the fences.

"No, but one did manage. Mind if I look around and see if I can find her."

"I suppose not. I'll just be here in the garden should you need anything."

"Great, I shouldn't be too long. You only have a few acres here."

She just grinned painfully and nodded. She knew that was a remark about the size of her place compared to his. It wasn't like she cared but Arjit certainly did. He boasted about having the largest spread around. His father was an old rancher from way back, and he inherited the land from his father, and his from those before him. She watched him look around the yard and fields, searching down the small paths that led through the junk piles. Aurelie grabbed the basket and continued with her small harvest, then stepped inside to wash the produce.

As she was standing at the kitchen sink, Arjit walked in and asked, "You got some coffee?"

Aurelie jumped again, this time slinging water all over her shirt front.

"Good grief, Arjit. Can't you announce your presence in some other way?" She aggravatingly dried her hands and wiped her wet shirt front.

"Sorry. Why are you so jumpy anyway?"

"I'm not jumpy. I'm just not used to having people sneaking around my property," she stated flatly.

"Oh. Well, coffee?" he stated.

She sighed and pointed to the pot on the stove. "Help yourself."

"Thanks. Are uh, you going to join me?" he asked, a small smile on his lips as he poured himself a steaming cup of liquid.

"I guess so. I haven't had mine yet."

"Maybe that's why you're so jumpy."

She glanced at him with irritation, rolled her eyes, and poured herself a cup.

"Did you find your cow?"

"What? Oh, um, no. She's not here." He leaned against the counter, crossing his legs at the ankles and blew on the steaming mug in his hands.

"Well, aren't you concerned about where she's gotten to?"

"Only a little. They usually find their way back. She's likely in an outer field somewhere."

Aurelie watched him closely. Had he really lost a cow, or was that excuse made up to come pester her?

"So, Aurie, what have you and the kids been up to lately?"

"Life. Why do you want to know?"

"Just making polite conversation. I uh, I hear that you all have been spending quite a lot of time around that Rennet fellow."

Aurelie blanched at his words. "Maybe we have. Are you spying on me Arjit?"

"No. I just wanted to make sure that the guy understood that you and I have an agreement."

"Do we now?" Aurelie sat her cup on the counter and crossed her arms over her chest as she looked questioningly at Arjit.

He grinned and set his cup on the counter. "Well, now Aurelie, you know I like you, and I figure you know that I'm quite a catch around here."

"Is that so?" She just continued to watch him, trying to keep her nerves steady and her tone flat.

"Come on Aurie, we've had this tension between us going on for years. You're just hesitant to take a chance."

She nearly laughed out loud at his comment. "Well, now Arjit," she copied his tone from earlier, "there has definitely been *tension* between us for years. But it is *not* the kind you think it is. I am not now, nor have I ever been, attracted to you in any way. I hope I'm making myself perfectly clear here."

Arjit looked sideways at her. "It's that Rennet fella' isn't it?"

"Good grief, Arjit! It has nothing to do with Rennet McCabe and everything to do with you. Look, I'm not trying to hurt your feelings here, but we have never had any kind of romantic relationship brewing. I have never thought of you in that way. And I have tried over the years to discourage your attentions. You're just too hard-headed to get it. I am not attracted to you."

His hands went to his hips and he paced a little. "Now Aurie, I don't understand that."

"I know you don't. That is part of the problem. Now I suggest you go on and find your lost cow. We have nothing else to discuss."

He dropped his hands and was about to take a step toward her when the girls appeared in the kitchen. They both stopped, surprised to find Arjit in their house.

"Good morning Mr. Arjit." Katie bounced in and sat at the table.

He stopped and turned to them, nodded to both girls, then turned back to look at Aurelie. She stood at the counter, her arms crossed defiantly across her chest, just calmly looking at him.

"This isn't over, Aurelie." He stormed out the kitchen door.

"Yes it is, Arjit," she called to his retreating back.

Birdie followed him onto the screened porch and watched him storm around the house to his side-by-side and take off down the road.

"Well that was interesting," she said as she came back into the kitchen.

"Interesting is right."

"What's not over?" Katie asked as she poured some milk into a cup.

"Nothing to concern yourself about, Sweetie. You and Birdie have your breakfast and get to your chores."

The girls ate while Aurelie drank her coffee, definitely needing a second cup. Not that the caffeine would calm her nerves, but the warmth of the mug in her hand and the rich taste gave her some comfort. Arjit Chiasson was growing quite bold in his advances and was beginning to be a real problem. She always figured he would get the message eventually and just let her be, but apparently he wasn't going to go away that easily. Surely after her admonishment a few minutes ago he would back off, but if he was true to his word, she was afraid that she *hadn't* heard the last of it.

Rennet and Baxter cut the holes in the walls where the windows were going to go. Baxter stood appreciating their work.

"That's some view, Rennet. Except for the few houses in front there, you almost have an unob-structed view of the water. The breeze is nice too."

"That's what I'm banking on. It's really hot here." Rennet stood beside Baxter and smiled at the scenery before him as he peered between the houses. The view of the ocean wasn't completely unblocked, but it was good enough. "Now, let's go get those windows and haul them up here so we can insert them."

They made their way downstairs, calling a hello to Sophanes and Anytos who were just a few houses over working on Sophanes' place.

"How's the build going, Rennet?"

"Great. How about yours?"

"Can't complain. I should be able to move into it next week."

"That's great, Sophanes."

Sophanes stopped his work and made his way down the steps and across the sparsely covered grassy area. "So, how did your meeting with Archie go yesterday?"

"Just fine. You know, he didn't even realize he was the one who hit me?"

Sophanes and Baxter looked at one another with surprise.

"Aurelie said it was because he was so intoxicated that he doesn't remember doing it. He did sort of apologize also."

Sophanes started laughing. "Well, I've never heard Archie offer an apology, so it probably had something to do with Aurelie fussing at him about it."

Rennet wondered if that were true.

Sophanes turned to Baxter. "So, it appears you have some help."

Baxter smiled. "Yes sir. Rennet has taught me a lot already about construction work and building. One day, I'll be able to build my own place."

Sophanes slapped Baxter on the shoulder. "Good for you, Bax. It's good to have a plan. Every man needs to think on his future."

Baxter smiled even bigger at Sophanes calling him a man.

Sophanes turned to Rennet. "What about you Rennet? Any plans on what you are going to do once you finish your place?"

Rennet shrugged. "Not yet. I'm just trying to get the basic necessities down, like food and shelter. Fortunately Aurelie gave me some provisions yesterday to tide me over for a while, but I need to get a small garden going."

"Well, Procne can probably help with that. The man's got a green thumb. Plus, he keeps some animals for the manure and ground fertilization."

"Thanks, I'll check with him."

"I'll need to do the same thing at my place so maybe you and I can go in together on some of the bartering for the fertilizer and plants we'll need."

"Sounds like a good idea, thanks Sophanes. You and Anytos have really been very helpful to me since I arrived. I don't think I've said thank you."

"You're welcome." He smiled broadly. "Anytime you need something Rennet, just stop by, Neighbor." Sophanes turned and went back to work while Rennet and Baxter did the same.

As the two walked back to Rennet's place, Rennet said, "We need to get the windows installed before I have to leave after lunch. I don't want to come home to a house full of mosquitoes this evening. But I think we can manage to install three windows before lunch."

"Right. How hard can it be?" Baxter shrugged and grinned at him.

"I guess we're going to find out."

The two hauled the windows one at a time up the stairs, then began fitting them into the wall from the inside. Rennet scratched his head about the fitting.

"These are supposed to mount from the outside. How am I going to hang these two? The balcony doesn't extend all the way around."

Baxter and Rennet peered out of the holes looking down at the ground, then up toward the roof line.

Rennet scratched his head again in thought. "I should have thought about this before I cut the holes."

Baxter offered, "Maybe we can drop them down from the roof?

"Whatever we used to drop them will get in the way of the installation. Maybe we should just walk over to Archie's and see if he has any ideas."

"Okay. If you like, I have my bike and I can just ride over there quickly and ask him?"

"All right, that sounds good. Thanks Baxter."

As Baxter ran down the stairs he yelled, "Be back soon."

While Baxter was gone Rennet cleared away some of the building waste making a burn pile in front of his house. Baxter was only gone for about ten minutes when he returned carrying two sets of very large, hand-held, suction cups.

"Hey Rennet, Archie said to use these. He said to clean the windows really well first, get these cups a little wet and place them on the windows. They should allow for an easier install."

"Well yeah, but how do I nail them in place? You didn't happen to see if Archie had a really long ladder I could use?"

"Nah, I didn't look, sorry."

"Well, you couldn't have carried it back on your bike anyhow. We'll have to walk down there and see."

They both left once again and walked the mile to Archie's building. Once they arrived they found Archie sitting on the small, covered, porch playing the harmonica's Rennet had traded to him.

"Hey Archie," Rennet called.

Archie stopped and turned to see who was approaching. "Rennet. You need something else?"

"As a matter of fact I do. You wouldn't happen to have a long ladder I can borrow do you?"

"I do." Archie stood and walked inside the building followed by Rennet and Baxter. The aisles of the building were packed tightly and it was a struggle to get through some areas. "It's near the back here. I've been meaning to organize in here for a long time, I just never got around to it. I figure that's what we will tackle when you come in to work this afternoon."

Rennet nodded. "Sounds like a good idea."

"Here it is." Archie slid some large pieces of old plywood around and pulled out a long sixteen-foot extension ladder. "This should do you just fine."

Archie hefted the ladder over his head to haul it outside of the jumbled and disorganized building. "You two can handle it from here." He handed it over to Rennet and Baxter who both took an end to carry it back to Rennet's.

Rennet turned to the man. "Thanks for this Archie. I'll have it back as soon as possible."

Archie just waved it off. "No hurry. It's not like I use it much anyway. I have a few of them lying around somewhere. That's just the one I saw recently so I knew where it was."

"Well, thanks just the same. See you in a few hours."

"Will do."

They carried the heavy ladder all the way back to Rennet's.

Rennet turned to Baxter and said, "Thank goodness you were here to help me haul this thing back here." They were both breathing hard from the exertion.

"Yeah. I figured it was lighter than it is since Archie just hefted the whole thing over his head."

They placed the ladder on the ground against a house pole and took a small breather.

"You have noticed the size of Archie's biceps haven't you? There nearly as big around as your head."

Baxter laughed. "Yeah, Archie's always been a big guy. Aurelie says that when she was little, before the collapse, she remembers him being a weight-lifter. He used to compete in beach muscle competitions."

"Well, he must still work out because he's still strong as an ox."

"Maybe you can figure that out when you go work for him later."

"Speaking of, we've already killed an hour and have three windows to install. Let's get to it."

They leaned the ladder under one of the cut-outs, then prepped the windows, and placed the large suction cups on the inside of it. Rennet ran outside and climbed the ladder, after which, Baxter handed him some nails through the opening and he stuck them in his pocket. He then hung the hammer from a belt loop and they commenced trying to install the window.

Sophanes and Anytos noticed the struggle Rennet was having and stopped what they were doing to go help. Sophanes also had a ladder which they hauled over. Anytos went inside to help Baxter to hold the heavy window in place while Sophanes and Rennet worked from the outside. An hour later, they had two of the windows placed in the wall. The third would be easier since they could stand on that part of the porch to reach it.

"Thanks again guys," Rennet said to the two men.

"Not a problem," Anytos stated.

"Would you like something to drink?" Rennet offered them some of the water he had.

"No, that's okay. We have our own water at my place. You keep that for yourself and Baxter," Sophanes answered.

"All right. But I do plan on having a little get together here when this is finished. Just to say thanks to everyone who has helped me."

They both smiled. "We're always ready for a party."

"Maybe another crawfish boil." Rennet stated.

Baxter put in. "Not likely. The season's done. But we can have a crab boil. I can even show you how to catch them."

"Great."

Rennet slapped the boy on the shoulder.

Sophanes and Anytos left while Rennet and Baxter installed the last window before eating lunch. Afterward, Baxter left for home and Rennet left for his shift at Archie's.

As Rennet walked down the road, he greeted and waved to anyone who was outside. He had neighbors and he was making friends which was something he hadn't really had since he had left home all those years ago. He took a deep, satisfying, breath, and grinned, adjusting his still full backpack which he carried everywhere because he never knew when he might need something. Just as he got near Archie's place, he saw Arjit standing outside speaking to Archie. When Arjit saw him coming, his stance straightened and there was a strange look on his face. One that told Rennet he might have a problem on his hands.

Chapter 10

Rennet approached Archie's as Arjit continued to stare him down.

"Afternoon fella's," Rennet offered.

Archie replied. "Afternoon, Rennet."

Arjit didn't respond, only glared at him.

Rennet nodded at him as he passed him by. "Archie, where can I stow my bag?"

"Just put it in the office or behind the front desk."

Their words caught Arjit's attention. "What's going on here, Archie?"

"What do you mean, Arjit?"

"Is that guy working for you?"

"Well, if it's any of your business, which it's not, he's working off the extra lumber he needs to rebuild his place."

"What place? He isn't from here."

"He squatted one of the abandoned cottages down on the beach."

Arjit's jaw clenched. "What's he staying here for anyway?"

"Why don't you ask him that. It ain't none of my business where the man wants to hang his hat. Can't say as I blame him though. We have a right nice community, and you can't beat the view."

"Yes, and we don't know anything about this guy. He could be dangerous."

"Nah, I doubt that." Archie stated. "Is there something you wanted this morning, Arjit?"

"Well, I need eight fence posts, and a bale of wire if you have it. I have some poles that rotted and need to be replaced."

"All right. I have some around back. I'll send Rennet out with them in a bit. What do you have to trade with today?"

"I have a few roasts and some rib meat. Will that do?"

"That'll do just fine."

Arjit watched Archie go back inside the building. He leaned against the side-by-side to wait for Rennet to make an appearance with his posts.

Archie rounded a corner inside just as Rennet was coming back to look for him.

"Arjit needs some fence posts and wire. Follow me and I'll show you where to find them. Then you can haul them up front to load on his trailer."

"Sure."

He followed Archie through the store toward the back of the building.

"What did you do to Arjit Chiasson anyway? The guy really doesn't like you."

"Just my appearance here I guess."

"Hmmm…" Archie shrugged and stopped in front of a pile of fence posts that were lying stacked on the floor. He then grabbed a large flat cart that was parked beside another wall and wheeled it over.

"Stack eight of those fence posts on here while I look for some wire. If you're done putting them on the cart before I return, just go ahead and haul them out to Arjit and load them on his trailer."

The Barter

Rennet loaded the required poles onto the cart and pulled them through a wider area of the building. He had to stop a few times and move things aside to get through. By the time he got the cart outside, Archie had already given Arjit the wire.

Arjit jeered. "What took so long?"

Rennet didn't answer him. He knew that no matter what he said Arjit wouldn't care.

Archie answered him. "The aisles are a mess in there. Rennet here is going to help me get things organized."

Arjit just nodded at him, then turned to eye Rennet as he loaded the poles onto his trailer.

"All right Arjit, you're loaded. When are you bringing my meat over?"

"I'll come back in an hour."

"I'll be waiting." Archie nodded and waved him off as Rennet returned the flat cart inside to the back of the building where Archie found it. He then went to the front where Archie laid out the plan for the day. Rennet suggested they start in the front, putting things where they belonged, and hanging or building needed shelving and storage areas to hold the wood straight up against the walls, making use of the ceiling height. Archie liked his plan. The men worked hard for the next five hours, getting nearly half the building organized and managed to build four wood storage bins.

"Well, Rennet McCabe, I'd say we did a good days work. I haven't seen this much of the floor for twenty years." Archie smiled at him.

"Yeah, the place looks nice, and it will be easier to find your stock this way."

"You want something to drink?"

"That would be great, thanks Archie."

Archie went to the office and returned with two bottles of water, handing one off to Rennet.

"Thanks." Rennet took a long drink of the cool liquid. "Well, I guess I'll be going now. I'll see you tomorrow?"

"Not tomorrow. We don't work on Sundays here."

"Oh, right. So does something happen on Sundays?"

"There's church services under the pavilion, as long as it don't rain."

"Got it. I guess I'll see you there tomorrow."

"Not me. I just don't get into the whole churchin' thing."

"Why not, if you don't mind me asking?" Rennet hoped he hadn't stepped on Archie's toes with the question.

Archie eyed him for a second before answering. He shrugged and said, "Just haven't been into it since Ma passed. She used to go all the time."

"How did she die?"

"Cancer. It ate her all up. She prayed and prayed about it all the time. So did I when I was young. It didn't do any good. I figured maybe we did too much bad stuff for God to listen to us."

"I don't know about that Archie. I believe all things happen for a reason. And no one is above salvation, no matter what happened in the past. Forgiveness is free to everyone who asks." Rennet finished the bottle of water and handed the empty bottle back to Archie, knowing it was likely reused.

The Barter

Archie took it and set it on the counter, not saying anything.

"Well, have a good night and day tomorrow, Archie. I'll see you Monday afternoon."

"Yep." Archie nodded, and Rennet grabbed his pack from the floor and slipped it on his back. He decided to walk the beach area instead of taking the slightly paved road home.

The air was warm and the breeze was a little stronger than it normally was. It felt as though a storm might be brewing somewhere. Rennet picked up a few larger shells as he walked, sticking them into a large outside, netted, pocket on his backpack. He waved and said hello to the others along the way, making it home in twenty minutes. He stowed his stuff and started a fire outside on which to heat some food. He found a large piece of log that had been cut off and rolled it over to his fireside. He sat down and watched the water break on the sand as he enjoyed the peaceful evening.

Foesy and Reesa Divins watched the young man go about the motions of life. Their granddaughter Reine watched with interest as well.

Reesa said, "I think we should go say hello, he is a neighbor now after-all."

Foesy replied, "But we don't know much about him yet?"

"How else are you going to get to know a body unless you introduce yourself." Reesa gave him a questioning look.

"True. But there ain't no rush. It appears that he is settling in for a while."

Reine dreamily said, "I hope he stays. I think he's handsome."

"Maybe so," Reesa said, "but he's far too old for you young lady."

"Why? It's not like there are many options, Memee."

"Well, understand he isn't one of them," Foesy stated plainly.

Reine crossed her arms defiantly over her chest and sat back in the chair.

"Besides, I think he's already set his sights on young Aurelie Haydel." Reesa grinned at Foesy and nodded to Reine.

Reine said, "Why do all the men take to Aurelie?"

Reesa turned to the girl. "Well, she's of proper age, pretty, smart, kind, and like you said, there isn't a lot of choices when selecting a mate now-a-days."

"So what am I supposed to do then?" Reine whined.

"The Good Lord will take care of the details when the time comes. Just like he did for Aurelie Haydel." Reesa smiled.

Foesy looked at his wife with a smirk. "You don't know that woman."

"I'm as certain of it as I am of you." She smiled brightly at him and winked.

Reine rolled her eyes at her grandparents obvious affection for one another. Though inside, she smiled, hoping that one day she would have that kind of marriage. Then she looked at Rennet McCabe and smiled again.

Rennet glanced over at the family who lived in the camp in front of his toward the beach. The Divins' home was off to the left a bit between his third row, and Sophanes' first row beach cottage. They seemed to be a nice family. He noticed the young girl smile coyly at him. He nodded at her and waved.

That's all he needed, one more young girl crushing on him. Emilie was enough, and technically, she was of proper age. But she was not the one for him. He thought of Aurelie Haydel once again. The woman seemed to invade his thoughts more times than not.

His food began to sizzle on the fire so he turned it over to brown the other side. He opened a container of beans Aurelie had left. There was rice and sausage with it. He sniffed the concoction and tasted it. It was good but needed to be warmed. He removed his meat from the pan to cool and dumped the beans, sausage, and rice into the pot. He ate his meat while it warmed, noticing the sky beginning to grow dark as large storm clouds rolled in. He started picking things up to move them inside while the beans continued to heat. By the time the beans were warmed enough, the rain began pelting the sand.

Rennet grabbed the pot from the fire and ran up the stairs into his house. He made it inside just before the skies opened and let loose their load. He stood at one of the large windows they installed that morning, watching the rain and enjoying the pot of beans; grateful they had gotten the windows done or else his house would have been full of water. He looked down at the pot of beans, also grateful for people who thought about his needs. Food here sure tasted different than it did in other places. There was so much flavor and the things they ate here were different than in other states. They were even a bit different when it came to northern and southern Louisiana. He was really going to like it here. He grinned at the smoky flavor with each bite and was surprised at how quickly his stomach filled. He looked at the pot noticing that there was still plenty of the red beans and rice left, so he scooped it back into the bowl he dumped it from and stored it in the largest Zeer Pot. He then took a chair and sat in front of the window again, enjoying the lightning, wind, and rain over the expanse of water.

As lightning flashed in the sky, he noticed movement beneath the Divins cottage. When it flashed again, he saw Foesy struggling with a ladder and a tarp. Rennet jumped to his feet and ran out the door, down the steps through the pouring rain, and over to Foesy's place.

"Mr. Divins, can I help you with something?"

Foesy jumped at the sound of his name. "Oh, uh, sure. We have a leak on the roof. Reesa told me to get this tarp up there before the next storm came through but I forgot."

"Well, I don't think it's a good idea to get up there right now to cover it. The wind's too strong. This tarp will act like a sail and pull you right off."

Foesy looked at the tarp in his hands. "I suppose you're right about that. Reesa's already madder than a cotton mouth."

"How about I come over to help you in the morning when the storm is over and we can better see?"

Foesy looked surprised at the offer. "Sure, that would be really nice, thank you, Rennet is it?"

"Yes sir."

"Well, just call me Foesy, Rennet."

"All right, Foesy. How long do these storms usually last?" Rennet peered out at the still heavily falling rain.

"That depends on the speed of the wind."

"Well it's whipping around pretty good right now."

"Yeah, it is. So I figure that in about another fifteen minutes or so, it'll be calm enough to climb up there."

"Yes, but it will also likely be slippery. That's a long way down." Rennet looked over at the height of his house which was just as tall as the Divins' place."

"True, but if another storm comes through tonight after this one, I'll have a mess on my hands when it's over."

Rennet looked at the older man, worry creasing his brow as he peered up at the underneath of his home.

"I'll tell you what," Rennet said, "as soon as the wind dies down and the rain slacks off, I'll climb up and tack the tarp down for you. Just tell me where to put it."

"Oh, you don't have to do that, I can take care of it. I just need someone to hold the ladder still."

"Let me do the climbing Foesy. I'm younger and stronger, and probably more sure footed as well. Besides, I don't have anyone to worry about should I get hurt. Your family needs you."

Foesy looked at him, a surprised look on his face. "I guess I never thought of it like that.

I guess living and being alone gives one a different perspective on things."

"Yeah, it does." Rennet stated, looking out at the slowing wind and rain.

"Well, regardless of whether or not you have someone to look after, you just be careful up there." Foesy grinned at him and nodded his thanks.

"Oh I plan on it," Rennet gave him a crooked smile. "Just because I'm single, doesn't mean I'm ready to meet my maker yet."

Foesy smiled at him. "Oh, it looks like it's stopping. By the time we get the ladder and tarp up the steps to the porch, the majority of the rain on the roof should be cleared off."

"Let's go then. I'll take the front of the ladder and the tarp. You grab the hammer and nails."

The two of them hefted the ladder and hauled it up to the second level of the porch. Reesa and Reine watched them from the living room window. Reesa stepped outside holding a small slicker over her head.

"You two be careful up there. It's dark and wet."

"We will Reesie," Foesy said. "Rennet here is doing all the climbing anyway. I'm just handing him stuff. You go on inside." Rennet climbed the ladder, tossing the tarp, hammer, and nails on the roof.

"I can hold the ladder down here if it'll help you and him to get the tarp down faster. You can pull the tarp from the lower end from the top of the ladder. Besides, you'll have to show him where to place the tarp."

"That's a good idea, Reesie. You sure are a smart one." Foesy kissed her appreciatively on the cheek.

"Just be careful on this ladder, Foesy. It's slippery." Reesa pulled the slicker on to free her hands, and grabbed the ladder on the sides, placing her feet at the base to keep it from slipping on the wet, aged, deck boards.

Foesy instructed Rennet where to put the tarp, and Rennet tapped the nails on the corners and edge of the tarp as Foesy pulled it into place from below, holding it down so it wouldn't blow around in the small wind gusts. Rennet had the tarp nailed in place within fifteen minutes and was slowly coming down off the roof when he slipped on the wet tarp, landing hard on his rear and right shoulder.

Foesy yelled, "You all right?"

Rennet gave him a thumbs up and scooted to the edge where the ladder was. They both climbed down off the roof, pulling down the ladder and laying it against the porch railing. Reesa ushered them inside the house just as the rain began to fall harder once more.

"Reine," she said, "run and get the men some towels to dry off."

"Yes ma'am." Reine hurriedly left the room.

"Come on in here to the kitchen and set down. I'll make a nice pot of hot tea. Or do you prefer coffee, Rennet?" Reesa looked at him.

"Tea is fine. I haven't had a cup of hot tea in ages."

Foesy and Rennet settled on the wooden chairs at the four-person table. The storm outside picked up once more as lightning flashed across the sky and the thunder boomed. Reine returned with the towels handing them off to the men. They thanked her and she grinned at Rennet, then sat down in a chair straight across from him, leaning her elbows on the table and resting her chin in her palm.

"Rennet, I sure appreciate your help with that. I couldn't have done it alone, not in this storm. What can I trade you for your services?"

"I don't need anything, Foesy. I'm glad I could help."

Foesy looked surprised by his answer. "Well, thanks again. If you need anything by way of solar powered equipment, you just let me know. I have just about anything you can imagine."

"Thanks, Foesy, I appreciate that. I need to figure out what I'm going to do for bartering first."

"No, I mean whatever you need is yours. You've done me a great service."

"Well, thanks Foesy, but I still have to barter with others. About the only thing I'm good at is minor repairs on things, and photography. I used to photograph nature a lot, but with traveling around, I couldn't exactly bring my darkroom equipment with me. I have a bag full of undeveloped film from my travels."

"Where do you get all the film?"

"Traveling through one of the larger cities I came across an abandoned electronics store. There wasn't much left in it, but I did find a really nice camera and a ton of film for it in the stockroom. I grabbed all I could. The only problem is that eventually I ran out of batteries for the camera, and those are very hard to find."

The Barter

Reesa returned to the table with the steaming mugs of hot water and tea bags. "Foesy here can probably turn that camera into a solar powered device. He's a whiz with electronics. Or he might have some batteries to fit it."

They both thanked the woman for the hot liquid.

"I sure can give it a try. I've never done it with a camera, but I've turned most other things into solar power."

"Thanks, Foesy. I'll bring it to you tomorrow."

Reine said, "I'd love to see some of your photographs."

Reesa agreed. "So would I. I bet you've taken some pretty interesting pictures while you were traveling all over."

Rennet sipped from the mug and nodded. "I have. The destruction was pretty intense in some places, especially the larger cities. But then the more I traveled, the more regrowth I saw. Especially in the countryside where nature existed the most. Every time I would see an animal, I would snap a photo, sort of trying to document what still existed after the collapse and wars. Walking down highway 27, I saw more wildlife than I had in a while."

Reesa said, "I bet you have some beautiful photographs. Too bad you couldn't figure out a way to develop those pictures."

"I'd like to see them myself, Reesa." Rennet smiled at her. They chatted for a little longer as they watched the storm howl outside. About thirty minutes later, the rain stopped and nightfall had arrived in full force. It was late evening when Rennet excused himself to go home.

"Come back and visit any time you like, Rennet." Reesa smiled at him.

"Thank you, Reesa, and same goes for all of you at my place."

Rennet walked out the door noticing the ladder still leaning against the railing. He carried it down the steps for Foesy, storing it where they had found it earlier. Foesy wasn't a feeble man, but he had to be in his late sixties. He walked the short distance to his place, climbed the steps and stepped inside. The large moon outside streamed light into his living room through the windows, illuminating the space enough for him to see without having to light a candle. He changed into some dry clothing, laid down on his bedroll, and quickly fell asleep.

Chapter 11

Aurelie awoke Sunday morning to even more rain. It wasn't a storm like it had been last night, but the rain was steadily coming down. She stood in her kitchen sipping on the coffee in her hand and watching the rain fall. Well, it looks like church might be called off this morning. The house was still quiet because she let the kids sleep in on Sundays. They only did the bare necessities on Sunday, and they had all been working extra hard the last two days helping Rennet, Sandra, and the extra work at home. She took her coffee and went to sit on the swing that hung on the front porch.

The air was cool and the mist from the rain lightly brushed her face and hands as she gently swung. She closed her eyes and just listened to the sounds of the rain on the metal roof. The way it hit the trees and trickled down each leaf. The thick canopy of trees around the house worked nearly like an umbrella, and the rain took on different sounds as it worked its way downward.

She looked over at the dog kennel. Chicken, which was the youngest of their dogs, was curled up near the back wall. The kids named her chicken because as a pup everything scared her. Maybelle, the mother hound, was nearing twelve. She was old, and with her last litter of pups; which was where Chicken came from; they had kept one. They knew that one day Maybelle would grow too old and pass on. Maybelle lay just inside the covered area by the doorway, watching Aurelie.

Aurelie smiled at all the memories that were popping into her head. The years she spent with Maybelle, hunting, fishing, and playing.

The screen door squeaked open and out stepped Baxter with a cup of coffee milk in hand. He was trying to grow up and therefore had been trying to get used to coffee. The extra honey and milk he added to his cup made it so sweet it was more like drinking sugar-water.

"Good morning, Bax."

"Morning, Aurie." He sat down beside her on the swing.

"So, how's building going over at Rennet's?"

"Really good. I've learned a lot. We installed three big windows yesterday. It's a good thing we got them in before all this rain started."

"That's great Bax. I'm glad you're enjoying your time with Rennet."

"Yeah. It feels good to build things with my own two hands."

Aurelie grinned at him, and he grinned back. They sat quietly, drinking their coffee for a while longer until the silence was broken once again by Birdie and Katie appearing with their morning beverages of coffee milk and orange juice.

They were fortunate to have many luxuries being in the country as they were. Their community had a nice array of fruit trees, livestock, and plant life, making things like orange juice a possibility.

They all sat quietly for a bit until the rain began to let up. Then they all went inside for breakfast and to get ready for Sunday services.

The Barter

Two hours later they were all seated in the side-by-side headed toward the pavilion. Birdie happily held the sheet music in her hands, ready to hand it off to the musicians. They always arrived a little earlier than the congregation due to Birdie needing to practice her songs with the others.

Aurelie, Baxter, and Katie took that time to walk along the beach a little, collecting shells for Birdie and Katie to make into crafts the kids would use to barter. Michael Guittreaux, one of the gentlemen in their community, would carve wooden toys in his spare time, mainly for the kids to have something fun for which to barter.

Katie excitedly picked up a large spiral shell, nearly as large as her hand. "Look at this one Aurie. Isn't it pretty?"

"It sure is. What are you going to do with that one?"

"Well, I think I'll make a wind-chime. I have many smaller ones like it at home."

"I think that would be a great idea."

Katie excitedly picked up more shells, tucking them carefully into the woven, net, bag she carried each time they came to the beach.

Aurelie smiled, watching Katie and Baxter looking for shells. She looked out over the elevated cottages to her right. She noticed that Sophanes' place was nearly finished, and she could see a large tarp over Foesy's roof that hadn't been there the other day. Right behind Foesy's was Rennet's cottage; the large windows and repair work he had done to the once run-down place made her smile. She always hated seeing homes abandoned and falling apart. It made her want to fix them up. Of course, there was no reason to do that. It wasn't like people were vying to move into them. Rennet was their only new visitor since her father had brought the kids home.

Just then, Rennet appeared on his porch, a coffee cup in hand as he stood looking out over the water. Aurelie quickly averted her gaze, not wanting him to think she was watching him.

"All right you two, it's time to turn back. Church will be starting soon."

"Okay." Katie announced, nearly skipping past Aurelie; she and Baxter racing in the sand toward the pavilion, laughing and teasing one another as they went.

Aurelie smiled at their relationship. Even though Baxter was trying his hardest to grow up, he still never balked at playing with the girls.

Rennet watched Aurelie on the beach. She and the kids turned around and headed back toward the pavilion. They were having church services today and Rennet hadn't been to a church service in years. There had been a few communities he had passed through in his travels where they had services, but not many.

He finished off his coffee, went downstairs to the makeshift, outside, shower he had constructed with some old lumber and a bucket, using the captured rainwater from yesterday's storm to clean up. He then went upstairs, found the best clothing that he owned, noting a few holes and tears in his jeans.

The Barter

As he was walking down the steps, he met up with the Divins, also walking to church. Reesa noticed the state of his pants.

"Rennet, if you bring me your clothing by later, I'll patch all of the holes for you. It's the least I can do to repay you for your help last night."

Rennet smiled at the woman. "No payment necessary, Reesa, but my clothes could use some repairs. I'll bring you some items after church."

She smiled, and the four of them chatted amiably as they made the mile long walk to the pavilion.

Rennet noticed that the crowd was nearly as large as it had been when he first came here. Of course, he didn't see Eloi or Archie in attendance, but it appeared that most everyone else was here, including Arjit Chiasson. That man seriously did not like him. He could only assume because he felt threatened by Rennet when it came to Aurelie; if what Emilie had told him was true.

Birdie and Katie smiled and waved to Rennet. He returned their kindness, and Baxter came over to shake his hand.

"Morning, Rennet." The boy smiled and stood beside him for services.

Rennet grinned at him and nodded. He looked around the pavilion. Nearly everyone he had met here made him feel welcome. No one pried into his past or asked him very many questions. Of course, he hadn't really spoken to too many people yet. He had only been here for five days, and had already found a home, friends, and quite possibly a future.

This last thought made him look at Aurelie who watched with pride as Birdie sang the hymns to begin the services. Directly after the music, Procne Crusenberry stepped up and opened a Bible and led services. Thirty minutes later, it was over, and people milled about visiting with one another. Many people came over to speak to him and introduce themselves. Jess Evanko was one of those people. As she stood speaking to Rennet, her gaze often shifted to Sophanes, who was visiting with someone else.

"So, Rennet, what made you decide to stay in our little town?" Jess asked curiously, just as nearly everyone else had.

"The scenery for one." Rennet nodded toward the ocean.

"Yes, well, I can't fault you there." She smiled. "I love the ocean. What else?"

"What do you mean?" Rennet looked at her confused.

"Well, you said for one." Jess said, nodding to the ocean.

"Oh, well, the people too I suppose. Everyone here has been really nice. Plus, I've just gotten tired of traveling. I wanted something more stable."

"I can understand that. I guess it's hard to make real friendships or relationships when you travel like you have."

Rennet noticed that her gaze shifted to Sophanes once again when the word *relationships* left her mouth.

"Yes, quite impossible actually."

"So you've never had a special someone?"

"I did, for a little while. There was another community that I nearly settled in, but I quickly came to find that it wasn't the place for me."

"Oh, well, I hope our little community will suit your needs."

He smiled at her words. "I think I will like it here just fine."

"Even after Archie accosted you the other night?"

They both laughed a little at the remembrance, their actions catching Sophanes' attention.

"Yes, well, Archie and I have gotten over that. I'm actually working for him for a little while to pay off some building materials."

"Yes, I've heard you've settled into one of the cottages down the beach, just near Sophanes' place."

"Yes. Baxter has been helping me build and repair a lot of the damage. Its dried in, but there is still a lot of work to do inside."

"Well, I'm a decent painter if you ever need help. My place is just down the beach on the other side of Archie's."

"Thanks for the offer, Jess, I appreciate that. Of course, I'm not sure where I'd get a decent can of paint now-a-days."

"Oh, well, Claire Rougeau makes milk paint. She uses natural materials to die the mixture."

"I've never heard of milk paint, but it sounds interesting."

"Come with me, I'll introduce you to her."

"Thanks."

Rennet followed Jess to where Claire was talking to others. He noticed that Sophanes watched the two of them with interest. Aurelie had said that Jess liked Sophanes, but that Sophanes was clueless to it or not interested. The man seemed to be curious enough about her right now. Maybe he just needed what he thought might be a little competition to get him to step up.

Aurelie watched Rennet with Jess, and how she took him over to introduce him to Claire. Both Jess and Claire were single, attractive, young women, but Aurelie didn't know why this seemed to pique her interest. She was simply observing the people around her, that's all. She did look over at Sophanes though, and he too seemed a bit interested in Jess and Rennet all of a sudden. She watched him excuse himself from his conversation with Procne and his wife Mary and walk toward Rennet's group.

"Good morning, Rennet," Sophanes interjected, stepping up between him and Jess, "how are you faring this morning?"

Rennet smiled at him. "Great, Sophanes, thanks for asking. Jess was just introducing me to Claire. I hear she makes milk paint. I'll be needing to paint my place soon, and Jess has offered to help." He watched the look on Sophanes' face turn to one of surprise.

"Is that so," Sophanes said, clearing his throat, looking between Jess and Rennet.

Jess smiled up at him. "Sure. Most of my days are free and clear. It'll be a nice change to help someone out."

"Oh, well, you can help me out as well if you like? I never thought about painting the inside of my cottage. It is nearly finished. I figure painted walls could brighten up the place."

"I'm sure it would, Sophanes." Jess smiled brightly at him. "I wouldn't mind helping you if you really need it."

"Sure, sure. I would appreciate that, Jess."

Sophanes turned to Claire.

"What sort of colors do you have in the milk paint, Claire?"

"Oh, just about any color you like. Most are a bit muted, but I can make them bolder."

"Well, I'm not sure about colors. I think that would require a woman's perspective. Jess, what do you suggest?"

Rennet grinned slightly at Sophanes' reaction to their talking. He also noticed how Jess brightened with surprise when Sophanes asked for her opinion.

"Well, why don't we walk over to Claire's place and have a look. You and Rennet can choose the colors you like and maybe Claire and I can help you both get the walls done."

Rennet smiled. "That sounds like a good idea to me."

Sophanes quickly interjected, "Yes, sounds good."

The four of them walked from the pavilion toward Claire's cottage, chatting and laughing. Rennet looked over at Aurelie who was watching them. He nodded and grinned at her, and she seemed slightly embarrassed to have been caught watching them. She gave a nod in return and then quickly turned to speak to someone else.

The exchange also didn't go unnoticed by Arjit, whose jaw clenched ever so slightly at Aurelie's obvious interest in the man.

Arjit watched Rennet and the others walk away. Perhaps the man would become interested in one of the other women, but he doubted that, especially after how he looked at Aurelie right before he left. Arjit would just have to make a visit to Mr. McCabe's place later and have a chat with the man. He would make sure that Rennet McCabe understood that Aurelie belonged to him; whether she accepted that or not. He always got what he wanted, even if he had to fight a little harder for some things. He would take on any man who dared try to take Aurelie from him. He grinned cockily. Rennet was no match for him, and from the way he ignored Arjit at Archie's yesterday afternoon, he was likely a coward too. Of course, the man did try to break up Eloi and Archie's argument at the party last week, but he never even tried to defend himself or retaliate when Archie punched him. Arjit grinned to himself once more. He figured Rennet McCabe would be easy to scare off since the man obviously had no spine or fighting skills.

Chapter 12

Sunday afternoon passed with the selecting of paint colors, and Claire and Jess walking down to see Rennet's and Sophanes' places. Sophanes and the women walked to his place last to view the nearly finished residence. Rennet excused himself to stay at his place, eat some lunch, and take the rest of the day to explore the surrounding area. He had spent so much of his time here simply working on his home that he hadn't really had a chance to see where people lived. The weather was nice even though it was a little on the hot side, but the ocean breeze cooled everything down. Rennet took to walking the street closest to the water. He waved and chatted with people who were outside their homes along the way, getting a feel for where everyone lived. He walked the length of the first street, then turned down another and walked it back to the end. He did this until he had walked all five streets. By the time he had finished, he knew where everyone lived, though he didn't know them all yet.

When he walked past Sandra and Marie's place on his return home, Sandra was outside sitting on the swing.

"Afternoon Rennet."

"Hello Sandra, hello Marie."

"Hi, I'm a seagull." Marie flew around the yard, flapping her arms and smiling.

"Yes, a very pretty seagull with large wings." Rennet smiled at the girl and walked over to visit Sandra.

"Well, yeah. I do fly you know." Marie continued on her path of play.

As Rennet sat down beside Sandra, she asked, "So, how's your nose healing up?"

"Great, I don't even think it went crooked."

"Well, fortunately it didn't break the bone, just the skin and some capillaries."

"Yes, I am grateful for that."

"Would you like a glass of sun tea?"

"That sounds great, thank you Sandra." Sandra got up and walked to the outside table, poured him a glass, and handed it to him. Rennet accepted the cool glass and drank appreciatively from it. "This is really good. I haven't had iced tea in a long time."

"It's so easy to make. I have tea plants, plus you can make tea from other parts of plants, not just the leaves."

"Really, like what?"

"Well, there are the seeds, flowers, hips, and roots."

"How did you learn to make tea from all of these things?"

"Books." Sandra smiled. "I love books as much as I love tea. Before the collapse I was dabbling in growing and making tea, so naturally afterward, I was glad that I had."

"I'd like to try and grow my own tea plants."

"Camellia bushes are the most common variety. I'll set you up with some plants when you're ready."

"Great, and what would you like in trade? I'm sure I can find something to give you or do for you in exchange."

The Barter

"Well, I have some repairs on my place that need doing. I'm not good with climbing and using tools at the same time." Sandra grinned sheepishly. "I'm always worried I'll fall. And then, what will happen to Marie?" She watched the girl fondly, concern evident behind her expression.

"Anything you need doing, you just say the word. I'll do repairs in exchange for you teaching me about growing and making tea."

"Deal," Sandra said, shaking hands with him as they smiled at one another. "I'll get a list together of what needs doing first since fall and winter are around the corner."

"I'll get started as soon as I'm done with paying off Archie with labor."

"Great, thank you Rennet."

"You're quite welcome. And thank you for this wonderful glass of iced tea."

He finished his beverage and said his goodbyes since the hour was growing late. It had taken him all afternoon to walk the area. He had gotten a good mental picture of the people, their homes, and the cottages that still sat empty and abandoned. He noticed that there were several young adults in the area who still lived with their parents. Perhaps they could start a beautification program and those young adults might be interested in rebuilding the abandoned places for some independence.

He sat down and sketched the area, trying to remember where the abandoned cottages were. Then he made a list of young people who were likely ready to be on their own. He knew of at least three right off. Emilie Comeaux, Adam Boudreaux, and Kester Bourgeois, although if Emilie were correct, Kester might be too immature. But what better way to grow up than to live alone and make your own way.

Leaving home had certainly made him grow and mature quickly. Of course, he hadn't just moved out, he toured the country on foot for a very long time. But he remembered that feeling of restlessness. Before the collapse, people had options. You could jump in a car, plane, or train and take off anywhere you wished. Now, people were stuck where they were born; especially in the out of the way communities such as this one. It might help with that longing in the single, young, people who wanted to do something or go somewhere. Perhaps living on their own would give them the excitement they needed, and perhaps squelch Emilie's need to leave. Certainly her parents would see the benefit in that? He would have to stop in and have a chat with them soon. There were so many abandoned cottages in dire need of owners. Plus, repairing them would help with safety issues where the younger children were concerned. If the whole community worked together they could repair all of them in no time and tear down the ones that were beyond fixing.

Maybe that was what he could offer as his bartering tool? He could be the local contractor. He doubted they had one since everyone here had probably lived in the same homes since before the societal collapse. The only other person he knew who was able to build was Sophanes. And from what Sandra said about needing help with repairs, there must be a need for a handyman, at least for the widowed and elderly.

The Barter

Rennet smiled and leaned back in his chair as he watched the sun set over the water. He looked up, giving thanks to God for the ideas, but soon found himself on his back.

The old reclining cloth and wood deck chair that he had found in a closet in his cottage, suddenly cracked and gave way under his weight. He lay there, deciding he needed to look into bartering with someone for some furniture. He might be able to rebuild homes, but making furniture was out of his league. He sat up just as the sun flashed below the water's surface, stood up, dusted himself off, and went upstairs to get some dinner.

He would sit down and draw up some plans for the properties in question for the next market day which would be coming up in three days. He took his food, and a notebook and pencil, and went outside on the deck to enjoy the little bit of daylight that remained. He did what he could until darkness settled over the area, then leaned back against the wall of his home and gazed at the star filled sky. That was something he enjoyed most, and it was something he noticed many people take pleasure in during his travels.

Star gazing was a lost art before the collapse. Large cities, and even country towns had so many lights that the night sky was never seen. City lights outshone the distant stars. After the collapse, there were no more lights to compete with God's creation. The stars shone brightly, and many people scavenged telescopes and learned to tell weather patterns based on the position of the stars.

He remembered an old saying his mother used to say pertaining to foretelling the weather based on the sky. "Red sky at night, sailor's delight, red sky at morn, sailor's be warned." He supposed the old farmers almanacs had become a staple for people in survival mode. People began reading anything agricultural to learn how to survive. The country folk already had a decent grasp on that lifeline in their livestock. But he remembered that the people who lived too close to the cities were hit harder than most. Many farmers were killed for their livestock and food storage by those who lived in the cities as people were desperate to survive. During his travels, he spoke with many people who had horrible stories to tell; if not their own, they were of people they had known.

He shook off the dark pictures that those reminders brought to his mind and watched the stars twinkle in the moonlit sky. The moon was waning, and soon there would be a new moon. He loved those night skies where the stars were at their fullest and the constellations were very visible.

It wasn't long before the local pests, mosquitoes mostly, began to buzz driving him indoors. Fortunately, his large windows provided a spectacular view. He decided that he would install another such window in the bedroom for future views and lighting. Right now, he could pull his bedroll over to the windows and fall asleep looking at the heavens. But once his place was finished, he would need to add furnishings and officially move his bedroll to the bedroom.

The Barter

Aurelie had watched Rennet talking with Jess and Claire earlier in the day, then they had all disappeared and she hadn't seen him again. No matter, he wasn't her problem anyway.

She and the kids had decided that since it was such a nice day that they would take a ride over to Little Florida Beach and the Peveto Woods Bird and Butterfly Sanctuary, which was only a short fifteen-minute ride in their side-by-side. Besides, it had been ages since she had spoken with Jen Grayson, the lady who lived at and took care of the sanctuary.

She remembered her father, Privat, taking her to the sanctuary as a child. They would spend hours just sitting and watching all the different species of birds that visited every year. The sanctuary was a forty-acre site once protected and maintained by the Baton Rouge Audubon Society. Now, Jen maintained it herself with a little help from some locals. She had been a teenager then, working the sanctuary with her parents; both of whom had succumbed to illness just years after the collapse. Jen lived there alone, except for the handful of people who lived there and helped out with the place. Aurelie had asked her once why she worked so hard to keep the sanctuary up and tend to the birds that would visit. She had said that now more than ever, they needed protecting if society as a whole were to survive. If the birds went extinct then the planet would suffer even more greatly than it already had. She and the others that lived and worked there with her, worked hard to restore the balance of nature, and help to replenish the animals.

One predatory animal they had to watch closely were the alligators. Living in the marsh areas of Louisiana, and the near depletion of animals in nature, the alligators tended to go hungry as they were not something that most people hunted, and over the last ten years, were beginning to be a problem around their area. If it weren't for most of the men in their community, the alligators would be out of control. These men set regular hunting parties to control the species and they used every part possible. The bones, like those of the regular fish that were caught, were crushed to make meal for collagen products to supplement diets for people and pets, and they were also used medicinally. The alligator skins were dried and turned into leather for boots and belts, using the teeth and claws as decoration in western style hats. Renauld Forester, the man in charge of gator hunts, was the one who ran a small factory type establishment where he processed all fish products for collagen production and leather tanning for clothing. He bartered his products at market, but the alligator meat, some unprocessed bone for boiling for soup stock supplies, and the dried collagen, were passed out to everyone on market days since he had too much to try to keep preserved.

To say people had learned to use nearly everything found in nature to benefit society was spot on. People here on the coast were a resilient bunch, learning how to survive quickly and efficiently. Many of the older people who had already lived through other wars of the past had much to teach the younger generations. And the collapse had made their knowledge invaluable.

They reached the preserve just around noon, setting their picnic lunch out on a blanket while they enjoyed nature. After they had their lunch, they all took to their regular activities when visiting the sanctuary. The girls liked to hunt for natural items to use in their crafts. Baxter liked to try and spot the many different varieties of birds and other animals. Aurelie usually just sat and listened to the different bird songs that filled the air. Sometimes the variety was so great the sound could almost be deafening at times. But today she had brought along her old sketching notebook. She decided she would begin drawing and writing again and figured that she could start by cataloging the many species of birds and butterflies they could find in the sanctuary. Along with Baxter's work, perhaps they could give the updated logs to Jen Grayson to help with tracking the different species that visited here.

They would go to visit Jen and the others for a few hours before leaving for the day. She didn't think that many people from the Holly Beach Community ventured this far from home. Not everyone had a side-by-side to run around in and explore since not everyone needed such a thing. Maybe she could talk Jen into coming to Market day on Wednesday to teach people a little about what they do out here, which might even get her a few more volunteers.

Chapter 13

Aurelie managed to wake up before Baxter did this morning. She put the coffee to brewing and packed him some lunch, then went out to harvest the garden produce to prepare for the Market in a few days. She walked the small orchard they had on the side of the house, her large basket hanging from her arm. She picked some apples and pears, a little concerned about all the rain lately which could harm the roots and cause rot. They would certainly have plenty to can this year. She then walked the fence which held the grape vines. They were doing quite well this year also. Several of the farmers at market liked to barter for Aurelie's grapes, not only for eating, but for making wine, the old-fashioned variety of muscadines grown for their unique flavor.

She lugged the full basket of orchard fruits toward the house. Upon entering the kitchen, she noticed that Baxter's lunch box was gone and in its place was a basket full of garden produce.

She took the items and placed all but what they would use into the underground storage boxes to keep until Wednesday's market. When she reentered the house the girls were already up. Birdie was making pancakes and Katie was pouring juice into glasses.

"Morning Aurie," Katie said excitedly. "Isn't Marie coming to play today?"

Aurelie smiled. "Yes she is, that is if we can get her to come over. I don't think she's ever been anywhere without Mrs. Sandra."

"I bet I can get her to come. She likes me, and I like her." Katie sat down at the table and took a big drink of her juice. She smiled and thanked Birdie for the pancake which she sat in front of her.

Aurelie watched Birdie who seemed to be maturing quite quickly as of late. "So, Birdie, what are your plans today?"

"I think I'll work on some seashell and drift-wood wind-chimes. We have a large quantity of stock. I want to have them ready for Wednesday's market."

"So I guess that means you three will be coming with me this week then?"

"Oh yes. We missed it the last few weeks. And last week Rennet showed up. I don't think I want to miss any more of them."

Aurelie grinned at her assumption that things would be exciting again. But in a way Birdie was correct. Jen Grayson was coming this week to talk about the sanctuary and the need for help. Plus, Rennet McCabe had joined their community. Aurelie was interested to know whether he found his own bartering tool?

"Let's finish up morning chores and clean up, then we will ride over and see about Marie."

"Can I go too Aurie?" Birdie asked. "I would like to see Rennet's place. I haven't been over there for a few days."

"Sure you can come. We'll go by Rennet's first then stop at Sandra's on the way back."

By nine a.m. they were on their way toward the beach and Rennet's place. As they approached, Aurelie noticed that Baxter and Rennet had already cut another large hole in the wall at the backside of the cottage and had installed a large window. They parked the cart and all piled out, climbing the steps to the cottage.

Aurelie knocked on the opened door and yelled, "Bax, Rennet?"

"Back here," came Rennet's reply. They stepped inside the cottage and walked to the back room which was the master bedroom. They were working on trimming around the new window.

"Good morning." Aurelie smiled at the work they had done, smoothing her hand over the beautifully grained wood trim. "You two do nice work."

"Thank you." Rennet smiled at her compliment. "So, what brings you three over today?"

Birdie answered. "I wanted to see what you had gotten done so far. It's starting to look really good. It looks like a house now instead of Swiss cheese."

They all laughed at her description of the cottage on day one and two when she had helped out.

Rennet looked at her in earnest. "It is looking much better, but I could use your help tomorrow morning with the painting of the trim."

Aurelie was surprised by this. "Oh Rennet, why paint this beautiful wood?"

"For protection and sealing. Living this close to the salt water and all the moisture in the air, it needs some kind of sealant."

"Well, I suppose I understand that. It's a shame to have to cover the wood grain in paint though."

Birdie, who was confused, said, "I didn't know Archie sold paint."

Rennet replied, "He doesn't. Claire Rougeau makes milk paint. It has a short shelf life, so when she mixes it for me, I need to use it up quickly. So, I'll need all the help I can get to have everything painted in one day."

"Well, I can help tomorrow," Birdie stated. "Painting might be fun. I've never done it before."

Rennet asked, "Aurelie, do you have a step stool of some kind we can borrow so Birdie can trim in the crown molding? I had to add it because of the irregularity of the squareness. This old cottage seems to have settled some. It's still sturdy, but a bit askew."

"Yes, I'll bring it over in the morning. The kids can ride their bikes so I won't have to come back to pick them up."

Rennet was a little put out by her comment. He rather liked getting every opportunity he could to see her.

"Great, thanks." He grinned at her, regardless of his feelings.

"All right girls, we need to get over to Sandra's."

"What's going on over there?" Rennet asked curiously.

"Nothing. We are picking up Marie for a play date at our place today."

"Oh. So you'll have to return later than to drop her back off."

"Yes, I suppose I will. Any reason you ask?"

"Perhaps you can drop that step stool then."

Aurelie nodded and grinned. "Sure, well, see you later then."

The Barter

"Thanks. And thank you for your help tomorrow Birdie. I'll check with Jess and Claire later to see if they will be able to help as well."

"Okay," Birdie happily yelled as she left the cottage.

Aurelie was a little put out that he hadn't asked her to help, but she supposed he had plenty of people for that. Still, she might have liked to help too. She shook off the feeling of being left out and they headed toward Sandra's.

"Good morning Marie, are you ready to come play with Katie today?"

"Well yeah!" Marie said excitedly.

Sandra smiled at Marie's exuberance. "She's excited, but I'm not sure what I'm going to do with my time."

Aurelie laughed. "I know. I had to figure out what I liked to do last week. I'm sure you'll come up with something."

"Yes. Maybe not today, but perhaps by the next one." Sandra grinned.

Marie loaded up in the cart with them, happy to take an adventure with Katie to the Haydel's home. She had never been there before and when they arrived, she was curious about all the large trees that sat on the property. Aurelie explained why they were there, then the girls played in the yard while Aurelie watched, wanting to make sure that Marie was okay being there. She sat on her porch swing and sketched the girls playing. Birdie stood at the porch railing hanging a piece of driftwood from thick fishing line and prepping the shells that didn't already have holes for the string to slide through.

Birdie walked over to Aurelie and sat down beside her, peering over her shoulder at her drawing.

"Aurie, you're really good at drawing. How come I never knew you could draw?"

"Well, I suppose it's because I never had the time before now."

"I bet you could do people's portraits."

"Maybe, but I prefer to draw nature. This is just for fun while the girls play. Something for a memory since photographs and cameras are no longer usable."

"All the more reason to draw the others in the community. For posterity's sake."

Aurelie giggled at Birdie's word usage. "Where did you learn such a big word?"

"Sometimes I get bored and read the old dictionaries on the bookshelf."

"Is that so? I've never seen you read them."

"I hide in my room because Bax would tease me constantly about it."

Aurelie laughed. "Too true."

"Well, I guess I'll get back to my wind-chime making."

Birdie stood up, picked up the shells that birds and sea creatures had already made holes in and began threading the string through them. By the time lunch had arrived, she had four wind-chimes done.

They all moved inside the house to eat, after which, Katie and Marie went upstairs to play for a while because the noontime sun was beginning to get stifling.

Aurelie and Birdie decided to tackle one of the repair jobs that needed doing. All the doors and windows in the old house needed to have new weather-stripping applied to the frames before the cold weather would set in. They scraped the old stripping off and applied the new rolls of stripping that Aurelie's father had stored away many years back, knowing the old house would need it with the lack of air-conditioning and central heat. They were working on the front door when Baxter returned from Rennet's. After he tended to his afternoon chores, he jumped in and helped them make all the seals air-tight.

It was nearing six in the evening, so Aurelie loaded her kitchen stool and took Marie home. When she arrived at Rennet's he was nowhere to be seen so she placed the stool to the side of his front door and returned home.

Rennet and Baxter finished up, ate lunch, and Baxter left for home. Rennet grabbed his pack and walked to Archie's thinking about the work he and Baxter had accomplished on his place. He would have to think of a way to thank the young man for all the help he had given him.

Rennet reached Archie's within thirty minutes, waving, and briefly chatting with others along the way. Archie was sitting behind the front desk just outside his office when Rennet arrived.

"Hey, Archie, how are things going?"

"Great, no problems to report."

"Good. Just let me stow my backpack in the office here and we can get started wherever you want." Rennet walked into the office and was taken by surprise by how clean and organized it was today compared to Saturday.

"Wow, Archie, you've been busy."

"Yeah, well, with all the work we managed to get done Saturday, I figured I could tackle the office by myself. I've been meaning to do it for years; I just lacked the motivation."

"Well, let's not lose that motivation. You ready to tackle some more of this place?" Rennet smiled at him; his eyebrows raised in question.

"Yep. I have to admit, it sure is nice to be able to find things quickly when people come asking for them. I always knew the general area before, but I usually had to dig for stuff."

"Well, once we're done, you shouldn't have to dig for much if anything."

"True. Let's pick up where we left off the other day. We can tackle the trim work section. There's a lot of that and the pieces are all long and narrow."

"We can use the walls of the building to lean them upright."

"Yeah, but they'll eventually warp if they stay bent."

"We can build the bottom out and taper the support boards back a little as we go up. That way the wood lays against something all the way up. It should keep the majority of the lumber straight."

"That's a good idea, Rennet."

"Thanks. We can also label all the bins, that way people can see what you've got and pull the lumber themselves. You won't have to do all the work."

The Barter

"Well, it ain't like there's a whole bunch of people wanting to build around here you know, just you and Sophanes lately. Most people just need lumber for light repairs, and only the necessary ones."

Rennet smiled. "Well, that may change soon. Let me tell you about my plan for the other abandoned and damaged cottages around here."

Rennet and Archie spent the afternoon working and talking about Rennet's plans to engage the young adults in the area. Archie agreed to take Rennet out on his cart after they finished their task and check to see how much wood they would need to repair the viable cottages, and to also see what could be salvaged from the ones that were beyond repair. They returned to the shop and made a list of needs per dwelling, which gave Rennet a good idea of the work involved for his spiel for Wednesday's market.

Rennet returned home and found the stool by his front door. He was a little sad that he hadn't had the chance to speak to Aurelie. He shrugged off the disappointment and grabbed some dinner, then decided to visit a few of the families in question, deciding to go by Adam Boudreaux's parent's home first. After dropping his clothes that needed mending to Reesa on the way out since she had asked for them once again; he walked up to the chest high fence at Adam's parent's place. Adam was outside feeding a few chickens that scratched and pecked at the dirt.

"Evening Adam."

"Hey, Rennet. What brings you by?"

"Well, I have a proposition I'd like to run by you and your folks."

"Sure, come on in."

Adam set the food on a nearby table and opened the gate for Rennet to enter.

"Thanks."

"Mom and Dad are upstairs seeing to dinner."

"I hope I'm not intruding?"

"Nah." Adam chuckled. "It's not like we get a lot of company. I'm sure they'll enjoy your visit."

"Well, that depends on how they take what I'm offering."

Adam gave him a curious look, his interest in what Rennet had to say, now piqued.

Adam introduced Rennet to his parents, even though they knew who he was already.

They offered Rennet some dinner which he declined as he had already eaten, but he told them to have their meal while they listened to what he had to say.

Adam was very interested in Rennet's plan, and his parents, although they weren't sure as to the need of Adam having his own place, understood the want of it. The abandoned camps would make for nice housing for the young adults and would give them something to look forward to.

Adam's father, William asked, "Where are the supplies to rebuild these places going to come from?"

Rennet stated, "Well, most of what is needed can be salvaged from the places that need torn down. We will leave the support beams standing since we couldn't unearth them anyway. Maybe we'll even build a little community fire-pit area. You know, roof the support beams with boards like a pergola, or use metal, and build a little seating area where people can gather and visit.

William nodded at Rennet's vision. "This is a good plan, Son. We've spent so many years just surviving, and we've gotten comfortable in our complacency. I believe this will be good for everybody, especially the kids that are near Adam's age." William looked at Adam, who smiled excitedly.

Adam said, "I can't wait to have my own place. I mean, no offense, Mom, Dad, you know I love you, but it will be nice to feel like I'm on my own. Even if it is only a little ways down the road here."

His parents laughed at his exuberance. William said, "Well, I'm glad you have something to look forward to, Son. I know you can't go too far, but this is a great start."

Rennet smiled broadly. "Great. If you want, we can all walk down now and look at the abandoned places and see which one you might want to claim."

Adam's smile was so big, Rennet thought it would touch his ears. "I'm game!"

The four of them walked around the area, looking at the camps in question. Adam chose one that was close to Rennet's, laughing and saying that the area would be known as the singles community. What Adam didn't know was that Rennet had no plans to remain single, but he supposed that for now, he most certainly was.

Adam asked Rennet, "How is this bartering going to work?"

"What do you mean?" Rennet asked quizzically.

"Who's going to rebuild it?"

"Well, I'll help in exchange for some supplies to start my place up. And Archie will supply the needed wood in exchange for bartering. You just need to discuss what that is with him."

Adam looked at his parents. He didn't really have anything himself. William smiled at him reassuringly, and said, "Not to worry, Son. We'll settle up with Archie on the lumber trades, but you will have to figure out what it is you're going to do with your time."

"I can still help you and mom." Adam said, not wanting to leave his parents to themselves.

"We can handle what little we do ourselves. We just need to figure out your talents and skills. You've been doing what we needed to survive ever since you were big enough to start helping. It's time you learned your own ways."

Adam looked a little nervous. "I'm not sure what that is?"

Rennet slapped him on the shoulder. "It'll come to you, especially once you have to think about it."

William added, "Not to worry none either. Until you get on your feet, your Mother and I will be right here to help you, and we'll get you set up with some seeds, chickens, rabbits, and whatever else you might need."

"Thanks dad; you too Rennet. I can't say that I've ever been this excited before. Except for last week when you passed Emilie Comeaux off to me at the dance." He smiled broadly at Rennet who smiled back.

"You're welcome. I was your age once, not too long ago either."

"This might even help Emilie to see me as an adult."

"I'll be talking to her parents as well. I'm hoping to hit up all the young adults, or those who want to strike out on their own."

Adam pondered. "This is such a great idea. I wonder why no one ever thought of it before?"

"I guess since people's needs have been what was important, wants weren't thought of anymore. I plan on pitching this idea at the market on Wednesday."

"I can't wait to see how that goes down."

Adam and Rennet smiled at each other, and the four of them stood making plans for Adam's new home until the sun went down.

Chapter 14

Tuesday morning's sunrise was bright and clear as paint helpers began arriving at Rennet's place. Not only did Rennet have Birdie and Baxter, but Claire, Jess, Sophanes, and even Adam showed up to knock the job out. They had so many people to help that they began getting in each other's way.

To alleviate the problem, Sophanes, Jess, and Adam decided to walk over to Sophanes' place to get started on his walls. Those left at Rennet's promised to walk over to help as soon as they had finished there.

On the other side of the beach road, Aurelie was dropping Katie off at Sandra's for the day to give her some help with her place and the chores. Sandra had told Aurelie when she picked her up last time, that Katie was such a big help that Marie was actually interested in doing her chores more because Katie made them fun.

Aurelie was glad of this. It made her heart happy to know the kids were all off somewhere in the community, helping others to live better.

She sat in her side-by-side and thought about what she would do that morning. She was curious as to what was going on at Rennet's and decided to ride over to check things out. Besides, she wanted to see the milk paint that Claire made. She might even decide to repaint her place. It could use some freshening up. It had been the same since as long as she could remember. She had some water spots from leaks that needed tending to anyway.

She steered the cart toward Rennet's place and pulled to a stop beneath his cottage, near the steps. The breeze off the water this morning had a cooling effect on her skin, and she stood there for a few minutes just enjoying the feel of the breeze as it tossed her hair about her head.

Rennet stopped his descent on the steps when he noticed Aurelie standing with her head tilted up, facing the wind; her shoulder length, sun-streaked, chestnut-brown hair, flying around behind her. She looked so peaceful, so calm and serene.

When Aurelie opened her eyes she saw a figure in her peripheral, making her jump. She hadn't known she was being watched.

"Sorry," Rennet quickly apologized, "you just looked so peaceful that I didn't want to disturb you."

Aurelie took a deep breath and grinned. "I love the ocean, the sound of the waves, and the nearly constant breeze. I couldn't imagine living anywhere else."

"I agree." Rennet smiled at her. "So, what brings you over today? I thought you were glad you wouldn't have to ride over this morning."

Aurelie's grin appeared to be a little forced. Rennet could kick himself. His words didn't quite come out the way he had wanted.

"I just dropped Katie off at Sandra's place and decided that since I was already here I would come take a look. I'm looking at repainting my place soon and was curious about the milk paint."

The Barter

"Sure, come on up. I'm glad you came by, Aurelie. I just need to wash these brushes out to change colors." Rennet tried to make sure she knew she was welcome at any time.

She nodded and passed by him on the stairs. He could tell she was agitated at his near accusatory words earlier, and he fussed under his breath at his own stupidity. She had willingly come to check his place out and he practically chastised her for it. Maybe she had just come over to check on the kids and it had absolutely nothing to do with him anyway?

Rennet shook his head to clear his thoughts, went about cleaning the brushes and rushed back up the steps to continue with the work.

When he entered his cottage, Claire and Aurelie were chatting about the paint while Claire worked. Baxter and Birdie were painting the rear of the house, while Claire and Rennet painted the living and kitchen area.

Aurelie said, "It's looking good in here, Rennet. I like the watery blue of the paint color."

"Thanks. I didn't want everything to be white. The trim work will stand out more being white, but the walls would look too stark the same color."

"Good choice. Well, I guess I'll let you all get back to work."

Rennet quickly added, "You can hang around if you like."

"There's no point in my being here. You seem to have plenty of help, I figure I would only get in the way. Besides, I think I'll head over to Sophanes' place and see how things are going over there."

Aurelie said her goodbyes, yelling to the kids that she would see them at home later. They both had their lunch boxes today, and she would be eating alone. She wasn't sure she liked time to herself. She felt like she was missing out on doing life with everyone else.

Rennet watched Aurelie leave and she looked a little dejected. He looked over at Claire who shrugged her shoulders, grinned, and went back to painting. He watched Aurelie's cart move across the grassy sand toward Sophanes' place. He wished she had hung around longer. He wished he could say things the right way.

Aurelie pulled up to Sophanes' place. It dawned on her that in all the years she had known Sophanes, she had never even seen the cottage he had rebuilt. She climbed the stairs, yelling her arrival.

"Good morning all!"

Sophanes smiled brightly. "Morning, Aurie. What brings you by here?"

Adam and Jess also announced their good mornings to her.

"I realized that I have never seen your place. Sophanes, this is really nice. I love the paint color you chose for the walls. This light coral accent wall in the living area, and the sea-foam green in the kitchen really gives the place a beach vibe."

Sophanes smiled, giving credit where it was due. "Jess actually picked those out."

Jess laughed. "Yes. Why the man let me choose what color his walls should be is beyond me? Of course the colors will keep the afternoon sun from bouncing off white walls and blinding him."

Aurelie smiled, thinking she knew exactly why. "Chalk it up to a woman's intuition, besides, you're right about the sun and the color white. Men usually have no sense of style or design. I'd say he did quite well allowing you to choose."

"Thanks." Jess smiled happily at Aurelie's praise.

Adam said, "You want to help us Aurelie? We have an extra brush, and these colors are going to require an extra coat anyway."

Aurelie smiled at him, "Sure. Sophanes, is that all right?"

"No need to ask my permission if you want to help." Sophanes laughed. "I'll take all the help I can get. I've figured out that I don't like painting."

Jess smiled at his honesty. "I love to paint. it gives new life to the drabness of existence. I feel like we are accomplishing something new, instead of trudging away in our sedentary worlds. My life has become dull and repetitive. I'm really enjoying doing this."

Aurelie took the brush that Adam offered her, noticing the look that crossed Sophanes' face at Jess' words.

Aurelie added; more for Sophanes' benefit, "Yes. I've come to realize that change can be a good thing. We've all become too settled in our own lives that we've taken those that we care about most for granted."

Everyone continued with their work for the next several hours, taking a break for a quick drink and to figure out what was next. They finished Sophanes' place before lunch and Aurelie left for home, picking up Katie in the process. The two of them had lunch together, then tended some chores while they waited on Birdie and Baxter to return.

Rennet thanked Claire, Birdie, and Baxter for their help as everyone ate lunch then headed home. Rennet then cleaned up the paint brushes, threw out the extra unneeded paint, cleaned up, and headed to Archie's for another day of servitude.

When he got there, Archie had already begun cleaning up and organizing the back portion of the building, which was all that they had left. They spent the rest of the afternoon putting things in their place. They finished earlier than expected and both sat down outside the large roll-up door, in the cool shade of the building's shadow, enjoying the ocean breeze and a cool drink of iced tea.

"Thanks for all your help Rennet. This place sure looks better and will be much easier to find what I need. Heck, I have stuff in there I didn't even know I had." Archie grinned crookedly and took a long drink of the cool tea.

"No problem Archie. I actually enjoyed doing it. It also gave me a good idea of what you have for all the cottages I hope we'll be redoing. Adam is already on board and excited to get started."

The Barter

"Is that right? Well, good for him. I guess we were all just so comfortable where we were that we didn't see that these young'uns needed a place of their own. I guess you coming to town stirred things up right well." Archie smiled at him and raised his glass to Rennet.

Rennet chuckled and repeated the action. As they both took another long drink, Arjit's side-by-side pulled up to the building.

Rennet eyed the vehicle and Archie eyed Rennet. He knew Arjit had a problem with the man, but he had no idea what that problem was.

Arjit stopped the cart and stepped up to where they both sat. He nodded to Archie, ignoring Rennet.

"Evening, Archie."

"Arjit." Archie nodded back, "Somethin' you need?"

"Yeah, about five more fence posts. I found some more rotten ones in another of my fields. With all the added rain, some of the posts just sit in the water too long. If it doesn't cause rot, then it makes them loosen up, sink, or the cows just push them right over."

"All right, I have them in back. You want to take a look for yourself and pick the ones you want? Rennet and I have gotten the place fixed up."

Arjit looked at Rennet with agitation, then back at Archie. "Sure, I suppose I can do that."

"Right this way." Archie stood and led Arjit to the fencing stock. Rennet trailed behind, causing Arjit to look over his shoulder at him. The look Arjit gave him was not a friendly one.

"Well, here they are Arjit. You pick the posts you want while I go get the cart to haul them out."

"Thanks Archie. You did a very good job of straightening up the place."

Archie yelled back as he left. "It was mostly Rennet's doing. The man's got a good head for organization."

Arjit looked over at Rennet, raking his eyes over Rennet in an unfriendly manner. Rennet decided that he had had enough.

"Look, Arjit, I don't know what I've done to you, but whatever it is, I promise you, it wasn't intentional."

"What exactly do you mean by that."

Rennet was confused by his question. "I just know that you don't like me for whatever reason."

"I think you know exactly why," Arjit seethed with aggravation.

"If I did, I wouldn't have asked." Rennet stated bluntly.

Arjit stepped up nearly nose to nose with Rennet. "I'll say this one time. Stay away from Aurelie Haydel."

Archie had started his return and overheard Arjit's words to Rennet. He stopped and just watched the scene play out, curious to how Rennet would react.

"When you say stay away, what exactly do you mean, Arjit? Because that's going to be nearly impossible to do with us living in the same community and the kids working for me."

Arjit's jaw twitched. Maybe this guy wasn't as cowardly as he first thought. "Aurelie and I have an understanding. I plan on marrying her one day soon, and you or no one else is going to stand in my way."

"From what I've seen of you and Aurelie's relationship so far, I'd say her understanding is much different than yours. She avoids you like the plague."

"Why you…"

"All right boys, take it outside if you want to continue with your squabble. We just got the placed fixed up and I'll not have you two bullheads messin' it up." Archie parked the cart in front of the fencing bin.

"Let's go." Arjit stated to Rennet, so close Rennet could smell the onions Arjit obviously had for lunch on his breath.

"Arjit, I have no intention of fighting with you over Aurelie Haydel."

"What's the matter, fellow, you afraid?" Arjit sneered.

"No. Just that Aurelie isn't mine to fight over, nor is she yours. She's not some prize to be won. And if you don't understand that, I doubt you'll have any more luck with her than you already have."

Arjit started to pull back to take a swing at Rennet but then noticed Archie step up behind Rennet with his arms crossed over his chest, staring at Arjit with a warning.

"Fine. I'll just get my fencing and leave. But one day soon, I'll catch up with you outside where Archie here won't have your back."

"Arjit, I don't need Archie's help. But I will say it again, I have no intention of fighting over Aurelie. She's a grown woman who can make up her own mind to like or date whoever she chooses." Rennet turned to Archie. "I'll see you later, Archie. I think it's time I leave." Rennet could feel Arjit's eyes boring a hole in his back as he walked away. He stopped at the office to grab his pack and head home.

Archie watched him go then turned to Arjit. "I suggest you take the man's advice Arjit. Aurelie ain't the type of woman who will take kindly to you warning others off her."

"Aurelie and I have an understanding, Archie. She's known for years that I like her."

"Just because you've liked her for years doesn't mean she likes you back, you idiot."

Arjit gave Archie a look of disbelief at his words, but no one, other than Sandra, argued with Archie.

"Well, if she doesn't, she will."

Archie stopped loading poles and looked disbelieving at the man. "It doesn't work like that Arjit. Who on this earth told you it did?"

"That's how my father got my mother to marry him. Persistence."

"Just because it worked for your dad doesn't mean it'll work for you. Your mother must have already had a thing for your dad. From what I've seen, Aurelie doesn't have feelings for you, at least not good ones anyway."

"Maybe, but I have a lot to offer any woman. I'd say I'm the catch of Cameron Parish."

Archie shook his head at Arjit's declaration. "I'd say you need a heavy dose of humility Chiasson. And one day soon, somebody's bound to give it to you."

"Whatever." Arjit waved off the words of warning.

The Barter

They finished the loading and Arjit asked. "What do I owe you Archie? I still need to pay you for the poles I got Saturday. I forgot to come back by with the meat I promised you."

"How about a young milk cow? I think I'd like to start raising some cattle of my own. Fresh milk, cheese, and butter sound awfully good. I might even try my hand at making milk paint."

Arjit's face contorted strangely with Archie's mention of milk paint. Then he said in disbelief, "A whole cow? Twelve poles and some fencing isn't worth that much!"

"That's my price, take it or leave it." Archie said, glaring at Arjit.

"Fine. But you're going to have to wait until market in the morning. It's too late to catch and load her tonight," Arjit complained as he pulled the loaded cart to his side-by-side.

Archie smiled. "Tomorrow will be just fine. That'll give me some time to build a pen." He stood and watched Arjit toss the poles and wire onto the trailer behind his vehicle. When Arjit was done, he sat down and sped away as fast as his side-by-side would go, the wood and fencing bouncing wildly on the trailer.

Archie just grinned and shook his head. Now, he had to see about a place to keep his new milk cow. He walked back into the building and began pulling the supplies to make a small barn and corral.

When Rennet returned home, Reesa was standing at the waist high fence around their property.

She waved him over, leaning over to hand him back the stack of clothing she had patched for him.

"Thank you Reesa, I really appreciate this. And let Foesy know that whenever he's ready to patch that roof to let me know."

"Well, you're very welcome Rennet, and I think Foesy said he was going to tackle that roof on Thursday. Tomorrow is market and it takes all morning and then afterward he usually has repairs to tend. Some repairs take him days to fix, but that roof really needs tending to before another storm blows through."

"I'm ready to help whenever he needs it."

"I'll be sure to tell him." Reesa smiled brightly and returned to her cottage.

Rennet smiled and turned with the armload of clothing, making the short walk, and taking the steps up to his place to put things away.

He grabbed some food to cook for dinner and went back downstairs to make a fire. One day, he'd find an old grill and gather wood to burn in it. That would be easier than cooking over an open fire. Perhaps he could find some lighter pine at the market tomorrow. The people who survived here for the last twenty years had surely figured out such things, someone was bound to have some.

Chapter 15

Wednesday morning started out with a bang as the sun shone brightly over the horizon. Market day was in full swing as everyone ran around preparing to barter their ready-made goods from the week.

Aurelie and Baxter set up the produce and fruit booth, while Birdie and Katie set about displaying their seashell wind chimes.

Jess, who helped with Sophanes and Anytos' fishing booth, waved to her, a bright smile on her face.

Kim and Kei Yamada were set up a few booths down and she smiled and waved to them, who replied in kind.

Kei yelled, "Good morning, children!"

They kids replied with smiles and giggles as the girls jiggled one of their windchimes.

"Save me a big one!" Mr. Kim replied.

The girls happily obliged, holding them up to let him choose before Katie ran it over to their booth.

Aurelie said, "Baxter, I'll be right back. I just want to go say hello to Jess."

"Okay." Baxter grinned, then yelled hello and waved to Rennet who responded in turn.

Aurelie turned to Rennet also, nodded and demurely waved to him. Rennet smiled more brightly than she had and gave a slight wave in return.

"Aurelie, good morning," Jess said, drawing her attention back to where she was going.

"Good morning, Jess." She smiled brightly at the woman.

"So, what brings you over this morning? Do you need some seafood?"

"Yes, but I just came over to say a proper hello. I enjoyed working with you yesterday at Sophanes'."

"Yes, so did I," Jess replied with a big smile. "We need to have a girl's night sometime. There are several young woman I think who would benefit from that." Jess noticed that Aurelie's gaze kept being drawn to where Rennet McCabe was setting up a table and a notebook.

"I agree, but there are also some older women who would as well." Aurelie thought about Sandra, and Procne's wife Mary.

"That's so true. We need to plan something for later in the week."

"Yes. Maybe we can have a get together under the pavilion one evening?" Aurelie looked toward Rennet once more.

Jess said, "He's a really great guy, at least from what I've seen so far." She smiled, waiting for Aurelie's reaction.

Aurelie's head snapped back around, knowing full well who Jess was speaking about. "Yes. He seems to be, but we really don't know much about him. I mean, who travels for ten years then picks here to settle down?"

"Well, he did say that he was going to settle in another community once, even had a budding relationship, but it didn't work out so he moved on."

Aurelie was surprised by her statement. She had asked Rennet once the same question and got little from him on the subject. Jess had known him for two days and she already knew much more than she herself did. Aurelie felt as though he didn't trust her; but did she trust him? She knew she was beginning to have feelings for the man or else his lack of inclusion and trust wouldn't bother her. She needed to get a handle on her feelings or risk getting hurt. Rennet McCabe may just decide to pick up and leave again one day when things didn't go the way he wanted. She not only had herself to consider here, but the feelings of the kids as well. Baxter especially had taken to Rennet like he had no other man in their community, other than her father Privat.

Aurelie shook herself from her reverie. "Good talking to you Jess. I better get back to my booth. I'll come by later for some fish and shrimp."

"Sure thing, Aurie, I'll set it aside." Jess smiled and nodded to her.

"Thanks."

As Aurelie walked back to her booth, she watched people at the market today. But for whatever reason, her attention kept being drawn back to Rennet. And it seemed nearly every time she looked his way, he was looking at her.

As market day went along, Aurelie noticed the parents of the younger people in the community gathering around Rennet's booth as he spoke to them, showing them a notebook and speaking very animatedly. Adam had also joined the conversation earlier and stayed by Rennet for the better part of the morning. Claire Rougeau even stopped by Rennet's booth and spent some time chatting amiably with him. Aurelie's curiosity was about to drive her crazy when Arjit stepped up, blocking her view of Rennet's booth.

"Good morning, Aurelie." Arjit placed his hands on the table and leaned forward, his face only inches from hers.

Aurelie quickly stepped back, her agitation with the man beginning instantly.

"Arjit," she said with a modicum of civility.

He glanced over his shoulder at Rennet, then turned to lean against her booth, crossing his arms and ankles as he relaxed.

Aurelie noticed him getting comfortable and asked. "Is there something you need Arjit?"

"I was just wondering, much like you are," he turned to look at her with a smirk, "what Mr. McCabe is up to? He seems to have everyone's attention."

"I'm sure if it were something important he'd fill us in. But whatever he's peddling, likely doesn't affect us in the least."

"That's good to know." Arjit turned back around toward her, a smile on his face at her words, which he twisted to suit his own needs.

"That is not what I was talking about Arjit and you know it. Look, I have customers, if you don't need anything will you excuse me?" Aurelie turned to walk away when Arjit's words stopped her.

"McCabe and I had a little discussion yesterday at Archie's. I informed the man that you and I had an understanding. He really didn't seem too worried about it. He wouldn't even fight me for the chance to date you; said you weren't his business. I guess that means he isn't interested."

The Barter

Aurelie began to seethe at the man's ridiculous assumptions. She turned back to face him, standing nearly nose to nose to get her point across and show him that he could not bully her into submission.

"First of all Arjit, I have told you before, *many times,* that there is *no* understanding between us, other than the fact that I *have had* it with your unwanted attention. Second, you and Rennet McCabe have no business discussing *anything* about me or who gets to date me. That is *my* decision and mine alone. Third, fighting is childish, and it wouldn't make me interested in either of you regardless. As a matter of fact, any man who settles his problems with his fists is a hothead and I don't need that in my life. And finally, and I want you to pay *very* close attention to what I have to say. I am not *now,* nor have I *ever been,* interested in you romantically in the slightest way. I will no longer put up with your *irritatingly,* incessant, *badgering* of me to date you. If you continue to bother me about this, I will be forced to deal with you in any manner I see fit. Do I make myself clear?"

Arjit stood bolt upright; confusion evident on his features. "Fine, but you'll regret this Aurelie Haydel. I'm quite a catch around here."

"So you keep saying!" Aurelie rolled her eyes at his declaration which angered him even more.

"And I can certainly make your life miserable if I choose to." Arjit jeered down at her.

"Nothing you do affects me in the least, Arjit, so I *seriously* doubt that."

Arjit turned abruptly and stalked back to his booth.

Aurelie saw Kim nod his head at her in approval as he eyed Arjit's departure. She also noticed that their heated exchange had garnered the attention of several others at the market. Some looked concerned, others amused by Arjit's obvious, final, rejection by Aurelie. She noticed that Rennet was also looking her way; glancing back and forth between her and Arjit. He grinned at her and nodded. She gave him an irritated look and abruptly turned away to do business with a customer.

Rennet wondered what that was about. What could he have possibly done to make Aurelie angry with him? He'd have to speak with her later after she had a chance to cool down.

Sophanes, Anytos, and Jess stood watching the argument between Aurelie and Arjit.

Sophanes said, "I hope Arjit doesn't do anything stupid, or else I'll have to interfere."

Jess looked up at him. "Like what?"

"I don't know, the man's got a temper."

"Perhaps, but I doubt that he would ever hurt Aurelie."

"Maybe not intentionally, but I've seen what happens when a man's passion takes control instead of him using his head. Passion can be a dangerous thing."

Jess sighed. "I don't know, I think it might be nice if a man felt that passionately about me."

Her words caught Sophanes' attention. She gazed up at him and continued.

The Barter

"Besides, Aurelie can take care of herself, and apparently, there are any number of men who would stand by her should Arjit get out of hand."

"Jess, I…"

"Excuse me, Sophanes', we have customers."

Jess walked away, the sadness and longing on her face tore at his heart. Did she think that he had a thing for Aurelie? It was time he spoke to Jess about his feelings for her before it was too late, especially with Rennet McCabe around. He liked Rennet, but he could see how woman behaved around him. Rennet was a very likable guy, along with being friendly and good-looking. Sophanes just might lose his chance with Jess if he didn't act soon, especially with the way Jess was watching Rennet at the moment.

Aurelie glanced at Rennet's busy booth as the young people and their parent's all surrounded him. Emilie Comeaux was particularly flirtatious and bouncy, much to Adam's disdain. The poor guy looked miserable as he watched her throw herself at Rennet. Aurelie had to admit that Rennet did seem to fend off her advancements, and often would put Adam between himself and her, much to Emilie's disdain. Aurelie smiled at the pout on Emilie's face at the last such action. Adam leaned down and said something to Emilie, causing her to look angrily at him. She glared at him and shot him a look that could kill, then stormed off like a spoiled child. Aurelie watched Adam take a deep breath and stand up taller as he watched her stalk away. She smiled at the action.

Finally the young man was beginning to stand up for himself when it came to Emilie. The young woman happily played Adam and Kester against each other for her own amusement. Aurelie figured she and Kester to be more of a match for one another personality wise than she and Adam. He was too mature for the young, hot-headed woman. She then looked at Claire Rougeau. Claire was only a year older than Adam, and their temperaments were quite similar, however, it appeared that Claire had her sights set on Rennet McCabe. Arjit's words about his and Rennet's discussion concerning her came back from earlier.

"Well, you can have him." Aurelie said out-loud in frustration.

"Who can have who?" Birdie asked as she watched the crowd of people who had Aurelie's attention.

Aurelie startled, "Oh, nothing. I was just thinking out loud."

Birdie shrugged and Aurelie asked her, "Do you know what's going on over there? Not that I care, I'm just curious is all."

Birdie said, "Sure. Rennet was telling us about his plans yesterday. He figures on fixing up the old cottages that are salvageable for the younger people in the community. He says that they all need something to call theirs."

"Huh." Aurelie said, watching the crowd.

"Seems like he has most of the parent's on board too." Birdie said appreciatively.

"Well, I guess that would be a good idea." Aurelie turned to the young girl and changed the subject. "So, did you and Katie trade up all your wind-chimes?"

The Barter

"Yes!" she said excitedly. "Mr. Michael had some really cool toys he said he found in an old, abandoned house a few miles out. They have a rubber ball and what he called Jacks."

Aurelie smiled. "I remember playing with those. I'll show you how they work later."

Birdie smiled happily until Baxter broke into their conversation. "Aurie, look at the sky out over the water."

Aurelie turned to take in the ominous storm clouds as far east to west as the eye could travel.

"That does not look good."

Baxter put in, "I think we need to start packing up and get home."

"I agree."

Aurelie and the others began packing, making sure to pass the word along to those who hadn't noticed the massive storm system heading their way.

Market day had come to an abrupt close and people were moving as quickly as humanly possible to stash their goods and get home safely.

Rennet rushed over to see if Aurelie needed help.

"What can I do?"

"We have it under control Rennet." Aurelie was curt and abrupt, continuing to move as quickly as possible with his interruption.

"Aurelie, have I done something wrong?"

"Rennet, this is not the time to discuss this."

"Well, I don't understand what I could have possibly done, but I have obviously made you angry somehow."

Aurelie stopped and looked at him. "Arjit told me about your fight with him."

"You mean the argument? I don't understand what the problem is?"

"I am not some object to be fought over. How dare either of you think you can decide between you who gets to date me?"

"Aurelie, I told Arjit the same thing. I said you weren't mine to fight over."

"I know. He told me. I'm glad you have your feelings straightened out Rennet and that I am not a consideration."

"I'm not sure if your angry or happy about thinking that I don't care for you." Rennet's hands flew to his hips in defiance.

"Well, it doesn't really matter does it?" She walked around him to grab another crate. Rennet started grabbing crates, following Aurelie who obviously wasn't going to stop long enough to speak to him. He placed the crate on the small trailer she pulled behind her cart.

"It matters to me, Aurelie." He stopped in front of her, making her stand still with the crate in hand.

"Why? What difference does it make?"

"Aurelie, I really like you, but if you'd rather me not bother you, I'll respect your wishes. I don't want you to think me a pest like you do Arjit."

"That's probably best. Besides, you'll likely just move on soon when things don't work out for you here, like you have before. At least this way, no one gets hurt."

"What does that mean?" He asked irritably.

The Barter

"Jess told me about your last relationship, and how when things didn't go well, you left."

"What difference would it make anyway, Aurelie, whether I stay or not."

"Rennet, my feelings aren't the only ones to consider here. The kids, especially Baxter, have really taken to you. As well as so many other people in the community. I saw the way they all interacted with you today. I don't want to be the one responsible for chasing you away should things not work out between us. But that isn't even an issue anyway. You've made it clear how you feel about me."

"Have I? I'm not sure what you think you know about my feelings. I just know that you are near impossible to talk to. You judge people before you even give them a chance to get to know you, driving everyone away."

"Everyone huh," she asked disbelieving. "Well Arjit seems to feel differently," she threw at him.

"Not after today." Rennet drove his point home.

Aurelie fumed, turned her back on him, threw the last crate on the trailer, climbed into the cart where the kids waited quietly while they fought, and they abruptly left.

Rennet watched her go. Not really sure what had just happened. He needed to get home and think about what she had said and try to make sense of it all. He took off toward home just making it to the bottom of his cottage steps when the sky let loose its load.

Before Aurelie and the kids could get home, the rain started hard and fast, soaking them to the bone. They had to spend another few minutes unloading the crates and taking them inside to the back porch for safe keeping. Aurelie looked at the kids who were drenched, and poor Katie was shivering.

"You three go get changed. We can finish with this after we're all dry."

Everyone went their separate ways and soon met back up in the kitchen to finish storing their goods. Afterward, Aurelie made some hot chocolate and coffee to warm them all up and they all took to the living room to wait out the storm which still raged outside.

Baxter looked out the window with concern.

"Do you think it'll be over soon, Aurie?"

"I have no idea, Bax. We can only hope and pray it will."

The storm raged on, growing stronger and more violent during the course of the night. The four of them curled up in Aurelie's room on her queen-sized bed, waking up to a loud creaking sound and a thud on the roof in the early morning hours.

Aurelie jumped up, followed by the kids, and ran up the stairs to the second story. In Baxter's room on the front side of the house, a large tree limb from the old oak that hung over their home had broken and fallen through the ceiling just over his bed. They all stood there in shock, realizing that Baxter could have seriously been hurt or killed.

"All right, everyone back downstairs, quickly."

The Barter

Aurelie pulled Baxter's bedroom door closed, hoping to shut out the storm that now raged in his room, ushering the kids down the steps and back to her bedroom. They all curled up together, huddling up as closely as possible. Katie began to cry as the storm outside continued in full force. The eerie sounds coming from outside scared them as tree limbs creaked, cracked, and broke. They could also hear things being blown into the side of the house.

"Aurelie, the dogs!" Baxter yelled. He jumped up and bolted from the room.

Aurelie chased after him.

"No Baxter, you cannot go outside, get back to the bedroom. The dogs will just have to make it on their own."

"But Aurie, they can't. They'll die if something hits the pen."

Birdie and Katie appeared behind Aurelie.

"So will you if something hits you."

"I'll be okay, I promise."

Aurelie stood and pondered what he said. If she didn't go out after them, then Baxter would.

"You stay here with your sister's. I'll see if I can get to the dogs."

"Aurie, I'm faster than you. Let me go."

"No, Baxter, if anyone is going out there, it's going to be me."

Baxter shook his head and the girls piled in around them.

Aurelie grabbed a raincoat and threw it over her head. She took a deep breath and threw open the front door. The wind was so strong the rain blew sideways. As lightning lit the sky, she could see part of the oak that had fallen into Baxter's room also lying on the ground in the yard. Lightning lit the sky once more and she could see the pathway to the dog's pen was clear.

"Lord, help me."

She dashed from the porch and ran as fast as she could against the wind that nearly toppled her over a few times. She grabbed at the dog pen fencing and pulled herself along toward the gate. The dogs were barking and yelping in fear. She called them to her and threw open the gate. Both animals bounced and yipped around Aurelie, following her toward the house. The dogs bolted up the steps and through the door. Aurelie had just made it onto the porch when lightning lit the sky, a loud crack was heard, and Aurelie heard Baxter, Birdie, and Katie all scream her name just before her world went dark.

Baxter and Birdie pulled Aurelie into the house as Katie continued to cry and the dogs both danced around worriedly, especially now that they could sense the anxiety in the children.

"Baxter, what are we going to do?" Birdie cried.

"I don't know. I can't go get help. It's too dangerous."

Katie cried, "What if she's dead?"

Baxter knelt beside Aurelie on the floor, feeling her wrist and neck for a pulse and checking her breathing.

"She's not dead Katie, just unconscious. Let's try to make her comfortable."

The Barter

Birdie said, "We can't move her. Just pulling her inside might have been a bad move. Katie, get some pillows off the couch."

Katie did as she was told while Birdie got a blanket to cover her with. Katie went to put the pillow under her head and noticed blood.

"Birdie, Aurelie's bleeding."

Birdie and Baxter exchanged looks. Baxter instructed, "Katie, go to the bathroom and bring back some rags and water, quickly."

Baxter turned to look at the dogs that lay curled up together on the living room floor, watching them anxiously and whining as if they knew what was happening. He then turned to look at the pale face of the still unconscious Aurelie. He swallowed hard, feeling very responsible for Aurelie's current condition.

Chapter 16

With the morning sun came the calm after the storm. Baxter had sat up all night, worry over Aurelie keeping him awake. The girls sat on the floor against the wall curled against one another fast asleep.

"Birdie," Baxter called in a desperate whisper, "wake up."

Birdie jerked awake, not really resting well at all. "What's wrong? Did Aurie wake up?"

"No. I've got to go get some help. Stay with her while I take the side-by-side." Birdie nodded and gently laid Katie over on her side. She crawled over to Aurelie, stroking the hair from her face as Baxter ran outside, pushed some tree limbs out of the way and jumped into the cart, taking off as fast as he could. He had to dodge a few downed trees and broken limbs but made it to the beach side cottages in record time. He looked at all the damage the storm had done to the places along the community roads. Most cottages appeared to have some sort of damage. He raced to Rennet's, the only place he could think of going to for help.

He quickly parked and ran up the steps, banging on Rennet's door.

Rennet opened the door and saw the look on Baxter's face.

"Please, Rennet, you have to come quick. Aurie's hurt."

Rennet grabbed his backpack and they both raced down the steps and jumped into the cart, racing for Aurelie's home.

"What happened Baxter?"

Baxter filled him in on the details, blaming himself for her injuries, crying as he explained.

"Baxter, it isn't your fault. Aurelie was doing what any parent would have done; protect their kids."

"Yeah, but she wouldn't have gone outside if I hadn't insisted on saving those stupid dogs."

"Baxter, she'll be okay. Don't worry. And don't blame the dogs either. Don't take your anger out on them. You were just being a good owner and taking care of your animals. Pets are like family; besides' didn't you tell me you use them for hunting? They are much needed tools for survival."

Baxter wiped at the tears that streaked his cheeks and simply nodded at Rennet's words.

They soon arrived home and Rennet took in the extent of the damage to the house as they ran inside. Baxter was happy to see Aurelie sitting up on the couch when they entered. Katie was in the kitchen making coffee and Birdie was sitting on the edge of the couch with Aurelie.

Baxter knelt on the floor beside Aurelie. "Aurie, I'm so sorry. It was stupid of me to want to get the dogs."

Aurie waved at him to calm down. Birdie said, "Not so loud Bax. She has a bad headache, and her leg is hurt. She couldn't put any weight on it. Katie and I had to help her to the couch."

Rennet sat across from her on the coffee table. "Aurelie, can you tell me everywhere you hurt?"

"I hurt everywhere," she said between clenched teeth.

"Can you be more specific," he asked a bit concerned.

"My head, and my left leg is the worst."

Rennet stood up to check her head. He winced when he saw the cut. "Well, you have a nice gash here, but at least you're no longer bleeding. It looks like the kids did a good job of cleaning you up." Rennet looked at Birdie who gave a grimaced grin at the memory of all the blood. "Let's take a look at your leg. Where exactly does if hurt?"

"Mostly around the ankle."

Rennet moved his hands along her shin and ankle, carefully moving the joint when she flinched and inhaled sharply.

"Well, I can't really tell if it's broken or just sprained. Either way, we need to immobilize it until I can get Sandra out here to check you out better."

Katie approached the couch with a steaming mug. "Aurie, here's your coffee."

"Thank you Katie. Could you also get me some pain medicine?"

"Yes ma'am." Katie rushed back to the kitchen.

Rennet looked at Aurelie. Her face was flushed, and her lips were rimmed in white. She appeared to not be in too much pain judging from how calm she seemed, but if her coloring were any indication, she was hurting much worse than she let on.

Rennet looked at the kids. "Baxter, Birdie, why don't you two gather up as many extra pillows as you can find. I'm going to carry Aurelie to her bedroom where we can make her more comfortable."

Both kids nodded and took off at top speed. Baxter raced upstairs and Birdie to a hallway closet then into Aurelie's room. Katie returned with the pain medication and a glass of water which Aurelie downed.

Rennet looked her in the eyes.

"Do you think you can handle me picking you up?"

"I can probably hobble into the room; you don't need to carry me." The pain that just her speaking caused was evident to him.

"Don't argue, Aurelie. Just throw your arm across my shoulder."

Aurelie did as she was asked, and Rennet picked her up. She inhaled sharply at the motion. Rennet stopped moving, just holding her in the air. "Are you all right?"

Aurelie nodded yes, and he slowly walked toward the bedroom as Katie led him. Birdie had propped as many pillows as she could against the headboard and Baxter came running in with more.

"Baxter, lay those along the bed there where her left leg will be," Rennet instructed the boy. Baxter did as asked as Rennet carefully laid Aurelie down. She clenched her eyes tightly against the pain.

"Now, I need you to go into town and see if you can bring Sandra back here. We need a professional opinion on Aurelie's condition."

"Yes sir."

Baxter was gone and the cart was started nearly before Aurelie was comfortable.

"Katie, bring Aurelie's coffee in here."

Katie nodded and looked worriedly at Aurelie before quietly leaving to get the mug.

Birdie stood there feeling helpless. "What can I do, Rennet?"

"Do you have any way to make ice?"

"A little. We have a small solar-powered generator we sometimes use for that."

"Good, Aurelie's going to need some for her ankle. Can you take care of that?"

"Yes sir."

Katie returned with the coffee mug and set it beside the bed. Her round, worried little eyes never leaving Aurelie's face. Rennet's heart bled for her. "Katie, do you think you can take the dogs back outside to the pen. They probably need to use the bathroom and are likely hungry as well."

Katie nodded her head, slowly backing out of the bedroom, then disappeared.

Aurelie's eyes remained shut to the brightness of the morning sunlight filtering into her room.

Now that the kids were all gone and busy, Rennet turned to Aurelie. "I have a feeling that you're in more pain than you're saying."

She opened her eyes slightly and nodded.

"Point to where."

She pointed at her ribcage.

"I need to see if there are any marks, okay?"

Aurelie nodded her approval and allowed Rennet to pull her toward him and lean her head against his shoulder. He then gently lifted her shirt up to her ribcage. He could already see light bruising. He slid her shirt back into place.

"I think you broke some ribs as well."

Aurelie sighed heavily. "What am I going to do, Rennet?" she squeaked out.

"You're going to rest while the kids and I take care of you."

"I'm sure everyone else in town needs help too. We can't be the only people who sustained damage."

"True, but they all live very near each other. Don't worry about that. You just rest and wait on Sandra to get here. I sent Baxter after her. They should be here soon."

Just then, Birdie walked into the room carrying a towel. "The ice will take a little while to make, but for now, here's a cool washcloth."

"Thank you, Birdie." Rennet took it from her and laid in on Aurelie's propped up ankle, noticing her wince from the simple touch.

"Now that we have Aurelie as comfortable as we can make her, why don't you and I take a look around the house to see about any damage."

"Oh, there's damage all right," Birdie said. "A large branch came through the roof upstairs last night."

"Show me where."

Birdie showed Rennet Baxter's bedroom which was now full of leaves, branches, and lots of water. Then they walked around outside, leaving Katie inside with Aurelie just in case she needed anything.

The damage to the trees around the house was extensive. It surprised Rennet that the house hadn't sustained more damage than it had. There was a part of the tree that went through Baxter's room, also laying across and partially through the front porch, which was obviously the branch that landed on Aurelie. Rennet was surprised that she was alive at all given the size of it. While they were walking around outside, Baxter had returned with Sandra and Marie.

Sandra entered the house through the back kitchen porch, being led to Aurelie's room by Baxter.

Sandra stepped into the room, took one look at Aurelie, and said, "Katie, why don't you and Marie go into the living room for a little visit while I check Aurelie over. You too Baxter."

"Yes ma'am," he replied.

Katie took Marie's hand and led her away.

Sandra heard Marie ask Katie, "Is she gonna' be okay?"

"I hope so, Marie."

Sandra looked at Aurelie and gave her an empathetic grin. "Now let's check you out." Sandra closed the door, and said, "Let's get you undressed so I can examined you, then we'll dress you in something more comfortable."

Sandra thoughtfully said, "I take back what I said the other day."

"What do you mean?" Aurelie asked.

"When I said we were all ready for any kind of excitement. I don't think anyone was ready for this."

Aurelie grinned ever so slightly.

After Sandra had finished wrapping her ribs and ankle and applying a few stitches and a small bandage to her scalp, she lay back against the thick pile of pillows, quickly falling asleep from sheer exhaustion. Sandra opened the door and stepped out to an anxious crew which sat in the kitchen awaiting her diagnosis.

"She'll be fine, it will just take her a while to heal. She has a concussion along with some stitches, several broken and bruised ribs, and a badly sprained ankle."

Everyone exhaled loudly at once, making Sandra grin. She then explained Aurelie's injuries further, along with instructions for her care.

"Now, I need to get back to the beach to make sure everyone else is all right."

"I'll take you," Baxter stepped up. "Rennet, do you want to ride back.

"No, I'll be staying here to help you out. There are a lot of repairs that need doing, and Aurelie is certainly in no condition to attempt any of them. I will give you a list of things to pick up later, but right now, just get Sandra and Marie back home." He then turned to Sandra, walking out with her to the cart. "Thanks for coming so quickly. I sure hope no one else has experienced any injuries. I know nearly everyone took some damage to their places though. I'll get back as soon as I can to help out, I just don't want to leave the kids here alone with Aurelie out of commission."

"No problem Rennet, I completely understand. Did your place have any damage?"

"Fortunately, no. But I did see Foesy and Reesa's house when I left with Baxter. Half of their roof looked like it had been torn off. What about your place?"

Sandra sighed exasperatedly. "Yeah, a corner of mine was removed as well, but only the outer shell. But with all the rain, I'll likely have water damage down that wall. But we're all alive and faring much better than poor Aurelie."

The Barter

Sandra sat down next to Baxter, waved goodbye, and they were soon underway.

Baxter took in the damage that was all around the beach area now that he could see better with the full light of day. Some people lost trees, some windows were broken, some pieces of roof were gone, and there was debris lying all over the place from anything that was loose. People milled about looking at the damage, and were already beginning to clean up, trying to salvage anything that was still good.

Baxter decided to stop by Archie's to see about getting some wood to repair the main roof. He knew some of what he would need to begin repairs. Baxter pulled up to Archie's, surprised to see a cow tied off to the interior wall braces and walking around the inside of the building.

"Archie?" Baxter yelled.

"Back here," came the reply.

Baxter followed the sound of Archie's voice, finding him pulling framing boards out of a very organized bin.

"Wow, it really looks good in here."

"Yep. Too bad the rest of the cottages along the beach didn't fare so well."

"Yeah. We had a lot of damage too. That's why I'm here. I came to let you know that I'll be back in a little while with our trailer to get a dozen framers, a few pieces of plywood, or tongue and groove boards if you don't have plywood, and some metal sheeting. We had a tree go through the roof in a few places."

"Everyone all right?"

"No."

Archie stood upright and looked at Baxter questioningly. He waited patiently for Baxter to answer, realizing the boy was trying hard to compose himself.

Baxter cleared his throat and looked at Archie. "Aurelie got hurt. She was trying to get the dogs inside and a tree branch fell on her. It was my fault."

"She just hurt, or worse?"

"She's hurt, but, pretty badly."

Archie walked over to Baxter and put a hand on his shoulder. Baxter threw his arms around the man's waist.

"It'll be all right, boy." Archie wrapped his arms around him and let him cry, patting his back for comfort. A minute later, Baxter straightened up, swiped his eyes with the back of his hand and looked up at Archie.

"Come on, let's take a ride to your place and we'll see just exactly what you're going to need."

Baxter nodded, not saying a word.

"I'll be back soon cow." Archie patted the beast on the rump.

"What are you going to name her."

"Cow. Figured I'd keep it simple." Archie smiled at him and Baxter grinned.

They both climbed into the cart and rode back home, taking in all the damage along the way.

Archie shook his head and sighed. "I sure hope I have enough wood to take care of all the needed repairs, and rebuild the cottages that Rennet wanted to undertake."

"Rennet's at our place. He was the only person I could think of to come help us."

"I'd say you made the right choice. Has Ms. Sandra been by yet?"

The Barter

"Yes sir. I just took her home before I went by your place."

"Good. I'm sure she took good care of Aurelie."

"Yeah, she did. But Aurelie will be unable to do much for about three to four weeks."

"Well, I guess she did it right then didn't she." Archie gave him a crooked grin.

Baxter grinned slightly at Archie's attempt to lighten his mood.

They arrived, and they met up with Rennet as the three of them took to cleaning up the yard, and pulling and chopping at the branches that were through the roof. By the time lunch rolled around, they had the branches off the house and porch and were assessing the damage and making repair lists.

Archie looked at Baxter. "You were right close to what you'd need to fix things here. I think you got a good head for figuring things."

"Thanks." Baxter managed a small grin.

"Well, let's go get that lumber. We need to get this roof sealed off before nightfall or the house will be full of mosquitoes and bugs."

They all three hooked up the trailer, took the sandwiches the girls made them, and headed to town. Birdie promised they would be fine until they all returned. Rennet borrowed Archie's cart to go and check on the Divins family. He pulled up and saw them sitting in their yard. Foesy's head was in his hands looking utterly defeated. Sophanes, Jess, Anytos, and the Yamadas were standing there with them.

"Reesa, Foesy, are you all okay?"

"Yes, but the house is nearly ruined."

Foesy's words were laced with hopelessness, and Reesa stood drying her eyes on an apron.

"Well, I have a proposition for you. I will be staying out at Aurelie's for a while to help out there. They had a lot of damage and Aurelie got injured." He quickly added at the looks of concern, "She's okay though, but will be out of commission for a while. I can't leave the kids alone. So, you three are welcome to stay at my place until we can get yours fixed up."

"That's awfully thoughtful of you Rennet. Are you sure?"

"Yes, I am. But there isn't much there in the way of furniture I'm afraid."

Sophanes stepped up. "Rennet, Foesy, my place is completely finished and ready to move into. I didn't have any damage except for a little outside trim. Why don't you all take my place? I'll stay at Rennet's or with Anytos a little longer."

Reesa started to cry again. "You boys are just wonderful. Thank you both." She stepped up and hugged the men.

Jess looked up at Sophanes, proud of the man whom she had fallen in love with so long ago. She only wished her feelings were reciprocated.

Sophanes looked down at Jess, unsure what emotion it was that had swiftly disappeared when he looked at her.

"Jess, do you think you can help me move my personal items over to Rennet's then get these three set up and made at home?"

"I most certainly can."

She smiled brightly at his request, taking Reesa and Reine by the arms and leading them inside their home to collect their belongings. She told them to pack, promised to return soon, headed back downstairs, and grabbed Sophanes pulling him to his place to ready the arrival of the Divins.

Kei asked Rennet, "Is there anything Aurelie or the kids need?"

"I don't think so, other than rest."

"Well, give her our love and let her know we'll be over to visit in a few days, and we'll bring food so you all won't have to cook."

"I certainly will."

Rennet smiled, went home to grab some of his own things, and headed back to Archie's. Baxter and Archie already had most of the wood loaded on the trailer and were ready to go.

"We'll need screws and nails too." Rennet placed his bags on the back seat.

"We have all that. Privat kept everything and has a shed full of the stuff. That is, if the shed survived last night's storm."

"Well, let's go find out. We three can work on the rebuilding while the girls focus on yard clean up." Rennet climbed onto the back seat leaving the front for Archie and Baxter. He looked out past the building and noticed a corral he hadn't seen before. In it was one lone cow, just watching him.

"Archie, when did you take up raising cattle?"

"Not cattle. One milk cow."

"Hmm. Any particular reason why?"

"The usual amenities; milk, cheese, butter, and paint."

Rennet smiled at him. "After last night, all four of those things might be needed in the coming days."

Archie climbed into his own cart. "I'll take my cart so you don't have to bring me back. Besides, I need to drive over and see how old Eloi fared during the storm."

Rennet moved to the front seat. "Baxter and I will drop the trailer and go with you, just in case you need help."

Archie nodded his thanks and the carts sped away toward Aurelie's farm, supplies in tow.

Chapter 17

Once they had dropped the trailer off at Aurelie's, Archie told them to climb into his side-by-side.

"No point in taking both. Besides mine does nearly sixty-five miles an hour, and old Eloi's place is a good five miles out from Aurelie's place."

Rennet asked, "Where does he live out here?"

"Near the old Pilots Boat dock."

"That seems pretty far away with the lack of traditional cars. Do others live there with him?"

"Nope. Old Eloi lives alone and likes it that way; stubborn old coot. I've tried to get him to move closer to the beach but he won't do it."

They arrived at Eloi's place which was void of trees, but there were a few metal buildings still standing, and a couple of old holding tanks. Eloi was outside walking around accessing the storm damage. He looked up at the sudden noise of the approach of Archie's cart and waved them over to where he stood.

"What are you fella's doing out here?"

Archie said, "We came to check on you. Just making sure you were okay out here after that storm."

"You mean hurricane."

"I figure it was at least a two."

"Yep, I reckoned that myself; closer to a level three though. Well, as you can see, I'm just fine."

"How did your place fare?"

"The house is all right. I was just out here at the boat slip making sure my air boat hadn't been blown or floated away when the surge reached near nine feet."

Archie noticed the boat was still parked where Eloi usually left it. "Well, glad you're all right. Guess we best be headed back. We have a lot of clean up to take care of."

"Anybody get hurt?"

"Aurelie's the only person I know of, but we've been busy. We haven't been able to check on everyone yet."

Eloi nodded. "Okay. I'll grab my tools and my airboat and meet y'all at Aurelie's."

"See you there." Archie turned the cart around and headed back to town.

Rennet was curious how Archie's airboat worked.

"Doesn't he mean he'll meet us at the beach?"

Archie looked over at him. "I guess you've never seen an airboat before."

"I saw the one back there. But no, I've never seen one in action."

Archie grinned. "Well, you're about to see Eloi's."

They arrived back at Aurelie's just before Rennet heard a loud whirring sound coming from the direction of the water. Cutting across the marsh and road in a big flat bottom boat was Eloi. The massive fan at the rear of the boat pushed him across the grass and sand. He stopped in Aurelie's driveway and climbed down.

Eloi whistled as he looked at the mass of tangled tree limbs, and debris.

"Is it all right if I go in and see Aurelie?"

Rennet answered, "Sure Eloi, I need to look in on her anyway."

Archie stepped up. "We'll all go. I haven't seen her yet myself. She was sleepin' earlier when I came by."

The four of them entered the kitchen door, and Rennet asked Birdie, "Is Aurelie asleep?"

"No, she woke a little while ago. Katie and I had a hard time helping her to the bathroom."

Archie said, "I have an old pair of crutches back at the lumber store from when I was a teenager. Of course, I was still bigger back then than Aurelie is now, so I'll need to likely cut them down. After we get the roof and porch dried in, I'll take care of that and run them over tonight."

Birdie smiled at him. "Thank you Mr. Archie. That will be very helpful."

Rennet asked, "Do you think she is up for some company?"

"I'll ask her." Birdie left the kitchen and walked into the room off the living area. She stepped back out the door and waved them inside.

The two older men entered the bedroom. Rennet stayed by the door, leaning on the frame to give Archie and Eloi more room to visit.

Archie and Eloi each went to opposite sides of the bed.

Eloi said, "Well, you don't look too bad off."

Aurelie smiled slightly at the man's observation. "Thanks. I suppose I feel worse than I look."

Archie said, "That's a good thing. I hear you'll be laid up for a while. I don't want you to worry about a thing. We'll take care of the repairs." He pointed to all of them.

"Thank you, Archie. I appreciate all that you're doing. Just let me know what I owe you when it's all done."

"Don't you worry about that either. Baxter and I will settle up. That boy sure knows his stuff when figuring job needs."

Aurelie smiled, and then looked at Rennet with a questioning gaze.

Archie took that as a necessary private moment. "Well, we're gonna' get to work so we can get back and take care of helping others."

"Did anyone else get hurt?" she asked, fear of the answer in her voice.

"I don't think so, but we haven't seen many others yet."

Aurelie nodded and they left. Rennet stepped up to the bed and sat on the edge.

"Did you have something to say?"

"Yes. Make sure Baxter understands that this was not his fault."

"I've tried, but he feels really guilty."

"I knew he would. Tell him I want to see him whenever he gets a chance."

"I will." Rennet took Aurelie's hand in his and smoothed his thumb over the back of her hand. "I'm glad you're going to be okay, Aurelie. I thought my heart was going to leap out of my chest when Baxter showed up this morning yelling that you were hurt and needed help."

She grinned at him. "Thank you for coming so quickly. I'm glad the kids have you to turn to when they need help."

The Barter

"Not just the kids Aurelie."

He picked up her hand and brushed the back of it with his lips. He then reached up and brushed a stray hair from her face, tucking it behind her ear.

Aurelie's breathing increased along with her heartbeat. They exchanged a brief look before he stood and said, "Well, I best get to helping Eloi and Archie or they'll both give me an earful. I'll come check on you later."

Rennet left the room, nearly running into Katie who was standing just outside the doorway, smiling from ear to ear. He gave her a chastising look for listening to his and Aurelie's conversation.

She looked up at Rennet and threw her arms around his waist. "Thank you Mr. Rennet."

"You're welcome Katie."

"I won't tell. It'll be our secret."

"Tell what, Katie?"

"That you and Aurie like each other."

She smiled again and ran out the living room door to help with cleaning up.

Rennet sighed heavily, then smiled to himself. It appeared that Katie might be right. Maybe Aurelie Haydel was falling for him. But it would have to wait until she was able to get around before they approached any sort of relationship. He wanted her to understand that he was there to help her without any strings attached regardless of how he felt. He knew they had only known each other about a week, but he also knew that he was falling in love with Aurelie Haydel.

Sophanes and Jess put his things in Rennet's house and returned to help the Divins put what they needed into Sophanes' cottage.

Reesa and Reine couldn't believe how clean and updated his cottage was. Foesy groaned knowing he would hear about it forever.

Reesa stated, "Maybe we can make our place over like this, Foesy?"

"Now Reesie, we may not have the resources to do all this. Sophanes has been working on this place for years little by little."

"Well, we're going to have to redo most of ours anyway. At least the living room and kitchen since that part of the roof was taken off."

"I don't know if I can manage to do what he's done here." Foesy said, feeling tired already just thinking about it.

"We'll help you Foesy," Jess added.

Sophanes agreed. "Sure we will. We'll see to it that the community is put back to rights before winter sets in."

"Everyone's got their own problems to worry about. You all don't have to fuss with ours."

"Now Foesy, you're not a problem; you're family." Sophanes smiled and slapped him on the shoulder.

Foesy nodded and grinned.

"Thanks Sophanes, I appreciate that."

"Now, Jess and I are going to let you three get settled in here and we are going to go check on some others."

The Barter

"Nope," Reesa stated. "We're coming with you two. We need to see if anyone else needs help. There will be plenty of time to rest later."

Foesy shook his head at his wife's determination. "You're a force to be reckoned with woman."

"That I am, and don't you forget it." She smiled and kissed him on the cheek.

The five of them left the cottage and traveled from house to house to check on their friends and neighbors. Many homes sustained light damage, but only a few of the houses had anything significant. The main problem was the debris and the damage to peoples livelihoods. Some animals were dead, others lost plants, harvests, trees were split and damaged, even a few had been uprooted from their overly large pots. Some of the wooden-fencing around people's properties lay split and strewn around the neighborhood. Some of those broken shards of wood protruded from the ground or out of another person's siding; stuck fast by a furious wind. Animal pens and fencing were bent from the powerful water surges pounding them for hours.

Procne and Mary, who lived off the beach in a higher elevation, drove around the area calling a meeting in the pavilion for later that night around dinnertime to discuss the damages and clean up. His and Mary's place had no damage and they decided to provide a meal for everyone who wanted or needed one. They would share it at the night's meeting. Sophanes and Anytos offered seafood to be made into shrimp or fish tacos. They had an abundance of seafood left over from yesterday's market and the abrupt, early, closing. Anytos' wife made tortilla's and had a lot of them in storage, and so they would provide that for the meal. The Yamada's offered yellow rice and beans, while others, who had anything of use, also offered to bring things as well to add to the meal.

Reesa informed Mary of Aurelie's condition and that they would need to drive out to the outer homesteads to let the others know.

Procne inquired, "Has anyone seen Archie? We'll need to discuss lumber needs with him."

Claire Rougeau, who lived near Archie's place, answered. "I believe I saw him earlier with Baxter and Rennet. They had a stack of wood behind Aurelie's cart. I figure her place must have been damaged pretty badly judging by the lumber they took with them and the hurry with which they were starting."

"Thanks Claire," Procne stated, "we'll head that way next, then over to Arjit's place."

"What about Jen Grayson? Has anyone checked on her?" Claire asked.

"I don't think so. Her place is a little too far for us to make and be back by tonight's meeting."

Sophanes said, "I'll go check on her and the others out that way."

Jess quickly added, "I'll ride with you. You may need some help if anyone is injured."

"Good point. Maybe we should grab some first aid supplies before we go?"

"I have an emergency bag at my place. I can go grab it," she said.

"Okay, you do that while I go get the side-by-side from Anytos."

The Barter

Everyone parted ways, setting about the cleanup, and trying to get some tarps or coverage of sorts over the homes that had no roof. Foesy's was one that was too far gone to be able to cover, but most everyone else's homes were still livable.

Sophanes grabbed the cart and headed to Jess's place to pick her up. He figured now would be as good a time as any to speak to her about his feelings. They had a fifteen-minute ride ahead of them, giving them plenty of time to discuss having a relationship. He pulled up to her place just as she was walking down the steps.

"Ready?"

"I think so. I should have whatever we might need. As long as the sanctuary buildings withstood the winds, they should have medical supplies handy, especially since they often treat wounded animals."

"How do you know that?"

"She talked about it at the market yesterday. I volunteered to help her out a few days a week."

"How will you get there?"

"I have a bicycle. A fifteen speed at that."

Sophanes smiled at her reply. "Jess, can I ask you a question?"

"Sure."

"I was just wondering if you would consider going out with me sometime?"

"Sophanes, I'm out with you now."

"I mean on a date. A real date."

Jess looked at him with surprise, then smiled brightly. "Sure, but why now?"

"What do you mean?"

"Did you suddenly discover you have feelings for me?"

"Well no. I've always had feelings for you."

"Really? Well why have you never mentioned that before. We've only known each other for the last fifteen years."

"Well, I suppose it was because I didn't have a place of my own until now, even though the Divins are using it. I never felt like I had anything to offer.

"Good grief Sophanes! Do you realize how much time you've wasted for the both of us? I have my own house you know. I don't need you to support me."

"I know, I just never thought about taking our relationship further until Rennet McCabe came into town. I saw how all the single woman, and even some of the married, act around him, and it got me to thinking."

"About what?"

"About what an attractive woman you are, and what a catch you would be for any man. I've taken you for granted over the years, and I'm sorry for that."

"Goodness. Your timing is terrible."

"Why do you say that?"

"You're asking me after a hurricane. I highly doubt we'll have much free time on our hands for a while with all the repairs that need tending to around town."

"You have a very valid point. So we don't waste any more time, marry me then."

Jess's head snapped around and she looked at him in shock.

"What did you just say?"

Sophanes pulled the cart to a stop and turned in the seat to look at her.

"Marry me, Jess Evanko."

"You can't be serious. We've never even been intimate. At all! How do you even know that you'll like kissing me, or feel romantically toward me?"

"I know what I feel, but if you want proof then let's find out. I've been wanting to do this for years anyway." Sophanes cupped her head with his hand and leaned over, planting a kiss on her lips. It seemed as though time stood still. When they separated, they both were a little breathless.

"I heartily enjoyed that. You?" he asked looking into her eyes.

Jess shook her head yes, unable to form words.

"Then I'd say we are very compatible and I am very attracted to you."

"I agree."

"I'll even venture to say that I'm in love with you, Jess."

Her eyes began to tear up ever so slightly. "Me too. I...I mean, I love you too."

Jess turned to face forward while Sophanes turned to steer the cart.

She asked, "Are we crazy for jumping into this?"

"I don't think so. Like you said, we've already wasted years unnecessarily. We spend nearly every waking moment in each other's company anyway."

"True." Jess sighed, as the weight in her chest lifted.

"So, when's the wedding?" He eyed her curiously.

"How about tonight, after the town meeting?"

"Sounds great!"

Sophanes and Jess smiled at one another and headed toward Little Florida Beach and the Peveto Bird Sanctuary; both happy and excited for the night soon to come.

Chapter 18

Evening came, and the light summer breeze, warm evening temperature, and the sound of the birds chirping happily in nearby trees mocked the destructive storm that had passed through in the early morning hours of the day.

Everyone in the area began gathering at the pavilion, many bringing fold out tables to put the food on and chairs. Reesa and a few other ladies rehung the string lights that encircled the canopy for gatherings and Foesy repaired the light's solar panel which had been damaged during the storm.

Many vendors from the market yesterday morning had excess product and brought food to help with the night's meal.

Anytos' wife Thalia and her two children, carried in trays of tortilla's while Sophanes and Anytos brought in the fried fish and steamed shrimp.

Procne and Mary brought barbecued pulled pork for sandwiches, while several others who baked bread brought in sliced loaves, sliced fruit and vegetable trays, and homemade dips to compliment the produce.

Sandra and Archie both brought several large pitchers of sun tea, and others brought water. Ice for the drinks was provided by Renauld Forester who had to continually make ice to keep his alligator processing plant up and running without the meat and collagen production going to waste.

Everyone attended the meeting, including Jen Grayson and the people who lived at and helped with the sanctuary. The only ones not in attendance were Aurelie, Rennet, Birdie, and Katie. Baxter had come to give Aurelie and Rennet news about the discussions. Even old Eloi was there.

After everyone had eaten, they all settled in for the meeting.

Procne began. "Well, we're glad to see everyone here; save a few people anyway. The storm that hit this morning has affected nearly everyone in some manner, but there are a few people who were hit harder than others. Foesy, Reesa, and Reine are living in Sophanes' place temporarily since half of their roof was taken. Sandra has a corner of her roof that needs fixing, and several others as well. Most of the damage was to the things we grow and the animals we tend that give us food. We need to make a list of damages, and anyone who needs help with repairs. Fortunately, there were no injuries other than the ones Aurelie sustained."

People gasped and began asking questions. Arjit was loudest.

"What happened to Aurelie?"

Sandra answered, "She's fine. She has a slight concussion, a few stitches in her scalp, some broken ribs, and a sprained ankle, all of which will take at least four weeks or more to heal completely."

Arjit was concerned about Aurelie, which caused him to look around the pavilion, noticing that Rennet McCabe was not present.

"I suppose that our squatter McCabe took off at the first signs of trouble? Couldn't handle the weather here?"

Archie glared at Arjit. "Actually he's not here because Baxter had the good sense to go for help this morning. Rennet was the first person he thought of, and the man is staying at Aurelie's place to help the kids take care of her and repair the damages her place took."

Arjit jumped to his feet, his temper beginning to escalate. "Why didn't I hear about any of this sooner?"

Archie jumped to his feet as well, prepared to handle Arjit should the need arise. "You didn't ask."

Arjit glared at Archie, who glared back. Arjit decided he'd best cool his temper and just listen to the rest of the discussions. He sat down and then Archie did as well.

Claire asked, "The damage at Aurelie's must be pretty bad. Do they need help with repairs?"

Baxter said, "No. It's mostly clean up now. Rennet, Mr. Archie, and Mr. Eloi all helped get the holes in the roof and porch fixed, and the trees off the house. We can handle the rest, but thanks."

Jess said, "Aurelie and I discussed having a girl's night yesterday morning at market. Maybe once she is feeling a little better, we ladies can surprise her with a visit? I'm sure she will be going out of her mind soon being laid up for so long."

Sophanes said, "That sounds like a great idea. Baxter, you'll have to keep Jess here apprised of how she is doing, and when might be a good time for that."

Baxter nodded as murmurs of excitement went around the pavilion, all the ladies chatting about what to do for the event.

Procne said, "Settle down now ladies, we still have matters to discuss."

It grew quiet again and Procne began. "It's been twenty years since the collapse, and yet fewer since the wars, but in all that time we went without a major storm or hurricane. People, I believe God has protected us for so many years. It's not like it used to be. When we got word or warning of a storm, we could load up in the cars and evacuate to somewhere else until it was over. Now, we don't even have a warning that a storm is coming until it's already upon us. I for one am grateful for God's protection."

Murmurs of the like-minded flitted through the crowd.

Procne asked, "I'm sure with everyone pitching in to help we can get those with the most damage fixed up quickly, then move on to the other places. As far as cleaning up the debris, we'll make a large pile on the center of the beach for burnable materials and have a bonfire later next week. Now, is there anything else we need to discuss other than the order in which we will manage repairs?"

Sophanes and Jess looked at one another and smiled. Sophanes said, "Procne, Jess and I would like to be married, right here, tonight."

The pavilion exploded with shouts, clapping, laughter, and hearty congratulations. Someone even yelled, "It's about time!" which caused even more laughter.

When things settled down, Procne asked, "Are you two sure you don't want a proper wedding?"

Jess said, "Thanks, but we've already wasted years waiting on the right time, we don't wish to waste any more."

Mary said, "Well, dear, we can still have it tonight, and with all these ladies present, we can have this place in tiptop shape within the hour. Besides, it's been fifteen years since we've had any kind of wedding to officiate."

Jess looked up at Sophanes who shrugged and grinned. "Whatever you want to do is fine with me. If we say no, I'm afraid they might all string us up."

Jess giggled and looked around at all the anxious faces who were nodding and begging her to let them do it up properly.

"Well, okay I guess."

The pavilion exploded again in excitement as all the women gathered together to make plans. Mary headed up and organized the wedding decorations and music. Kei planned the food and cake, while Claire, Reesa, Reine, Emilie, Thalia, and Sandra all gathered around Jess, fussing over what to do with her hair and where to find a dress that would fit her. Many of the older ladies had their old dresses hanging in the closet at home or packed in a protective storage box.

Sandra stepped up, "You look to be the same size I was when I got married, Why don't all you ladies come to the house and we can take care of the bride to be?"

Everyone agreed as they followed Sandra and Marie home. Marie wasn't sure what to make of all the ladies and the fuss. Jess explained to her what was about to happen.

"Mr. Sophanes and I are going to become a family. Husband and wife."

"Like mom and dad were?"

"Yes, just like that."

"So are you gonna' have kids like me?"

Everyone laughed, and Jess said, "Well, maybe someday but not right away."

Sandra put in, "These things take time, Marie."

Jess looked at Marie and asked, "Would you like to be my flower girl?"

"Yeah! What does a flower girl do?"

"You walk in front of me and toss flowers on the ground."

"Okay!"

Sandra smiled at Jess's thoughtful, sweet, heart to include Marie in her big day. "Marie, we'll have to find you a pretty dress too."

Marie bounced up and down, clapping her hands in excitement. Sandra walked to the closet and pulled out a sealed box.

"I had my dress preserved, just in case my daughter wanted it when she got older." The sadness that flit across her face was brief but understood by all those in the room. They all knew Marie would never experience marriage. "But I'm glad I did, because, if you like it, it's yours."

Sandra tore open the box, breaking the seal, and pulled out her dress, bouquet, and shoes, all of which were in pristine condition.

Everyone gasped.

Jess said, "Oh Sandra, it's beautiful."

The empire waisted dress was covered in a beautiful, small patterned, old-fashioned lace, three-quarter inch fitted sleeves bordered by a scalloped lace, a thick white ribbon that tied in the back where the faux button pattern which conveniently concealed a zipper ran from the shoulder-height, opened-back, down to the waist. It had a small three-foot train that followed behind, with a small elastic band that attached to the wrist for dancing. Her veil was a ring of silk white and peach colored flowers and green leaves and a long white, thin ribbon that was tied in a bow and hung down the back.

The ladies excitedly began getting Jess ready. Emilie and Claire, feeling in the way, decided to go to Jess's place and get it ready for the newlyweds. They cleaned and straightened up the place; which was already neat and tidy; and got the small house prepared for a night of romance. They found as many candles as they could and placed them around the bedroom and kitchen. They found Jess's transistor radio, tuned it to one of the channels that broadcast some soft music from somewhere in the world, and left, happy with their work.

Emilie said, "We'll sneak back before they leave for the reception and light the candles."

Claire giggled. "This is so exciting. It's about time Sophanes stepped up and married that girl."

Emilie grinned at her. "I had no idea they even liked one another."

"I've known it for simply years. It was so obvious."

"I don't notice things like that." Emilie shrugged.

"You need to pay more attention, Emilie. There is one particular fellow that is head over heels for you."

"You mean Kester, or Adam?"

"You mean to tell me that you know Adam likes you?"

"Well, yeah. He hangs around like a lost puppy. Well, at least he did until yesterday at the market."

"What do you mean?"

"Well, I was flirting with Rennet. I don't know why; I know he has a thing for Aurelie. Anyway, Adam leaned down and whispered that I was behaving like a silly little schoolgirl and that I should have more respect for myself."

"Really?" Claire asked astonished.

"Yep. I was pretty angry, until I realized he was right. I also realized that I totally respected him for keeping me in line. I think I was just trying to make him jealous. Being around Rennet sure seems to have given him more of a backbone."

"I suppose so. But why try to make him jealous? He already likes you."

"Yeah, but a little competition never hurt anyone."

They both giggled at Emilie's words and over-the-top attitude.

Anytos pulled Sophanes to his house and dug out his old tuxedo. The only problem was that Sophanes was much larger than he was.

The Barter

Sophanes looked at his appearance in the mirror. "What am I going to do. I don't have any sort of suit to wear. We should have just gotten it over with and not fussed with all this."

Anytos said, "Surely we can find something for you to wear."

"All of my clothes are in my new place. And The things that I need for everyday are at Rennet's. We don't have time to run all over the place looking for something descent for me to wear.

"I have an idea, come with me."

They left Anytos' house and headed toward Archie's place.

"What are we doing here?" Sophanes asked.

"Just wait and see. You and Archie are about the same size, right?"

"I guess. I've never really compared myself to him, but we sort of see eye to eye. I can't imagine him having a suit though."

They knocked on Archie's door, hoping to find him home and not off helping to prep for the wedding.

Archie opened the door and his eyebrows shot upward.

Anytos said, "We need help." They stepped past Archie into his living room.

"Cold feet?"

"No!" Sophanes rejected quickly. "I don't have anything to wear, and Anytos thought you might."

Archie looked at them thoughtfully. "Wait here."

Archie left the room and soon returned with a rather smart-looking suit.

"Where on earth did you get that?" Sophanes asked.

"I've had it for more than twenty years. Still fits too. It should do quite well for you. Just don't mess it up. This suit cost me a pretty penny back in the day, that's why I keep it in a clothing bag."

Anytos chuckled, "It's not like you'll ever use it again."

Archie glared at him with raised eyebrows again. "How do you know? It's coming in handy right now isn't it?"

Anytos swallowed hard at the look Archie gave him and simply nodded and grinned.

Sophanes smiled at the look of fear on Anytos' face. "Thanks, Archie. This will do quite well. And I promise to return it to you in pristine condition. I'll even wash it."

"Don't do that, just send it back when you're done. I'll clean it myself. It needs a special touch."

"Let's just hope it fits right."

"You look to be the right size. Head on into my bedroom there and change."

Sophanes went into Archie's room, soon returning, decked out in the black fitted suit.

"Dude, you look good." Anytos stated in appreciation.

Archie nodded. "It fits you well."

"It does, thanks again Archie."

Anytos asked, "What about a tie?"

Archie disappeared and reappeared with several in hand.

Sophanes and Anytos both looked at each other, surprised by Archie's hidden wardrobe. They had both only ever seen the man in leather, jeans, or t-shirts.

He stopped and looked at them. "What, you don't think a man has a right to have some nice clothes?"

They both only nodded yes quickly not wanting to anger him, especially since he was the one helping them. Archie picked a tie and even tied it for Sophanes, who had no clue how to do so.

"How you fellas' ever navigated the world of women before the collapse I'll never know." Archie stated. He stepped back and looked Sophanes over. He and Anytos exchanged looks and shrugged.

"It's okay?" Sophanes asked nervously.

"You're no me, but it'll do nice enough." Archie stated.

Sophanes and Anytos shook their heads in amusement to Archie's statement and the three of them walked to the pavilion.

Back at Aurelie's Baxter was excitedly telling everyone about the meeting and the wedding to take place soon.

Aurelie said, "I wish I could attend; I just don't think I could handle the ride over."

Birdie thought a minute. "What about if we blow up the old air mattress and put it in the trailer? We can layer pillows and blankets all around you and drive really slowly."

Rennet said with apprehension, "I don't know, Birdie, Aurelie's injuries are very fresh and new. This could cause her a lot of pain."

Aurelie added, "Not to mention the fact that I can't wash my hair where the stitches are."

"I'll wash everything else for you avoiding the stitched area, and you can wear one of your pretty summer hats." Birdie offered happily.

Aurelie looked at Rennet, who could tell she was fighting with the decision. He knew she really wanted to go.

"We can try it if you want to Aurelie. Whatever you want to do."

"Both Sophanes and Jess are my friends. I would like to try."

"All right then, everyone get ready to attend a wedding." Rennet grinned down at Aurelie who worriedly grinned back.

Everyone scattered, except for Birdie who patiently and carefully washed Aurelie's hair. She then picked out a pretty sun-dress for Aurelie to change into. One that hung and wouldn't bind around her ribcage. She then found a loose-fitting pair of decorative flip-flops that matched the dress and that wouldn't interfere or bind the wrapping around her ankle. When she was done, Birdie opened the bedroom door. Rennet was sitting on the couch waiting for them. He stepped into Aurelie's room.

He smiled at Aurelie, then turned to Birdie. "You did a wonderful job, Birdie, of fixing up our cripple."

"Thanks, I'm just going to run upstairs and change."

Rennet looked over Aurelie's appearance. "If it weren't for the bandaged ankle, no one would even know you were hurt. You look beautiful."

The Barter

Aurelie smiled at him. "Thanks, I hardly feel it though. Could you get me some more pain medication before we leave? I think I might need it."

"Absolutely." He walked to the kitchen, grabbed the medicine, removing the necessary dosage and placing the rest in a pocket. He returned to her room and handed the pills and a bottle of water to Aurelie.

She downed the meds and sat the water on the bedside table. "I guess I'm ready."

Baxter entered the room. "I got the mattress ready, and put some blankets, the couch pillows, and the girls' bed pillows on top. Mine are soaked from the roof damage."

Aurelie smiled at him. "Thank you Baxter. I'm sure whatever you have rigged up will be fine." She looked up at Rennet who then bent down and gently scooped her into his arms.

Rennet stopped moving, hearing her sharp intake of breath. "Are you all right?" He asked her, looking directly into her eyes, not taking another step until she answered.

Aurelie, shyly nodded then braved to look back at him. "Yes, I'm fine." The caring that she saw there was enough to take her breath away. This stranger that she had met just a little over a week ago made her feel completely safe.

Rennet nodded. "Are you ready?"

She said, "I think so."

He carefully carried her outside and placed her on the air mattress, tucking pillows and blankets all around her. He then looked at the kids. "We will attempt this, but you all need to help me keep an eye on Aurelie. If she appears to be hurting any worse, then we all come home immediately."

Everyone agreed to do their part and they all climbed into the cart. Katie being the lightest, climbed on top of the mattress with Aurelie to keep watch over her. Rennet drove the cart and trailer, which moved painstakingly slowly for the two-mile ride to the beach.

Baxter commented, "We could likely walk faster than this."

Rennet looked over at him. "Probably so, but we don't want to risk jarring Aurelie around at all. Some spots in the road have ruts and pot-holes.

Baxter nodded, and looked back at Aurelie who was chatting with Katie. "I'm just glad she feels up to going. Not that I wanted to go or anything, I'm just glad she's going to be all right."

Rennet nodded. "But, we'll still have our work cut out for us when we get there. We have to make sure people understand that they can't hug or touch her."

Baxter nodded. "I'll handle that."

Rennet grinned at the boy's look of determination. "I'm sure you will.

Chapter 19

Rennet pulled the cart and trailer up beside the side of the pavilion, giving Aurelie a good view of the front where the bride and groom would stand. Everyone, dressed in their absolute best, suddenly encompassed the trailer; all questioning Aurelie all at once.

Baxter stood between her and the approaching crowd, his hands raised in the air to halt the assault.

"Please everybody, Aurie is still hurt and sore, she just wanted to see Jess and Sophanes get married. No body touch or try to hug her."

Everyone respectfully agreed, they all just expressed their happiness at seeing her in good health then departed to find a seat for the big event.

Arjit saw Aurelie sitting on the trailer, and Rennet propped up on the side sitting beside her along with the kids who encircled her protectively.

He decided to find a seat near the back of the pavilion, not wishing to cross paths with Aurelie in her current state. He was still angry at her for her words on market day and the fact that Rennet McCabe was staying at her place was the hammer driving the nail, especially since he had witnessed their argument when the Market suddenly closed before the storm. He thought he had placed a wedge in whatever budding relationship that was beginning between them, but

Aurelie's unfortunate accident seemed to have repaired the rift he had created.

Arjit looked over and nodded to an attractive woman sitting a few chairs down whom he had only seen a handful of times before.

She smiled, held out her hand, and introduced herself.

"Hello, I'm Jen Grayson."

He nodded and accepted her hand.

"Arjit Chiasson."

"I've heard some about you. You've quite the reputation around here."

"Is that so? Exactly what have you heard?" he asked, curious to what people were saying about him.

"Only that you have quite the spread. Cattle, farmland, good crops, and that you're quite the eligible bachelor. I'm also a good friend of Aurelie's." She smiled at him making Arjit sit a little taller, grinning back at her. Not sure what her last statement meant.

The music began as Sophanes stepped up to the front of the congregation. Everyone stood as Jess began her walk down the aisle between the rows of chairs that flanked both sides. When she reached the front and turned to face Sophanes she saw Aurelie off to the side. Jess grinned brightly and waved. Aurelie mouthed that Jess looked beautiful.

Procne officiated the ceremony which was short and sweet. After Sophanes and Jess made their return walk down the aisle as Mr. and Mrs. Leos, they both quickly made their way over to Aurelie. Rennet and the kids had walked off to get everyone some party food and beverages.

Jess smiled, and put out her hand to Aurelie, who gladly took it. "Aurie, I'm so surprised to see you here, but happy too."

"I didn't want to miss your and Sophanes' big day. Jess that dress is absolutely gorgeous on you."

"Thanks, it belonged to Sandra. She gave it to me. But I suddenly realize now looking at the state in which you were brought here, that perhaps we should have waited until you were well enough to attend."

Aurelie gave her a disbelieving look. "Hold your tongue woman. Absolutely not. This day has been coming for you two for a very long time." She smiled brightly at them both.

Sophanes said, "We'd hug you but from what I understand Baxter has made it perfectly clear that such actions are off limits." He laughed at the boy's spunk.

"Yes. He's ever so protective of me in this state." She laughed with them, wincing in pain.

They both looked concerned as jess asked, "Are you all right?"

"Yes." She inhaled deeply and exhaled slowly. "Busted ribs make it hard to do a lot of things that we often take for granted."

Sophanes nodded. "I've been there and completely understand. But, when you're better, you owe me a dance."

Aurelie smiled at her friend. "Deal, although now you have a wife to consider."

Jess smiled broadly at her. "I guess we had better get to that ourselves now that everyone has moved the chairs back. We'll see you soon,

Aurie." They turned and walked to the dance floor.

Rennet and the kids returned with plates and cups in hand. Birdie handed Aurelie a plate of snack foods, Baxter set down a dessert plate and Katie placed the glass of iced tea on the tire's fender. They sat and ate in silence for a minute as they watched everyone having a good time dancing.

Aurelie watched the kids, knowing they were itching to go dance.

"Baxter," she said, "why don't you, Birdie, and Katie go have fun. I'll be just fine right here for a little while."

"I don't feel like it Aurie," Baxter shrugged.

However the girls were more than happy to join in the dancing. Birdie and Katie set down their plates and happily ran to the middle of the floor.

Aurelie sighed and noticed that Reine Divins was watching Baxter.

"I think you should go ask Reine to dance."

Baxter's cheeks flushed red. "Aurie," he said under his breath, "she's older than me."

"Only by a year. Besides, she looks like she wants you to ask her."

Rennet looked over at the girl who was shyly grinning and gazing in Baxter's direction.

"I think Aurie's right. Besides, Reine is cute."

Baxter looked mortified.

Then Rennet looked at Baxter and said, "Baxter do you see Sophanes and Jess?"

"Yeah," the boy answered, looking at the two happily dancing.

"Well, from what I've gathered, they have liked one another for nearly twenty years. They waited so long to tell each other how they felt. It wasn't until Sophanes feared losing Jess to someone else that he realized that he was in love with her. Don't waste your life because of your fear. Life is about taking chances, no matter the outcome."

Baxter nodded, chancing a look at Reine. He looked at Aurelie with a questioning stare.

"Go. Have fun."

"But I feel bad that you're stuck here in the trailer."

"Bax, honey, you are not to blame. I don't want you to feel like you can't have fun. Besides, I take no greater joy than watching you and the girls enjoying life. Please, go enjoy the evening."

Baxter sighed, and looked at Reine again, who was watching him and smiling.

Rennet leaned over and squeezed his shoulder in encouragement. "Go get that girl, young man."

Baxter stood up, grabbed Aurelie's hand, giving it a shake and walked over to Reine.

Rennet watched the joy that lit Aurelie's face.

"Thank you for figuring out how to get me here, Rennet."

"It was actually Birdie's idea, remember." He smiled down at her.

She giggled and winced. "Yes. Those kids are awesome little humans."

"That they are."

They exchanged looks of agreement, and then Aurelie quickly glanced back at the floor.

"Rennet, you don't have to just sit here with me. Go dance, enjoy yourself. It's not very often that we have a wedding after all."

Rennet looked down at her. "I'm quite content where I am."

The look on his face made her heart race a little and her cheeks felt as though they were flushed. She grinned demurely and turned to watch the people on the floor. They ate and chatted for a little while, watching their friends and family enjoying the evening.

Rennet said, "Watching everyone now, it's hard to believe that just this morning we were all cleaning up after a hurricane."

Aurelie smiled, though her eyes were showing pain in contrast to her encouraging words. "We're a resilient bunch here on the coast."

"I agree." He watched her face for a minute then said, "I'll be right back."

Rennet stood, taking the plates and drinks and placed them on a table. He walked over to Baxter and the girls and whispered something. He then spoke to Archie, who amazingly enough seemed to be staying sober even though Eloi was already a few sheets into the wind. When he returned to Aurelie's side he said, "I think it's time to get you home young lady."

"No, the kids are enjoying themselves. I don't want to cut it short."

"That's why I asked Archie to bring them home. And I told them the same thing."

The Barter

"Are you sure they'll be all right. Archie is known to tie one on."

"Yes, they'll be fine. He isn't drunk at all tonight."

Rennet made sure she was comfortable before starting the slow drive back to Aurelie's. She lay in the trailer, looking up at the star-filled sky. The night was so clear she could make out the Milky Way. She inhaled as deeply as her aching ribs would allow and smiled happily. She may not be in the best physical condition right now, but her life seemed brighter than it had in a very long time.

Sure she had always been happy so to speak, but she always felt like she was just living instead of thriving. Now, for whatever reason, be it the kids growing up, their community pulling together like never before, Jess and Sophanes' wedding, or Rennet McCabe's presence in her life, she truly felt content at this moment in time.

She thought about Rennet. The man had gone out of his way to make her comfortable and take care of her family. She had to admit, even if only to herself, he stirred feelings deep inside her that she didn't even know existed; but she wasn't completely ready to just give herself over to her feelings. She had the kids to consider, and Rennet was basically knew to the area. She had no idea if he would actually stay around; he may grow bored one day and decide to just pick up and leave here.

When they arrived at home, Rennet carefully picked Aurelie up and carried her into the house.

He laid her on the bed removing her flip-flops and hat.

"Rennet."

"Yeah?"

"I need to use the bathroom."

"Oh, okay. If I help you to the door, can you manage from there?"

"Yes."

He went to pick her up again and she said, "You don't have to carry me. I can just lean on your arm."

"What? And give up the chance to have you in my arms?" he grinned mischievously, wiggling his eyebrows as he hefted her into his arms once more. She giggled and then groaned.

"Sorry, I'll try not to make you laugh again."

"That would be wonderful, at least for a little while."

He carried her into the bathroom and set her down by the toilet.

"I'll just be outside."

"I think I may take a bath. Well, at least a sink bath anyway."

"Do you need to wait on Birdie to return?"

"I think I can manage by myself, but I can't turn on the generator to heat the water."

"How do I do that?"

"Just off the kitchen porch is a generator tied into the electrical panel. Switch it on, then go to the breaker box on the living room wall and turn on the breaker that says water heater."

"Sounds easy enough. If you need me I'll be right here."

The Barter

"Thank you, Rennet." Aurelie looked up at him with sincerity.

"You're welcome, Aurelie."

She could feel the meaning behind his words.

He left the bathroom and pulled the door closed behind him. Rennet had never felt this way about someone else before. Sure he had thought what he had a few years back was the real thing, but that quickly proved to be untrue. He was glad of that change, because he now realized that the feelings he had for Madison was nothing compared to what he now felt for Aurelie. This had to be real. This had to be what true love felt like.

Rennet decided to flip the breaker on the water-heater first, then found the generator and turned it on. He noticed that he had forgotten all about the pillows and blankets on the trailer and pulled everything inside, leaving the inflated mattress on the porch. He took care of the few dishes in the kitchen and put on some coffee to brew. He definitely needed a cup and figured Aurelie may want one as well.

When the coffee finished brewing, he took his cup and went into Aurelie's room just in case she needed him. He had just set his mug down when she cracked the bathroom door enough to speak to him.

"Rennet, I didn't grab any clothes before I came in. Can you look in the bottom drawer of my dresser and hand me a pair of sleep pants and a t-shirt?"

"Sure, anything else?"

"Yes." She gave him a pained smile, figuring he knew what else she needed.

He grinned at her with that crooked, dimpled grin. "I got it. Where are they?"

"Top drawer."

"I promise not to look too hard or long."

"Thank you."

Aurelie was quite embarrassed having to ask him to send her underclothes as well. Having a man dig in her unmentionables drawer was tough to swallow. Perhaps she should have waited for Birdie to return. But she was growing quite tired and just wanted to crash. She really needed some pain medication again too.

Rennet knocked on the door, and she pulled it slightly open, sticking her head around the corner. "Thank you, Rennet. I'm sorry you have to do all of this."

"Aurelie, it's not a problem. I told you, whatever you need, I'm here." Rennet looked her in the eyes once again as they held each other's attention. He then asked, "I made some coffee. Would you like a cup?"

"No, I don't think so, but I will need another pain pill and some water."

"I'll have it here when you're done."

She closed the door and got dressed, brushed her teeth, and tried to brush out her hair a little, which nearly brought tears to her eyes, deciding that would have to wait for a while longer.

She pulled open the door to find Rennet sitting on the edge of her bed waiting on her to appear. He stood up and took her hand in his. She hobbled to the bed slowly, not wishing to hop because of the jarring it would cause to her ribcage, and her head.

The Barter

Rennet helped her to sit down and handed her the pain pills and water. Once she had taken them, he then helped her scoot back against the pillows propping her ankle up and covering her with the blanket.

He leaned over her one last time and asked, "Do you need anything else?"

"No, thank you. I'm really tired. I think I'll just try to sleep."

"Well, if you need anything, both Baxter and I will be in the living room. Tomorrow, after we get his room dried in and repaired, he and I will put his room back together. His mattress should be dry by then and he'll be able to use his room again."

"What about you Rennet? Are you planning on living on the couch?"

"I've slept in much worse places before." He smiled at her concern.

Aurelie grinned at his humor. "Goodnight Rennet."

"Goodnight Aurelie."

He stood and walked out of the room, pulling her door closed but not completely just to make sure he could hear her if she needed anything. He went to sit on the couch, suddenly realizing how exhausted he was. It had been an extremely long day. With everything that had taken place over the last two days, he couldn't help falling asleep as he waited on the kids to arrive.

It was nearing ten-thirty when Archie returned the kids home, leaving the cut down crutches for Aurelie with them. Baxter heard the generator running on the side of the house and turned it off.

The kids entered the house, realizing it was quiet. Baxter shushed the girls, not wanting to wake Aurelie or Rennet. He placed the crutches beside Aurelie's bed where she would see them if she needed them, then they all crept upstairs to change. He grabbed a clean pillow and blanket and pulled the air mattress off the porch where Rennet had left it, dragging it into the living room and onto the floor. He covered the sleeping Rennet with a spare blanket then curled up on the mattress and fell fast asleep.

Chapter 20

Aurelie woke in the early morning hours. Her head hurt and she felt a little stiff from where she had lain in the same position for most of the night. She put her hands underneath her and pushed her weight up, wincing and groaning in pain; her ribs causing the worst of it. Her head throbbed but it was manageable, and her ankle didn't really hurt unless she put her weight on it. She needed to use the bathroom but didn't want to disturb anyone. She sat there for a minute just sinking into the bed pillows at her back. The soft support they lent was heavenly, but she was so tired of lying around. It had only been one full day and she was already about to go crazy. How was she supposed to do this for several weeks? She looked around her room as the pale moonlight lit the interior furnishings. Her eyes suddenly fell on something leaning against the headboard beside her bed. She squinted into the dim light trying to make out what it was. Crutches! Where did those come from? She didn't know, but she was certainly glad for them. She pushed back the sheets and carefully scooted to the edge of the bed as the pain began to pulse everywhere. She saw the bottle of water and pain medication Rennet had left for her and she took a few of the pills to ward off any excessive pain her moving about would undoubtedly cause. After that, she reached for the crutches and slowly pulled herself to a standing position with their support.

She smiled at her accomplishment so far and tucked each crutch beneath an arm. The weight of her body and the position of the crutch pad did cause some discomfort in her ribs, but she would figure out how to position it eventually. She took a step forward, then another, and another, until she was in the bathroom. She smiled happily at her new freedom. At least now Rennet wouldn't insist on carrying her everywhere. His arms were feeling too familiar and comfortable, and she was not ready for that.

"This will do quite nicely," she said to herself.

She took care of business and decided that she wanted some coffee. She slowly and quietly made her way through the living room, noticing Baxter on the air mattress and Rennet passed out on the couch. She continued into the kitchen and put on a large pot of coffee. While she waited on it to brew, she decided to walk out the kitchen door to view the destruction the storm left behind. Fortunately the back porch was undamaged. It was still a little dark outside, but the sun would come up shortly and bathe her farm in dappled light. Of course with the extent of tree damage, that dappling might now look like full on sunshine.

She stood on the screened porch, listening to the early morning bird calls. All seemed right in the world; nature seemed undisturbed by yesterday morning's hurricane. If only her world was just as undisturbed. She thought about Rennet who slept just a mere thirty or so feet away. She appreciated every effort he had made with her and the kids' comfort in mind, but she could likely handle things now that she could get around on her own.

The ocean breeze began to blow a little harder as the sun began its ascent over the horizon. Aurelie stood, her face in the wind once more, enjoying the fresh smell of the ocean air, and smiling at all that God had given her. She might be bruised and battered, but she was here. The tree that had fallen on her could have killed her, and then the kids would be all alone. She knew she should have simply put her foot down and not gone out after the dogs, but Baxter had been so determined. She couldn't imagine him being hurt instead of herself.

She glanced around at the larger branches on the ground. It appeared that all the smaller debris had already been taken care of. She knew Archie, Eloi, Rennet, and the kids had all worked most of yesterday to repair necessary damages, but they had also cleaned up the yard. She wondered how the garden and orchard had fared and hoped that neither had too much damage.

The smell of the coffee brewing filtered out the screen door. Figuring it was done, she went back inside, surprised to find Rennet standing in the kitchen. His hair was a disheveled mess, and he stood their yawning and stretching. She must have startled him because he jumped when she entered the kitchen.

She smiled at him. "Sorry, I didn't mean to surprise you like that."

"I just wasn't sure who was coming through the door. I expected one of the kids." Rennet was surprised by the progress she was already making. "Well, look at you. I guess Archie sent those crutches back with the kids last night."

"Yeah, they're great. This is so much better than lying around on my backside."

"Well, it doesn't mean you can run all over the place. You still have to keep your ankle elevated to reduce swelling."

"My ankle is the least of my worries."

Rennet gave her a look.

"All right, all right. I promise to be good. But lying around will drive me crazy."

At the look he gave her and to stop whatever it was he was about to say, she held up her hands and added, "But, I promise to take it easy."

"Good, because I'm going to be here to make sure of that."

"Rennet, I truly appreciate everything you've done for me and the kids. But, now that I can get around, you don't have to stay here."

She noticed he seemed a bit taken aback by her words. He ran his hands through his hair and said, "Well, until you can lift and carry things on your own, I'll be here, okay."

She sighed heavily. "Okay." She nodded and stiffly grinned at him.

He stepped closer to her and said lowly, "Aurelie, if I've made you uncomfortable in any way, I apologize. I promise to keep my distance if that makes you feel better. I never want you to feel like I'm pushing myself on you. As soon as you're well enough, I promise, I'll leave you to your life."

He walked out of the kitchen and off the porch out into the yard as she stood there, figuratively kicking herself.

The Barter

"Great job, Aurelie," she chastised herself for apparently hurting his feelings somehow. She must have come off as unappreciative, or uncomfortable with him. When he came back inside she would have to explain.

She poured herself a cup of coffee and sat at the table to drink it. It wasn't too long before she heard the generator start up and Rennet appeared in the kitchen. Before she had a chance to say anything, he looked over at her and asked, "Do you mind if I take a shower?"

"No, not at all."

"Is there another bathroom?"

"There is one upstairs, but you're welcome to use the one in my room."

"Thanks." He walked over and grabbed his pack and walked into her room. She could hear the door click and the shower turn on.

Yep, she had definitely put her foot in it somehow. But before she would get the chance to speak to him about how her answer had come off, Baxter woke up and walked into the kitchen.

"Good morning, Aurie. I see you found the crutches." He grinned sleepily at her, walking to the coffee pot for a cup.

She smiled at him. "Yes, thank you for bringing them home, and make sure you thank Archie for me when you see him."

"I will. I plan on going into town after chores are done. Several towns people are going to start working on Foesy Divins' place. Half the roof is gone." He sat in a chair at the table with her, adding honey and cream to his cup.

"Goodness, was anyone hurt?"

"No. It's all good. Sophanes is letting them stay at his place until it's fixed."

"Well that was kind of him."

"Yeah. I guess he really doesn't need it now."

"True, but with his place being so new, I'm sure he and Jess will move into it once the Divins' place is finished."

"Yeah, his place is bigger than her smaller cottage. What do you think she'll do with hers?"

Aurelie thought for a second and shrugged. "I'm sure I don't know. Perhaps one of the young adults would like to move into it as a starter place."

"That's what I figured. With all the repairs and cleanup needing to be done, Rennet's plans to restore the other cottages will have to wait. I wonder if any of the already damaged and vacant places have more damage now?"

"Probably so, Bax. I would think that if structurally sound places have damage, than those empty places with holes in the walls and rooves certainly have more."

Rennet appeared from Aurelie's room, set his pack on the floor by the couch and walked to the kitchen.

"Morning Bax." Rennet headed for the coffee pot and poured himself a cup.

"Morning, Rennet. You can leave the generator on. The girls and I need to shower, so I'll turn it off later."

"So," he asked, leaning back against the countertop crossing his ankles and looked at Aurelie, "What's first today? I know there are a lot of chores that need doing along with finishing the cleanup."

The Barter

Aurelie said, "Well, I usually tend to the orchard harvesting and the garden, but I'm wondering how everything handled the storm."

Baxter answered, "Several of the garden plants are broken and damaged. A few tree limbs did end up in the garden. I removed the branches yesterday, but we might not get much off the plants now."

She sighed, "Well, it is getting to the end of summer anyway. I guess we should start the seedlings for the Winter in the greenhouse so we can have some fresh produce over the fall and winter months.

"I can do that," Rennet stated.

"No, the girls can tend to that when they get up. I'm sure your skills and strength can best be used elsewhere."

"True. Baxter and I will walk the orchards and gardens and inspect damages. We can try to repair any broken limbs or plants or remove them to allow the trees to heal."

"I wish I could go out with y'all instead of just sitting here."

Rennet looked at her, realizing that this period of being an invalid was going to drive her insane and likely make her cranky. He also noticed the painful look on Baxter's face at her words.

He gave her a look and nodded to Baxter, then said, "Maybe in a day or two Aurelie. It's only been twenty-four hours so far. Give yourself time to heal."

She looked at him, a look of regret on her face at her words. "You're right; I know I'm being unreasonable. Besides, I'm sure I can find something to occupy my time. I've been getting back to drawing lately. This time will give me the opportunity to explore my writing and drawing again."

"That's the spirit," Rennet stated exuberantly, mostly for Baxter's benefit.

The boy's countenance did seem to change some based on Aurelie's tone. She noticed it as well. She would have to make sure she didn't complain so much, if for nothing more than Baxter's conscience. He already felt responsible, and she certainly didn't want to make him feel any worse.

Rennet asked, "What's for breakfast, and where do I find it to cook it?"

Baxter grinned. "The Zeer pots on the porch here." He stood up to show Rennet where to find eggs, and bacon. When Baxter returned, Aurelie asked him to give her all the ingredients to make biscuits. She could do that sitting down. He obliged, then added wood to the oven and lit it. The three of them talked about the day's chores, the mending of the dog pen which did sustain some damage after all, the wedding from the night before, and the budding relationship between Baxter and Reine Divins.

The girls eventually appeared in the kitchen, feigning starvation and the smell of the food making them hungry. Aurelie told them it was their job this morning to tend to the damaged garden plants and to pick anything that survived. Afterward, if everything there at home was taken care of, they would all maybe go with Baxter into town to see about helping out with clean up and damage repairs.

"Aurelie, how are you going to manage that?" Rennet asked her.

"Y'all got me there last night."

"Yes, but we also stayed with you. We'll be running all over helping people with repairs."

"So, just set me in a swing under a cottage somewhere and leave me be. I'm sure I'll be just fine."

Rennet looked at her questioningly. "And what happens if you need a bathroom. Climbing all those steps to any one of the places for that will be a challenge."

"I'll go to Archie's if I need the bathroom. Sandra's place isn't too far from there, and she does need repairs done. Plus she is the nurse, and Katie and Marie will both likely be close if I need anything."

Rennet shook his head in frustration. "Fine, but I hope you don't regret all this running around that you're doing."

"Like I said, Sandra is a nurse. I'll be fine. Besides, I know you all want to go help everyone else, and that you won't dare leave me here alone, so this is the only option."

Rennet said, "Fine. When we are done, we'll come back here, eat lunch, pack a snack and beverage basket and head to the beach area."

"Deal," Aurelie said, as she slowly kneaded the bread, realizing that the motion and pushing actually made her ribs hurt, but she wasn't about to tell anyone. Instead, she simply encouraged Katie to have a turn at the process and learn to make biscuits. Katie excitedly accepted, listening to Aurelie's instructions carefully.

Birdie and Baxter went out to tend to a few chores until breakfast was done.

Rennet stood at the wood burning stove cooking the eggs and bacon while he watched Aurelie and Katie at the table. He smiled at the scene before him. He could really get used to having people in his life daily; especially these people. He had already grown quite attached to the kids, and his heart was already fully attached to Aurelie Haydel. He wasn't sure she felt the same, especially after the look on her face earlier when he had said he would be here until she could manage on her own. He felt he was in her way, maybe she even saw him as a nuisance? But, if he could manage it, he would do his best to win Aurelie's heart. He had no desire to go anywhere else. He had found a home in this community, even if Aurelie Haydel wanted nothing more than his friendship.

Chapter 21

Chores and added cleanup around the Haydel farm was finished, lunch was eaten, and the whole crew loaded up in the side-by-side and trailer to head over to the beach for more storm cleanup and repairs. Rennet and Baxter loaded up tools, ladders, and anything else they thought someone might need to repair and replace damaged items. They also grabbed drinks and snacks to help fuel them for the remainder of the day, and Aurelie's pain medication just in case she needed it.

They pulled up to Sandra's house, got Aurelie settled on the swing and everyone went in separate directions to help someone in need.

Katie and Marie pulled Marie's wagon around and picked up trash and smaller debris while Rennet and Baxter went down the road to help repair the roof on Foesy's place.

Sandra approached the swing from behind and asked, "Aurelie, how have you been feeling?"

"Not too bad. Some headaches and rib pain but that is expected."

"Yes, it is." Sandra leaned down to inspect the stitches in her scalp.

"Are you sure you'll be all right here by yourself?"

"Yes, Sandra, I'm fine. Go, help someone else. Rennet left me the cart. If I need a restroom, I'll drive over to Archie's place. These crutches are very handy."

"Yes, well, no trying to go too fast, especially on your own."

"I promise," Aurelie said, holding her hand up with two fingers pointed toward the sky and her other hand over her heart.

"You were a scout back in the day?"

"Nope. I just figured it was a binding contract." Aurelie looked up at her and grinned.

Sandra smirked at her as she walked toward her gate. "If the girls come back and need anything, just tell Katie she knows where everything is and to help themselves."

"Sure thing."

Aurelie smiled at the woman who had become a very close friend as of late. They had all lived in the same community, spent time together weekly, and even at special events during the months, but they had only recently really began spending time together on a personal level.

Aurelie sat swinging in the cool, breezy, shade of Sandra's overhead cottage. She watched as people moved about the area, all waving hello to her. Kei blew her kisses and waved while Aurelie returned the gesture.

It appeared that everyone was here cleaning and repairing after the storm. The ground looked like ants all scattered about, working tirelessly on different things. She wished she could help somehow, but even though that was not a possibility, she was glad to be here right now in the thick of things. This was much better than sitting at home bored out of her mind. The happenings along the beach reminded her of television shows when she was a little girl. People watching was certainly entertaining as they laughed and chatted, fussed and cussed about hammering a finger, or argued over the best way to repair something.

She smiled and looked up toward the sky. "Thank you Lord for sparing our little community and those that live here."

The workday continued well into the evening hours as people began to slink away to their homes for nourishment and rest. The beach area had been cleaned of debris, and Foesy, Reesa, and Reine's home had been reroofed. The men decided to replace the entire thing to make the structure solid and sound, especially since the other half that was still intact was missing many shingles, and Archie had more than enough pallets of shingles stored up in the back of the building to replace them all.

As dusk settled over the area, Aurelie's crew returned and they all piled up in the side-by-side for the trip home. The tired crew of workers, and one worn out invalid who was exhausted from just sitting, ate a sparse, quick, dinner, then cleaned up, changed clothing, and everyone crashed in their respective beds.

For the next several weeks, life was busy both at Aurelie's farm and in the beach community. It was the same routine nearly every day. Wake, eat, farm chores, trim broken branches, replant replacement plants for the ones that were destroyed, lunch, then off to the beach to help someone else.

The Divins' place was finished, and people in the community who had extra furniture stored away somewhere gave what they could to help replace damaged and waterlogged pieces. Michael Guittreaux, who was the toy maker, also made furniture and fashioned a new wooden couch frame, while Reesa and several other ladies made new cushions by stripping the old fabric off their old ones, drying out the wet foam, and recovering the cushions.

Aurelie was healing well and quickly. For the first week or so she sat and drew a lot, keeping her ankle elevated and giving her ribcage time to mend. Her head healed nicely and at one of the visits to town, Sandra was able to remove the stitches. Aurelie happily took a long, luxurious shower that night to wash any residual blood from her scalp. By the second week, she was able to put weight on her ankle and walk, still having to elevate it in the evening hours to minimize swelling from the day's use.

With her new-found freedom, she was able to take care of things inside, and go out and help pick fruits and vegetables, but she still could not carry the baskets; her ribs taking the longest to heal.

By this time, the ladies decided it was time to have their girl's night and everyone surprised Aurelie by showing up and bringing snacks. They sent Rennet and the kids off to the pavilion to spend time with the men and other kids. The women spent the better part of the night talking, giggling, and teasing Aurelie about Rennet staying there.

By the third week she was all healed up and Fall was in the air. The crisp cool mornings, hot afternoons, and warm to cooling nights ushered in the need to hunt. All the places in town were repaired and everyone got on with life once more; meaning Rennet would soon return home.

The Barter

She still had not been able to speak to him about their conversation and her reaction to him staying here, and how his advances toward her, though light as they were, were received. For the last three and a half weeks, he had been true to his word. He was kind, attentive, helpful, and did anything that needed doing, but the playful flirtations had stopped. He still joked with the kids and her, smiled and laughed, played games, and acted silly. But other than an occasional look her way or at times when she would catch him watching her; which would make her insides feel like a bowl of shaking gelatin; he never said another word about how he felt.

One quiet Fall morning, as the sun peeked over the distant tree-line, she was sitting on the front porch swing with her coffee cup and her sketch pad when Rennet walked out with his mug of coffee and sat beside her on the swing.

They smiled at one another but there always seemed to be a tension hanging in the air between them. Aurelie couldn't handle the quiet politeness any longer.

"Rennet, I know you have to get back to your own life and home. I just want you to know how much I appreciate everything you've done for us; for me."

"You're welcome, Aurelie, I…" He stopped speaking and she could see he was trying to figure out what to say. "I've enjoyed staying here with you and the kids. It's like having a real family. I haven't had that since my mom died. So, thank you; for allowing me to stay here and basically trusting me with your lives." He smiled, knowing he had been a complete stranger.

Someone they had known only a week when he had moved into her home to help her.

She smiled back, giggling at his words.

Rennet watched her. How he loved her smile and the sound of her voice and laughter. He wasn't sure how he was going to go back to living alone, but it was time for him to move out. Aurelie was doing very well, and they really didn't need him anymore.

Aurelie noticed that his smile suddenly changed to a look of seriousness and sadness. She reached over and took his right hand with her left, linking her fingers in his. She had come to value him far above any other man currently in her life and she didn't want to lose that once he moved out.

The shocked look on his face at her actions made her smile and even giggle a little. He looked down at their intertwined fingers and smiled. Probably one of the biggest smiles she had seen yet. He squeezed her hand and looked over at her without saying anything. She could see what he felt in his eyes as he looked at her.

She sighed heavily and said, "We're going to miss you around here."

"I'm going to miss being here."

He brought her hand up to his lips and brushed a kiss across the back, smoothing the skin with his thumb.

"You can always come to visit and hang out whenever you get the notion."

He smiled brightly. "Be careful what you offer. I might not leave."

"I'd be okay with that."

He looked at her with such intensity, causing Aurelie's heart to beat so hard in her chest that her healing ribcage ached a little. Rennet took their coffee cups and sat them on the side table. He turned to Aurelie, and his right hand slid up her neck and settled at the back of her head, his fingers sliding into the silky strands of her hair. His left hand caressed her cheek as he pulled her slightly forward to meet his approaching lips.

The kiss was sweet, tender, and lingering; both of them shaking a little at the contact. They pulled apart and looked at one another, gazing into each other's eyes. They both leaned back in for another kiss, but this time Aurelie's hands stretched out and wrapped around Rennet's neck as the kiss intensified. Her insides were on fire, her heart raced, and she could feel the warmth of his hands at her neck and the small of her back.

Rennet suddenly broke contact with her, and they both were breathing harder. He looked into her eyes and leaned his forehead against hers.

"We need to stop, Aurelie. I don't want to, but if I don't I won't be able to."

She shook her head in understanding. It wasn't just the two of them here; the kids were just inside. They sat there for just a few minutes, enjoying the touch of one another, and trying to control their emotions.

Little Katie stood just at the edge of the living room windows, looking out, a smile big as the sun on her face. She was giggling quietly and happily at the scene before her when Baxter and Birdie came down the steps.

Baxter asked, "Katie, what are you giggling at?" His question was answered as he looked at what had Katie's attention. He smiled brightly and looked back at Birdie who was smiling as well. The three of them all shared more giggles and high-fives.

Baxter said, "All right you two, we have to keep it quiet that we know they like each other. We don't want anything to mess this up."

Katie giggled and clapped. "I like games. This will be another fun secret to keep."

Birdie looked down at her. "What do you mean by 'another secret'?"

"I already had a secret. I guess I can tell you and Bax since it's almost the same secret anyway. I heard Rennet talking to Aurie when she first got hurt. I already knew they really liked each other. Now, I guess their liking turned into love." She smiled brightly at them.

Baxter ruffled her hair playfully. "It looks like that might be true. What do you say we be quiet, grab a quick breakfast, and sneak off the back porch to do chores? Rennet and Aurie need some privacy."

Katie and Birdie smiled brightly.

"Deal," they said in unison.

The kids all grabbed some pieces of fruit and bottles of water, being careful to stay away from the front of the house; even though Baxter had to pull Katie away to keep her from sneaking around the outside of the house to watch Rennet and Aurelie.

The Barter

Aurelie and Rennet split apart, both realizing the kids should have made an appearance by now. They both stood and went into the house.

Aurelie yelled up the staircase. "Bax, Birdie, Katie?"

No answer.

Rennet had walked into the kitchen to wash their coffee mugs he had grabbed off the porch railing, glancing out the kitchen window toward the yard and the orchard in the distance.

"Aurelie, the kids are already outside."

"What?" She walked over to the sink to peer out the window. "Well, I wonder why…" She suddenly stopped her words. "You don't think they saw us do you?"

Rennet smiled broadly. "I think that perhaps they did. And...," he said, turning to her and pulling her into his arms, "since there were no protests, assuming they disappeared to leave us alone, I'd say they are all for us being together."

She smiled at him as he wriggled his eyebrows, leaning into his arms. "I would have to agree. Besides, they already adore you; especially Baxter. He needs a man around."

"What about you?" he asked, gazing down into her eyes, his hands locked together behind her waist. "Do you need a man around?"

Aurelie grinned slightly at his question. "No."

Rennet looked confused by her answer.

"I don't necessarily *need* a man, but I do want you," she answered in all seriousness.

He grinned at her answer and leaned down for another long, agonizing kiss. When they pulled apart once more, Rennet groaned. "This is going to drive me crazy. I'm going to head into town now and try to rationalize living in my little cottage on the beach, but I know all I'll be doing is thinking about wanting to be here."

"I'm sorry. If it's any consolation, we will certainly miss you too."

"It's not." He grinned at her, kissed her once more, and broke away, going into the living room and grabbing his backpack.

"I'll drive you back to your place." Aurelie said as they walked outside to the side-by-side.

"You don't have to. I can walk it."

"Rennet, it's two miles."

"Aurelie, I've walked across the states for ten years. Two miles won't kill me. Besides, if you drive me, I'm going to be tempted to kiss you goodbye, and everyone else will see that we are now an item."

"So?"

"I've been living here for nearly a month. I don't want anyone to get the wrong idea. I'm not ready for people to know that we've progressed to affection just yet, only because I don't wish to tarnish your reputation. People can talk, and the kids don't need to hear things that are untrue."

Aurelie was surprised by his thoughtful, considerate, answer; so much so she took his face in her hands and gently kissed him.

"Thank you. I would have never thought of that being an issue, but you're right."

The Barter

"Well, I better get going. I'm sure there's work still needing to be done. I know Sandra's place needed some work before the storm, so I'll likely be there today taking care of that."

"We'll drive over later for a visit. Besides, Baxter is going to want to get back to helping you again."

"Okay, I'll see you later."

Rennet adjusted his backpack and began walking toward the beach, yelling, and waving to the kids as he left.

The kids waved back, running back to the house toward Aurelie.

Baxter asked, "Where's Rennet going?"

"Home," Aurelie said, looking at them all.

Katie said, "We thought he was gonna' stay."

"Why do you say that?"

"Because you and Rennet love each other."

"Oh, Katie, Rennet and I do care a lot for each other, but we are still getting to know one another."

"Oh." Katie thought for a minute and looked up at Aurelie. "Okay, I think I understand."

Aurelie grinned at her. "Good."

Baxter asked, "Can I go over later and see if Rennet needs help again working on his place?"

"Yes. I told him you would want to do that and we would go over later."

Birdie asked, "He didn't want a ride home?"

"Nope. He said he was used to walking. Now, what do you say we go in and have a good brunch."

"Yeah," Katie said happily.

Aurelie and Baxter both laughed at the small girl's insatiable appetite.

Rennet passed by Sandra's place and noticed the woman out in her yard.

"Good morning, Sandra."

"Hey, Rennet. You've got your pack on. I guess this means you're moving back to your place."

"Yeah, Aurelie can get around fine now, so I'm really not needed there any longer."

Sandra smiled knowingly. "I doubt that."

Rennet smiled back at her. "Well, I do need to get back to life here. So, when do you want me to start on that list of repairs for you?"

"Well, some of it was done with the storm repairs, but there are still some things inside that need doing. How about this evening?"

"Sounds good. I'll come over around two p.m."

"Okay, see you then."

Rennet continued on to his place, looking out over the places that he had wanted to start rebuilding for the younger crowd. Some of them weathered the storm okay, but a few were destroyed even further, making them unlivable.

He made it home, went upstairs to store his pack, and surveyed his surroundings. After staying with Aurelie and the kids, what once felt like his home now felt foreign to him. It was just a house, and a shell at that. He hadn't even had the chance to get any kind of furniture before the storm. He stood looking out of the large windows that faced the shoreline. The waves were lapping at the sand, flowing in, and washing back out in a rhythmic dance. He could see Reine Divins sitting outside on their swing, and Jess working in their yard in Sophanes' new place. It appeared that life in Holly Beach was back to normal for everyone, including him, and he did not like it one bit. He wanted so badly to be back at Aurelie's. He shook off the feelings of self-pity and got to work on his place again. Most everything had been finished, now he had to redo the counters and some of the cabinets. He had plenty of wood left from the rebuild to fix what needed repairing, so he got to work, taking some cabinet doors he had already removed and walked over to Foesy's place.

He and Foesy visited and worked on Rennet's cabinet doors until lunch. Reesa insisted he stay and eat with them, knowing he had little to nothing at his place since he had been gone for so long. After lunch, she sent him home with some extra provisions, and he got to work hanging the cabinet doors. After that, he headed to Sandra's to make the necessary repairs to her place.

Aurelie and the kids drove over to Rennet's to return some clothing he had left drying on the clothesline outside.

They walked up the steps but Rennet was nowhere to be found.

Baxter said, "He's likely out helping someone else with something."

Aurelie looked around at the sparse furnishings. "Yes, likely so. I forgot how barren this place really is. Rennet needs some furniture."

Katie came bounding out of the back of the house. "He doesn't even have a bed."

Aurelie spied Jess and Sophanes outside below their home, working in their yard when an idea struck her.

"Let's go visit Jess and Sophanes until Rennet gets back."

They all walked over to the Leos' home, and Aurelie struck a deal with Jess concerning the unnecessary furniture she had left in her old place.

They took the cart, went home to get the trailer, and met Jess and Sophanes at Jess's old place. They loaded her bed, some sheets, the dresser, the couch, her small kitchen table and living room furniture onto the trailer and took it back to Rennet's. When they arrived, he was home working on the cabinets once more.

Rennet heard a cart approaching his house and walked down the stairs hoping to see Aurelie. He was very surprised by what he saw.

"What's all this?" he asked Aurelie when the cart came to a stop, followed by the Leos's cart.

"Well, Jess no longer needed any of this, so we traded some things for her furniture so you'd have some stuff."

"That's really great, thank you, Aurelie."

"You're welcome."

Rennet leaned over and whispered, "I'd kiss you, but people would start to talk."

They coyly looked at one another and smiled.

Sophanes and Jess helped them unload the trailer and haul everything upstairs.

Rennet said, "Thanks for this Jess, and thank you both for all the help."

Sophanes smiled. "Well, I didn't figure Aurelie and the kids could lug this queen-sized mattress and box-spring up these steps."

They got the furniture moved in just as darkness settled over them.

The Barter

Jess and Sophanes said their goodbyes, and Rennet, Aurelie, and the kids settled onto the couch and chairs for a few minutes before they had to leave.

Rennet walked them out to say goodbye, stopping at the cart.

Aurelie turned and looked at Rennet. "We'll see you tomorrow afternoon. I'll bring you some lunch."

"Thanks, that would be most appreciated. I forgot how much work there still needs to be done here, and how little supplies I have. I've gotten spoiled living at your place."

Aurelie smiled. "We'll get you fixed up here. I'll have the girls bring some of the extra, mature, potted plants over for your garden. Although with fall already here, there isn't too much growing season left."

"Yeah, and I don't really have a warm place to store them yet. I guess I should build a garden shed of some kind down here to protect food stores for the winter."

"Yes. I don't know what winters are like in other areas, but here on the edge of the ocean, it gets very cold, especially with the wind."

"Understood." Rennet grinned at her, not wanting them to leave and feeling a bit awkward not being able to hold her and kiss her goodbye.

Aurelie felt it as well.

He smiled and said, "We're going to have to do something about this situation soon. I know it's just the first day, but I already don't like not being able to publicly show my feelings for you."

She grinned painfully, "I know. I feel the same."

Aurelie leaned over and kissed him on the cheek. They grinned at one another, and she and the kids climbed into the cart and headed home.

Katie turned to watch as Rennet faded into the darkness. "Aurie, why can't Rennet live with us again? He acts like he wants to."

Aurelie thought about her question.

"Well, Katie, Rennet's real home is here. He only stayed to help me until I was better."

"But his house is only a house, and there isn't anything there that he really needs to live. He could live much better with us. I can tell he wants to."

Baxter replied, "Rennet can't live on our couch forever, Katie, and Aurie and Rennet aren't married."

"But they want to be; right?" Katie asked, looking at Aurelie.

Aurelie smiled down at her, not answering. She pondered the simple wisdom of children and could see that adults often complicated things with so many other thoughts and worries. She knew Katie was right, about several things, and Aurelie would pray about the thoughts going through her mind at Katie's surprising revelations.

Chapter 22

The crisp fall mornings and cool nights were a nice change, although the afternoons and evening temperatures still had not changed much except for a few cooler and breezier days.

The meat storage had gotten lower than expected, especially since Rennett had been staying there, so Aurelie decided it was time to get to hunting and preparing for winter. It may not snow here in the south, but they certainly didn't want to be running around in the humid, windy, cold temperatures, up to their hips at times in water. Her fathers' old airboat took them through the swamps pretty quickly, but it would be a tight fit for all of them, plus any prey they managed to kill.

"Birdie," she said as they finished breakfast one morning, "Baxter and I are going hunting, and Rennet is coming along to learn. You and Katie will have to stay here."

"Okay. Katie and I will start stacking the firewood Baxter has been splitting by the front door and gather any kindling out in the fields."

"That would be great, thank you. Just watch for snakes, you know how they like to hide in the oaks and amongst the fallen leaves."

"Yes ma'am, we'll be careful."

Rennet showed up soon after breakfast, and Aurelie, Baxter, and he, all carrying arm-loads of supplies, walked out through the orchard to the back of the property and loaded up the airboat with their provisions for the day. Guns, ammunition, ropes for hauling prey if needed, knives for gutting, and food for lunch and snacks.

"Aurelie," Rennet stated, "I've never been in an airboat before. As a matter of fact the first time I saw one was when Eloi came over. I don't see any sort of solar panels on here to power the engine. How do you make it run?"

Aurelie and Baxter smiled at one another.

"Well," she said, "the airboats need a certain level of power to move the way they do. A solar panel large enough to give that sort of power wouldn't fit on board. So, we use Eloi's moonshine."

"Moonshine? For fuel?"

"Yep. Have you tasted Eloi's homemade moon-shine yet?"

"No," Rennet said skeptically, "and if it powers small engines, I certainly don't want to."

Baxter and Aurelie laughed at Rennet's observation.

They loaded up, got situated on the boat seats, and Aurelie warned, "Hold on tight."

Rennet was unsure what she meant, especially since rough water tended to make him sick, but as the engine started and the large rear-facing fan began to spin, he could feel the force and vibration through the metal of the boat. As Aurelie revved the motor's rpm's the fan turned faster growing louder, and the boat began its trek across the grassy yard toward the waterways not far off. The ease with which the boat moved about on land surprised Rennet, and once it hit the water, the resistance was lessened and the boat flew across the surface with ease and at great speed. Rennet was not prepared for the release of the resistance from grass to water and was thrown backward, quickly grabbing at the seat beneath him so as to not tumble over backward.

Aurelie and Baxter watched Rennet with amusement, both laughing when he nearly went heels over-head backward from his seat.

Rennet turned to look at Aurelie, a look of surprise on his face. She smiled at him and he nodded and smiled back. He turned to watch the marsh waters speed by as they flew out over the waterways, moving from pond to pond over small roadways or banks looking for signs of animal crossings, his stomach lurching each time the boat was slightly airborne. He had never traveled this fast, except by car, and that was so long ago he barely remembered the experience at all. Aurelie soon backed the boat motor down until they were stopped and settled in an area where they could hide a little. Rennet took some time to calm his churning stomach.

Aurelie pulled the boat up to the edge of the bank, secured it so it wouldn't move, and they erected a lightweight camouflaged mesh over and around them to hide from their prey.

Aurelie grabbed her rifle, handing Rennet one as well, showing him how to load the gun, aim, and shoot.

"Geese will be flying over soon. The Speckle Bellies are the best tasting. They don't have that gamey taste."

"How do I tell them apart? Don't they fly pretty high?"

"Sometimes, just shoot, we'll figure out the rest later."

"How do you store whatever meat you kill?"

"By smoking, salting, or canning."

"I've seen a bit of the process while traveling, but I haven't stayed in one place long enough to learn it from start to finish."

"Well, depending on which type of meat you're preserving depends on the process."

They quietly hunkered down and waited. A few hours later they had one deer, and about a dozen geese. They went back home to clean the meat and begin the storage process. Rennet was given a portion of the kills, dividing the meat equally between all of them, and putting what they would barter with aside for Market day.

They hung the deer and cleaned it, while the girls plucked the geese. After the long day of working, they stored what they could and went inside for dinner. Afterward, they retired to the porch to enjoy the cooling, fall, temperatures. Darkness had descended and visibility tonight was very low due to the waning crescent moon.

Aurelie asked, "Want me to drive you home?"

"Yeah, I'm too tired to walk it tonight," Rennet stated, stretching his long frame on the porch swing, and propping his feet up on the handrail.

Baxter and the girls all stood up, excusing themselves to have showers and to get ready for bed. Aurelie smiled at them as they bid each other goodnight.

"Poor things." She grinned as she watched the kids drag themselves inside. "Every year at the beginning of hunting season they get worn out. There is just so much to do to get ready for the Winter months, even though they are more moderate here than in the northern states."

"Yeah, all of this would be harder to handle in eight feet of snow." Rennet laughed, remembering his wandering days.

"We've gotten snow a few times here over the years, but just a small dusting over everything. It didn't last more than a few hours before it melted."

Rennet smiled and stood up, reaching out and pulling Aurelie to her feet.

"I hate to leave, but we're both going to end up falling asleep out here and becoming mosquito bait."

Aurelie smiled at him and allowed him to pull her into his arms. They shared a kiss before pulling apart and walking hand in hand toward the side-by-side. They climbed in, started the cart and were off to Rennet's home. When they arrived, Rennet leaned over, pulled Aurelie toward him and they shared another kiss; this one lasting longer.

Someone whistled lowly, drawing their attention as they looked around, unable to see who or what made the sound. Just at that moment, Adam walked out of the darkness toward their cart.

Rennet and Aurelie both jumped at his sudden appearance from the shadows.

"Dude," Rennet said, "give us a little more of a warning next time."

Adam chuckled, "Sorry, I didn't mean to scare you."

Aurelie asked, "What are you doing out here at this time of night anyway?"

"I was just working late on my place and got caught up in some details and didn't realize how late it was."

They both nodded and looked at each other, both feeling a little awkward at being caught together.

Adam noticed the exchange.

"You know, you two don't have to hide the fact that you're dating. Everyone knows."

"What?" Rennet asked surprised.

"Well, it's obvious how you two feel for one another, even though there have been no public signs of affection, save the one I just witnessed."

Adam smiled from ear to ear.

Rennet turned to Aurelie. "Well, since our cover is blown." He planted a huge kiss on Aurelie's lips, wriggled his eyebrows at her making her giggle, and climbed out of the vehicle.

Adam said, "You really didn't think you were fooling anybody did you? I mean, you spend nearly every free, waking, moment with each other, and Baxter told Reine, who told Reesa and Foesy, who told everybody else."

Aurelie smiled. "That figures; small community and all."

"Yep. Everyone has known for the last month."

"We've only been together for the last two."

"Exactly. You can have no secrets here." Adam shrugged by way of apology. "Well, see you two tomorrow. I'm going to head to my parent's place and get a good night's sleep."

The Barter

"See you tomorrow, Adam," Rennet said, waving to him.

Rennet turned to Aurelie and asked, "Walk me inside?"

"Do you think I should?"

"Well, there's nothing to hide now." He chuckled and waved his arms around at the houses nearby.

"True, but if I come inside, I may not want to leave." Aurelie answered honestly.

Rennet took her hands and pulled her up from the seat. He wrapped his arms around her waist and pulled her to him, planting another kiss on her lips. They stood there in an embrace for a few minutes, then he slid his hands down her arms, and took her hands in his.

"Goodnight, Aurelie," he whispered, releasing her hands to fall to her side.

"Goodnight, Rennet." Aurelie watched him go up the stairs as they locked eyes until he was out of sight.

Aurelie let out a deep sigh. "Lord, I do think that I am in love with that man."

She slid back into the seat of the cart and took off for home, the contrast of the night air cooled the warmth that emanated from her skin at the intense feelings she had for Rennet. She made it home, took a shower, and climbed into bed, thanking God for all she had; her family, community, and now one handsome, thoughtful, honorable, breath-stealing man.

Rennet stood at his bedroom window watching Aurelie drive away into the night. He watched the tail-lights of the cart until they disappeared.

Parting from her was becoming harder and harder; and now that everyone apparently knew they were in a relationship, it would be even more difficult since they no longer had to hide their emotions or actions.

He sat down on his bed to think. No one had ever stirred such deep emotions in him before. He thought he had loved Madison, but even his feelings then did not compare to what he now felt for Aurelie. He was so glad that relationship had fallen to the wayside or else he would have never come here and found his home. He had spent much more time in the other community wooing Madison and yet she had never even really acknowledged his feelings. She had simply used him to make another jealous and had played her part well. Madison's immaturity was completely apparent to him now, especially seeing how Aurelie behaved and treated him. She was thoughtful, caring, and responsible; she didn't play games with his emotions.

He fell backward onto his bed, sighing heavily as his emotions wreaked havoc in his body.

"Lord, what am I supposed to do? I don't want to rush our relationship, but I also don't want to spend any more time away from her. This everyday separation is getting harder and harder. Give me the strength to do what's right, and the wisdom to know when and what that is."

The Barter

Rennet stood and went to clean up in his cold, outdoor, shower. He was going to have to see about getting the indoor shower fixed and a solar-generator to heat the water or else the cold winter weather was going to make showering brutal. He also needed to figure out better food storage because his portion of the meat from the day's hunt would not fit in the Zeer pots. Tomorrow morning he would talk to Foesy and see what he used for such purposes, and where Rennet could acquire such a device.

Rennet awoke the next morning to Foesy knocking at his door. A meeting had been called at the pavilion in an hour to deal with a pest situation and everyone was to attend.

Rennet arrived at the pavilion along with everyone else. There was a buzz of activity and questions as everyone wondered what was going on. When it appeared that the community had all arrived, he noticed that the local alligator man, Renauld Forester, who was in charge of controlling the species, stood up to speak.

"Settle down everyone," Renauld said. "Procne and Mary, whom you all know live on the village outskirts, have noticed a little more gator activity than normal. Arjit has even reported that a few of his cows have gone missing. And not from the outer fields, but the ones closest to our community. It's time for us men to take to hunting the gators again."

Mr. Kim asked, "Has anyone else seen anything close?"

Everyone looked around, shaking their heads and muttering no.

Renauld nodded. "All right then, we'll start the search by Procne and Mary's place. Men, get your guns and meet back here in thirty minutes."

Everyone dispersed with Rennet stopping Archie to ask, "What do we use if we don't have a gun?"

"I don't know, but I don't recommend hunting alligators without a gun."

"Let me see if I can borrow one of Aurelie's." Rennet ran to catch up with her before she left for home.

"Aurelie!" He waved her down just as the cart was about to pull out. "I need to borrow a gun."

"Rennet are you planning on going on this hunt?" she asked, surprised.

"Well, yeah. I'm one of the men in the community. I figure I have to do my part." He climbed into the cart as she headed for her house.

Aurelie looked at him with trepidation. "I assume you've never done this before."

"You assume correctly," he exhaled loudly.

"Of course you can borrow a gun, just do me a favor."

"What's that?"

"Stay very close to Archie or one of the more experienced hunters. Gators can be very tricky. They hide well and are faster on land than you think. I would hate for you to get eaten."

"Well, that's very reassuring, Aurelie. Thanks for that visual." Rennet stated, rubbing his eyes with one hand.

"Sorry, I just need you to understand how dangerous it is."

"Point taken. Now, get me a gun and some ammo woman, so I can tame the wild frontier."

Aurelie threw her head back in laughter at his joking, gallant words, and posture.

"You crack me up."

They arrived at her place and gathered the needed supplies, then headed back to the pavilion. She turned to him in earnest before leaving.

"Rennet, all joking aside, please be careful."

"I will, I promise. I don't know much about this, but I'll do my best to stay safe."

Aurelie placed both hands on either side of his face and kissed him. Many onlookers smiled and some even whistled.

Arjit was not as pleased as the others. His jaw twitched at the public show of affection. He knew they liked each other, but he didn't know their affection for one another had grown so quickly.

Renauld said, "All right everyone, split into your usual teams. You all know what to do."

Rennet, unsure who to join up with looked around and noticed Eloi, Archie, Foesy, Kim, and Sophanes waving him over. He also noticed that Arjit was in the same group.

Rennet approached and nodded, gripping the rifle with both hands. "Fellas."

Archie said, "We're all going on Eloi's and Arjit's airboats to the other side of the marsh across the road there." He pointed northwest. "Eloi's been hunting out that way lately and has noticed more gator activity. That's also near Arjit's front fields where his cows are going missing."

"Okay, so who do I ride with?"

Arjit spoke up and said, "You can ride with me, McCabe."

Rennet looked surprised and looked at him in question.

Sophanes and Foesy looked at each other and nodded. Sophanes said, "Foesy and I will ride with Arjit too."

Archie said, "Good. Arjit's boat is a little bigger than Eloi's. See you boys out on the bayou."

With that, Archie, Eloi, and Kim walked away. Arjit said, "Load up in the side-by-side boys and lets head to my place to get the boat."

On the ride over, Rennet asked Sophanes, "Where's Anytos? I haven't seen much of him lately."

"Home," Sophanes answered, "Thalia's due to give birth any day now, he can't really leave her alone."

Rennet nodded and the rest of the ride was relatively quiet. When they arrived at Arjit's place Rennet noticed the size of his property, and how well he kept the place up.

"Nice place, Arjit."

"Yeah, it is. It's a lot of work, but it's worth it."

They all followed Arjit to a gate where a bayou ran through a pasture. They all climbed into the boat that sat docked in the narrow channel.

"McCabe, you might need these."

Rennet turned to see Arjit tossing a hat and glasses at him.

"The sun reflecting off the water can be pretty bright. These polarized sunglasses will help you to see what's beneath the water, and the hat will protect your head from overheating and sun exposure."

"Thanks, Arjit." Rennet wasn't sure what to make of the man's sudden, unexpected kindness. Rennet figured Arjit had wanted him to ride with him so he could leave his body in the swamp somewhere.

Arjit just nodded and started the boat.

Sophanes leaned over and whispered to Rennet. "Hold on tight."

The boat and passengers took off across the bayou. Without slowing the boat, Arjit jumped across roadways and smaller pieces of land that jutted out between waterways.

Rennet nearly lost the gun at one point and was glad he hadn't loaded it yet. He decided to stow the weapon on the floor beneath his feet during a smoother point in the ride.

Arjit grinned broadly at Rennet's fumbling during the ride. Here at least he could cause some chaos in the man's life.

Sophanes and Foesy had buckled down. Years of experience had taught them that Arjit could drive crazy when it came to his airboat; and hunting gator's seemed to excite the man.

Rennet was glad that he had already experienced riding in an airboat with Aurelie, but Arjit was just plain dangerous, causing his stomach to do more flip-flops.

They traveled for a good fifteen minutes before they saw Eloi, Archie, and Kim just on the other side of another body of water. Arjit slowed the boat, driving it up onto the shore and cutting off the engine.

Everyone filed out; guns in hand. Rennet nearly tumbling out due to his wobbly legs. They all cautiously walked the banks of the water in the same direction. Rennet noticed that there were ponds and bodies of water all around them, all linked by small grassy levees about the width of two airboats sitting side by side. Along the edge of the ponds were areas of tall grass and reeds which spilled onto the bank but sat mostly in the water. Places of hiding for small animals like frogs, snakes, and some fish. Some ponds even had tall grasses and reeds out toward the center, perhaps marking the area as shallower water.

Rennet could see Archie and the others walking toward them, with everyone soon converging at one point on the banks.

Arjit asked, "Any movement yet fellas?"

Archie looked at him with annoyance. "Don't you think you would have heard a shot?"

"All right, all right, Archie. All you had to do was answer yes or no."

Eloi cackled. "Don't ask stupid questions, Arjit."

The men passed by each other, all continuing on their inspection of the pond's banks. Archie's group headed back toward their boat on the south side of their pond, and Arjit's group headed north toward his.

The Barter

Rennet walked slowly, his gun pressed into his shoulder and ready to fire at the slightest movement. Sophanes and Foesy walked a little ahead of Arjit and Rennet.

Arjit took the opportunity to speak to Rennet.

"So, you and Aurelie huh?"

Rennet wasn't prepared for the question but answered with, "Yeah, it looks that way."

"I thought you said you weren't interested in her."

"I never said that. I said she wasn't mine to fight over, and at the time she wasn't. But now things have changed, and if push comes to shove, I will fight for Aurelie."

Arjit looked at him sideways.

They walked a little further and heard something stir in the water. Rennet turned to look but saw nothing. He then turned back around to see Arjit's gun pointed straight in his direction.

Chapter 23

Rennet's eyes grew wide with fear then clamped shut when he heard the shot from Arjit's rifle ringing in the air.

Rennet stood there breathing heavily, realizing he was still alive. He patted his body trying to feel for injuries. His eyes popped open and he looked to where Arjit had walked past him. There on the bank of the pond, facing in his direction was a very large alligator.

Rennet jumped at the sight of the massive creature lying only a few feet from him, then slumped forward breathing hard, his hands resting on his knees; his gun lying on the ground where he had dropped it when Arjit's gun went off.

Arjit looked over at him with a strange expression.

"Did you think I was aiming my rifle at you?" Arjit asked, surprise in his voice.

"Well, yeah," Rennet stated honestly.

"I may not like you much, and only because I always thought Aurelie and I would get together, but I'd never shoot you. What do you take me for?"

"I don't know what I was thinking, sorry."

Rennet stood up straight just as the others all came running.

Sophanes stated in awe, "Look at the size of that monster."

Foesy said, "It looks to measure twelve feet in length from snout to tail tip."

Rennet said, "Yeah, and I was almost alligator food. Arjit saved my life."

Arjit's head snapped up to look at him. Rennet nodded and said, "Thank you, Arjit. I shudder to think what becoming alligator food would have been like."

"Not a problem. It's not like I did it cause I like you or anything. I was just doing my job."

Rennet watched Arjit stand up and walk off toward the airboat to pull it closer so they wouldn't have to drag the alligator so far. What he didn't see was the smile that split Arjit's lips.

Arjit drove the boat up beside the alligator, and the men lashed a rope around its head with each man grabbing an area of the body and hauling it onto the boat.

Rennet asked, "Now what? Do we head home?"

"Not yet," Foesy stated. "We need to keep checking the ponds. With all the attacks lately, there are likely several more of these out here. One gator won't store that much food, especially with Arjit here missing several cows."

Arjit looked down at Rennet. "Rennet, this time, keep your gun in your hand. It won't do you any good lying on the ground."

The smile on Arjit's face told Rennet that the words, though true, were meant in fun, even though Rennet dropped his gun when he thought Arjit had shot him, not because of the alligator. Rennet laughed along with the others but did decide that he had better keep his eyes trained on his surroundings in the future. He had turned his back on the alligator and wouldn't be here if not for Arjit's skills and spot-on shooting.

The Barter

By mid-afternoon when all the men had returned from hunting, the collective results for alligator control was a whopping twenty alligators between the seven boats and thirty men that had gone out for the day.

The processing plant where Renauld Forester lived was on a bayou. The large building had a covered patio area where there was one large table which sat under the cover beside the water. There was a gasoline generator likely moon-shine powered, sitting by the open bay door with a thick hose running to some very large tanks inside that likely held fresh water. Several smaller water hoses were attached to the generator's pumping tank which likely forced the water out of the larger tanks more quickly, for purposes of washing the marsh water from the meat and hides.

Rennet stood looking over the line of alligators that were laid out under the covered portion of the wash down and processing area. The one that Arjit had saved him from was by far the largest.

People began showing up in droves to help with the processing, each bringing some sort of dish or platter of food for supper, lining up the platters on a few long foldout tables which sat against the building's wall. Rennet assumed that meant it was going to be a very long evening.

It wasn't long before Aurelie and the kids appeared with the crowd. She was wearing the blue, half-cable-knit sweater he had bartered to her on his first day here. That day had been the start of something beautiful. A new life for him, with a woman who he knew he loved without a doubt, and he didn't wish to spend any more time away from her or the kids. Today had taught him that life was fleeting, and it could have been his last on this earth.

He noticed that Aurelie had stopped to speak with Sophanes. Her expression soon turned very serious as her eyes locked on him. She then turned to listen to Sophanes once more. Rennet could imagine what he was saying, especially when he started laughing. Aurelie's eyes grew large, and she only cracked a worried grin, during Sophanes' obvious, elaborate tale. She soon excused herself and walked straight toward him, deliberation in her steps.

Rennet figured he was in for a tongue lashing, but when she reached him, she surprisingly threw her arms around his neck. Rennet was taken aback and he wrapped Aurelie in a hug, and the two of them stood there for a minute in their embrace.

Everyone watched the scene with interest; some with curiosity and some knowing exactly why Aurelie was being a little emotional. Arjit watched them as well; a small grin graced his face at the scene. He nodded to Rennet who looked over at him, then turned to find Jen Grayson chatting with Sophanes and Jess, as Sophanes regaled yet another willing listener to Arjit's bravery and heroic deeds of the day. Jen Grayson, who was standing with her arms crossed listening intently, looked over at Arjit and smiled brightly, wriggling her fingers at him in a gesture of greeting.

Arjit smiled broadly and nodded back at her, then turned to get on with the work to be done concerning the cleaning and processing of the alligators. He did, however, sneak a few looks in Jen's direction, noticing that she was doing the same to him as well.

As the evening went on with everyone busily tending to the business at hand, Aurelie managed to catch Arjit alone inside the building while he was looking for some more coolers for meat storage.

"Arjit." She announced her presence to him as she entered the building.

"Aurelie, did you need something?"

Aurelie approached him and hugged the man, then placed a small kiss on his cheek. This took him completely by surprise. He stood motionless, not knowing what to say.

"Thank you, Arjit, for saving Rennet's life today."

Arjit grinned down at her. "It wasn't anything I wouldn't have done for anyone else. I was just hunting, Aurelie."

"I know. But if it hadn't been for your quick thinking and amazing shooting skills, Rennet might have been hurt, or worse."

Arjit grinned down at her. "You're really in love with the guy aren't you?"

Aurelie giggled slightly. "Yes, I believe that I am."

"You know, we would have made a great couple; leaders in the community."

Aurelie smiled at his playful attempt at reason over his feelings for her.

"Social status isn't a thing anymore Arjit. I know you're used to getting what you want, but we both know that I'm not it. We would have made each other miserable. I'm much too stubborn for you."

"Yeah, but see, that's partly what I like about you." Arjit smiled brightly at her.

"Perhaps, but I think you would have changed your tune if that same stubbornness came from your wife. You would have expected me to change, and I would have expected the same of you. It just wouldn't have worked between us. Then there is still the whole attraction thing. Even though I like you as a friend, I'm not in love with you or attracted to you."

"Which I've never understood. I'm a good-looking man who has a lot to offer. I know that sounds conceited to you, but it's true regardless."

Aurelie shook her head at his words, knowing he was being serious.

"Well, maybe so Arjit, but I can't just materialize feelings that aren't there. Like you said, you can have nearly any other woman around; and I think we both know who that is. I've noticed a certain lady who seems very into you. And she is age appropriate, head-strong, and absolutely gorgeous."

Arjit smiled broadly. "You're right on all counts there. You know, I never even considered anyone else. I was just so sure it had to be you. I guess God brought Rennet McCabe here for more than just you."

"That He did, Arjit. Again, thank you for taking care of him for me."

She tiptoed up to kiss him on the cheek once more, clasped his hand with a squeeze and then walked from the building. Just as she disappeared around the corner, Jen Grayson walked in with two plates of food in her hands and a few bottles of water tucked under an arm.

"Hey handsome." She smiled brightly.

"Hey." Arjit smiled back.

"Would our local hero mind having dinner with an admirer?" She held the plates higher offering him one of them.

"Not at all." Arjit took the offered plate and bottle of water.

The two of them found a place to sit on some small crates and have dinner as they chatted, getting to know each other better.

With the cleaning, skinning, and cutting up of the alligator meat finished, the community commenced with the meal and the fellowship continued late into the evening. The musicians who brought their instruments played and Archie even pulled his harmonicas out of their case to join in, much to the surprise of everyone there.

Rennet stood against a nearby awning pole looking around at all the people laughing, chatting, and dancing—which included Arjit and Jen Grayson—a contented grin forming on his face.

Aurelie, who was sitting at a table next to him, noticed the look, stood up, and asked, "What are you grinning about?"

"This," Rennet said with a nod, "all these people gathered together, helping each other out."

"This is normal for this event. Well, except for Archie and his harmonicas." She smiled watching the man happily playing along with the others. "There is a lot of work to be done on days like this, and the meat gets divided equally between everyone who shows up to help. Renauld's processing also helps the community in many other ways. It's just what we do."

"You do know this isn't normal. I've seen people helping others in some of the other communities I've traveled through, but not one where the entire community gathers together like this regularly."

Aurelie smiled at him. "Rennet, it's not like you haven't seen this before since you've been here. First was Birdie's birthday, and then again after the hurricane."

"I know. It just still takes me by surprise though."

"You'll get used to it. Besides, you're partly responsible for some of our gatherings," Aurelie accused.

Rennet asked, "What do you mean?"

"Well," Aurelie turned to look at him directly, "since your arrival, people have been more helpful without expecting a trade of some kind. You're willingness to jump in and help whoever do whatever seems to be contagious."

Rennet puffed out his chest in mock cockiness. "Well, just doing what I do little lady."

Aurelie laughed at him, wrapping her arms around his waist, and leaning her head against his chest.

Rennet smiled, leaning his head on top of her hair. "Now I can get used to this; public displays of affection and all."

"I hope so, because I don't plan on stopping any time soon." She pulled back a little to look up at him.

Rennet leaned down and planted a sweet kiss on her lips, those nearby whistling lowly and some even clapping.

They broke apart, both smiling because of their admirers. They looked at each other and laughed.

Katie ran up to them giggling and clapping, throwing her arms around them both and smiling up at them.

"So when are you getting married?" she asked happily as though it was a completely natural question.

Those sitting nearby stopped what they were doing and looked at them, waiting for their reaction, now feeling invested in the conversation.

Aurelie stammered, "Oh, Katie, just because Rennet and I are in a relationship doesn't automatically mean we're getting married."

"Why not?" came several questions simultaneously.

Aurelie's head snapped up from Katie's question to Rennet's.

"What?" she asked surprised.

Rennet smiled at her. "Why not get married? I know that I'm in love with you, and I assume you feel the same way."

"Well, yes, but…"

"But what, Aurelie? I could have died today, and that made me realize that we are waiting for something. I'm not sure what that something is, but I'm ready if you are?"

Aurelie's mouth hung open, unsure what to say. She looked at all the kids who were happily nodding yes and then back to Rennet. She sighed happily and smiled. "Okay."

"Okay, you'll marry me?" he asked with a tilted head.

"Are you asking properly?" She smiled questioningly at him.

Rennet smiled and dropped down to one knee, drawing the attention of everyone.

"Aurelie Haydel, will you marry me?"

Gasps of excitement and breathless waiting wafted through the area.

Aurelie smiled brightly, waiting a few seconds before answering, adding a little more anticipation to the event.

"Yes, Rennet McCabe, I will marry you!"

Roars of applause and joy floated on the night air out across the bayou and marshes, drowning out the croaking and chirping of the murky, watery, nightlife. Congratulations flew around the room as everyone made their way over to congratulate the happy couple and the kids.

The proposal which added to the night's revelry made the evening last longer as people stayed later than usual to celebrate Aurelie and Rennet's engagement.

The stars twinkled above the water, glistening like little lights on the surface. Even the mosquitoes seemed to sense the special evening as they too gave a much-needed respite from their normally, incessant biting; which truthfully was mainly due to the cooler weather; but blissful none the less.

Chapter 24

The next morning, Rennet had slept a bit late due to last night's activities. The night hadn't ended until well past midnight by the time things were cleaned up and everyone had left for home. He set his coffee to brewing and walked out on the porch to look out over the water. Kim and Kei Yamada were walking along the shoreline, gathering seaweed, shells, and driftwood. Foesy was quietly working in his outdoor shop under his cottage, and Adam was working on his cottage with a helper who surprisingly turned out to be Emilie.

Rennet watched the two with interest as they poked and teased each other like a couple of school kids just realizing they liked each other. Rennet was happy for Adam. The young man had stood up to Emilie and had put his foot down, making her realize that he wasn't going to play her games anymore, and it looked as if she finally settled her spirited sights on him.

Rennet walked back inside to get his coffee and took it outside to drink. Just as he had settled into his chair on the porch, Anytos came running up to his place. He was waving and yelling in a panicked state.

"Rennet, I need your help man."

"What's wrong?"

"Thalia, she's having the baby. I don't know what to do!"

"Haven't you seen this twice before? You do have two other kids."

"I never watched! Sandra and Jess always took care of it; I just sat in the living room and waited!"

Rennet set his mug down and took off down the steps. As the men ran across the beach toward Anytos' home, Rennet said, "Anytos, I've never delivered a baby before either. I have no clue what to do. We need to get Sandra."

Anytos said frantically, "I tried, but she's not home."

"Well what about Sophanes and Jess?"

"They're not home either. They signed up to help at Peveto Woods, and I guess this is one of those days."

"Oh man, now what do we do?"

Archie, who was sitting outside watching their panicked state decided to see what was happening.

"Hey fellas, what's going on?" he yelled to them.

Anytos yelled back. "It's Thalia, the baby's coming, now!"

Archie stood up, set his mug down, and walked over to them. "Either of you boys know how to deliver a baby?"

"No!" came the collective replies.

Anytos said, "And, I can't find Sandra."

"She and Marie are out with Michael this morning."

Anytos just shrugged and nodded, the words lost on his panicked state.

"All right, let's go." Archie trotted back to his shop and jumped in his cart. Anytos and Rennet looked at each other and shrugged, then jumped in the cart with Archie when he stopped beside them. They made the short trip back to Anytos' home, quickly moving up the steps. As they entered the house, they could hear Thalia yelling in pain from the bedroom. Archie went to the sink and washed his hands, giving instructions to the others.

"We need some clean towels, hot water, and a pair of sharp, sterilized scissors or a knife."

Anytos nodded quickly, getting to work on the orders. Rennet looked at the other two kids who were sitting in the living room looking a little scared.

"Hey, you two, what do you say I take you over to Foesy and Reesa's to play with Reine for a little while?"

The kids nodded and grinned slightly. Rennet used Archie's cart to make the trip quickly, explaining the situation to Reesa and Reine. He left to return and crossed paths with the Yamada's on the beach.

Mr. Kim asked, "Rennet, is something wrong?"

"Thalia is having her baby and Sandra is nowhere to be found."

Mrs. Kei smiled happily. "Well, delivering a baby is easy and natural. We'll help."

They stowed their finds in the top-mounted, front basket of the vehicle, and climbed into the cart.

They soon arrived and entered Anytos' house to yells of pain, and Thalia's rapid speaking in Greek and Anytos' unrecognizable replies back to her.

When they entered the bedroom Archie was standing at the foot of the bed and Anytos was holding Thalia's hand.

Thalia who looked haggard already, seemed to smile thankfully at the presence of Kei Yamada.

Kim and Rennet went out to the kitchen to grab the water and other supplies and returned to the bedroom.

Archie and Kei stood at the end of the bed, giving Thalia instructions.

Kei excitedly said, "I can already see the baby's head. Push Thalia."

Thalia pushed, screaming in pain as Anytos screamed right along with her at the crushing pain of her squeezing his hand.

Rennet stood off to the side with Kim behind Archie and Kei.

As the baby made its way into the world, Rennet yelled and winced at how painful it appeared. Anytos, who had noticed Rennet's reaction, walked to the foot of the bed to see the progress, and quickly passed out. Thalia was waving Rennet over to her, so he stepped over Anytos' prostate body on the floor and walked over to hold her hand in her husband's place while Kim Yamada tried feverishly to wake Anytos.

Thalia's grip on Rennet's hand was so tight that with each contraction and push she had, he thought she might break it as he yelled right along with her; the pain almost bringing him to his knees. He now understood why Anytos was screaming earlier.

What felt like an eternity to Rennet, in reality, had only been about fifteen minutes when Thalia slumped back against the pillows as Archie and Kei smiled brightly at her, and the new baby took its first breath and cried.

Archie said, "Meet your daughter."

The Barter

Kei took the baby from him and carried her to her mother who was now smiling and speaking rapidly in Greek once again as her baby was laid in her arms.

Rennet stood back and watched, completely in awe at what had just happened.

Kim managed to bring Anytos back to reality and he stood up off the floor and rushed to Thalia's side, kneeling on the floor beside the bed.

They both smiled and laughed at the sight of their newest family member.

Thalia looked up and said to everyone in the room, "Thank you all so much. My Anytos panics and can't handle the pressure, as you all noticed." She looked at Anytos with raised eyebrows and gave a pained grinned.

Archie nodded, "Not a problem. Glad everything turned out all right. Well, I'll be going. I figure Kei here can handle the rest."

Kei smiled and nodded at him, bowing slightly.

Rennet followed Archie out of the room.

"Archie, how do you know how to deliver a baby?"

"Well, when you live out in a remote place like this, it's good to know how to do a lot of things. I've helped Sandra over the years a few times with other deliveries, plus, I read a lot."

"Really?" Rennet asked, shocked to think of Archie sitting somewhere reading medical journals.

"Is the thought of my reading so surprising to you?"

Rennet smiled at him. "Let's just say that you are sort of an enigma to me."

"Fair enough."

Archie grinned and the two went to the Divins place to collect the children and returned them home. They then left for Archie's house.

When they arrived, he invited Rennet to sit on his porch and have a drink.

"I think after what we just participated in we might need a little something to take the edge off." He went inside and came out with a dark colored, glass, canning-jar.

"I have a little something special here that ought to take care of those nerves." Archie handed Rennet a glass and poured some of the liquid into it. He did the same for himself, then sat down and toasted.

"To new life." Archie downed the liquid in one gulp.

Unsure what to expect Rennet sniffed the glass first, noting a strong alcohol scent. Archie watched him closely.

Rennet downed the beverage, and inhaled sharply, coughing a little, even though the smoothness settled quickly.

"Wow, what is this?" Rennet coughed again and asked as he sniffed the now empty glass once more.

"I take Eloi's rotgut moonshine and add my own flavors to it. This one is a butter and pecan flavor. It's better if you sip on it slowly."

Rennet nodded. "You could have mentioned that before I downed it. It's actually really good, just a little strong to drink all at once." He coughed again, still feeling the warmth of the liquid coating his esophagus.

Archie chuckled. "Well, remember, I'm used to drinking Eloi's moonshine-slash-engine-fuel straight up. This stuff is nothing, and it tastes a lot better."

Archie poured them both another glass and toasted again.

"To new futures."

Rennet raised his glass, knowing he was referring to his and Aurelie's soon to come wedding.

"To new futures."

The men sipped on the second glass for the next few minutes making small talk, then Rennet stood up and excused himself to head home. He realized on his walk home that he was feeling a little lightheaded. He then realized that he had not had breakfast yet and had been drinking on an empty stomach. When he reached home, he quickly ate some bread, hoping to counter the effects of the alcohol, if there was any left in his stomach for the bread to absorb. He then walked over to Adam's place to see if they needed any help with the building process.

Adam was happy to have more help and the three of them spent the remainder of the morning working.

At noon, Aurelie and the kids showed up at Rennet's, noticed he was helping at Adam's, and walked over. Rennet filled them in on the events of the morning.

Aurelie said, "I am going over to see the new baby. Anyone else want to come?"

All the kids replied yes.

Emilie stated, "I want to go as well."

"Sure, you can ride with us," Aurelie offered.

They left, returning within the hour to have lunch before continuing with their day.

While eating, Katie looked at Aurelie and asked, "Aurie, are you going to have a baby?"

Aurelie and Rennet both nearly choked on their food. Adam and Emilie both chuckled lowly, and Baxter and Birdie smiled hopefully.

Aurelie said, "Well, perhaps one day. But that is for God to decide."

"Well, aren't you and Rennet getting married?"

"Yes, but not everyone who gets married has babies, Katie. Some women can't have a baby."

She seemed to ponder Aurelie's words and then shrugged.

Aurelie and Rennet looked at each other with raised eyebrows and slight grins.

Rennet couldn't help but wonder what their baby would look like should she get pregnant one day. And after what he witnessed this morning he now had a greater respect for the opposite sex. He never knew how intense childbirth could be, especially now with the lack of medical advancements and medications. He only hoped that if Aurelie did eventually get pregnant, that he wouldn't pass out like Anytos did during delivery.

After lunch, Rennet and Baxter continued helping Adam. Birdie went to help the Yamada's and to learn about the use of herbal medications, and Emilie left with Aurelie to head over to

Sandra's for Katie's and Marie's play date, and to discuss wedding plans. .

Aurelie and Emilie chatted as they drove to Sandra's.

Emilie said, "Another wedding soon to come. I never thought I'd be the one to get excited over weddings. I have always wanted to leave and go exploring."

Aurelie smiled. "You don't want that anymore?"

Emilie giggled. "Nope. Life around here is actually more exciting than I thought. I just never really got involved enough to see it. I was always stuck in my own selfish world. Now that Adam and I are exclusive, my plans have changed."

Aurelie smiled at Emilie's happiness. "Yes, I noticed yours and Adam's budding relationship. It's about time; that boy has pined over you for years."

Emilie giggled. "Yes, and I sure tortured him enough, poor thing. And yet he still wants me after everything I've put him through."

Aurelie smiled at Emilie's confessions and her obvious contentedness. She then changed the subject.

"I heard that Jess offered you her place to live in."

"Yeah. Adam and I are planning a future together, but we aren't in a hurry. I figure I'll live in Jess's old place until that changes; if and when it changes."

Aurelie smiled and said, "I figure that will be sooner than you think, especially since Adam has liked you since you were both little."

They arrived at Sandra's and Katie and Marie took off to play while the ladies sat on Sandra's swing drinking sun tea, talking about the arrival of the newest member to the community, and wedding plans for Aurelie and Rennet.

Aurelie said, "Kei wants to make the wedding cake, and I still have my mother's dress hanging in the back of my closet."

Sandra smiled. "Oh Aurelie, that's wonderful."

"It's a little old-fashioned, but I think Reesa might be able to tailor it to my needs."

Emilie asked, "Is anyone going to give you away?"

"Yes. I've asked Mr. Kim to do the honors."

Emilie squealed with excitement. "I can't wait till the wedding. Have you set a date yet?"

"Well, we figure we need to give Reesa a little while to alter my dress and take up my father's old suit for Rennet."

Emilie sighed dreamily. "I think it's really cool that you'll both be wearing something that belonged to both of your parents."

Sandra chuckled at her wistful expression. "Emilie, you're a romantic at heart."

"Yeah, who would have ever thought."

The women all laughed at her remark. They discussed more plans for the remainder of the afternoon; plans for the wedding, and Emilie's ideas for making over Jess's old place. Before they realized the time, dusk was beginning to set over the area.

Aurelie said, "Goodness, I didn't realize how late it was getting. Sandra, I'm sorry if we kept you too long."

The Barter

Sandra dismissed her comment with a wave of her hand. "Oh, posh. How often do we girls get together to discuss such things."

"Never really."

"Exactly. I'm like Emily. I cannot wait to see you in your mother's dress. You'll have to bring it over tomorrow and let us have a peek at it."

"I'll do that; besides, tomorrow is Katie's day to help you out here. And after we've monopolized your time today, I'm sure you could use it. Besides, I need to take the dress over to Reesa's for a fitting anyhow."

"Great, I'll see you tomorrow. Emilie, will you be coming as well?"

"I wouldn't miss it!"

"Okay. Then I will make us some hot tea and cinnamon cakes tomorrow morning, say ten a.m.?"

Both women agreed, and Aurelie yelled for Katie. They climbed into the side-by-side and went to pick up Birdie from the Yamada's, and Baxter from Adam's place.

Aurelie invited Rennet over for dinner since they had been working all day. She had put a roast in the crockpot before leaving at noon, knowing they had a full afternoon ahead of them. She was so grateful for the solar panels her fathered had installed shortly after the collapse. He had watched world events with interest and studied what was taking place. Even then, he had started collecting and trading up items for panels and batteries. Her home had electricity for cooking and hot water because of it. The trees had overgrown so much over the years that the solar panels were barely of use, but since the storm had broken many of the old oak tree's branches the panels were now able to receive more light, and their power was more plentiful as of late. It was something that had happened so gradually over the years she didn't even realize that the trees were the problem. She had just thought that the panels had outlived their usefulness, especially since many of them were already used when her father had acquired them twenty years back. She would have to make a plan to move them into a more direct stream of light to prevent having to use the generator so often.

After dinner the kids all said they were tired and went to bed, and Aurelie and Rennet took advantage of the quiet time to be alone, sitting on the screened porch to talk. Rennet leaned back in the small wicker love-seat with his arms wrapped around Aurelie who leaned back into him.

"So," Rennet said, "we discussed a lot of things about the wedding over dinner tonight, but what about the honeymoon?"

"I was wondering about that myself. Maybe the kids can stay with someone else that night?"

"How about we leave them here and use my place as our honeymoon cottage?"

"That is a wonderful idea! I never thought of that." She kissed him to show her appreciation for his thoughts. "What will you do with it afterward."

"Well, I figured on keeping it for Baxter. It's only going to be a few years before he's going to want to strike out on his own."

"Oh, I didn't think about that, but you're right. It would make a wonderful place for him."

"Especially with Reine being right next door." Rennet wriggled his eyebrows at her.

Aurelie laughed. "Yes, and Foesy and Reesa will be right there to keep an eye on them both. But that's not for several years still. Let's not rush it."

"Speaking of rushing, are you okay with the speed in which our lives are about to change? I'm just asking because Katie really put us both on the spot the other night."

"Yeah, I know. Are you?"

"Absolutely. I would not have proposed if I wasn't ready. But if you need more time, Aurelie, I can wait."

Aurelie loved his patient heart, and she sat up and turned to look him in the eyes.

"I am. I think I've been ready to have someone in my life for a long time, I just had to wait for God to bring you to me."

Aurelie leaned in and kissed him. She couldn't wait until next week when he would never have to leave again.

Rennet's heart raced and his pulse quickened. He knew he had to stop or else, so he reluctantly pulled away.

"Okay, time for me to go." He set her at arm's length and stood up. "But you are going to have to drive me back tonight."

"Just take the cart. I won't need it until about 9:45 when I have to go to Sandra's. You can return it in the morning."

"Good idea." Rennet pulled her into one last hug then set her away from him.

"Good night fair maiden."

He bowed majestically, sweeping his arm in front of himself.

She smiled at him playfully, batting her eyes and fanning herself with her hand, pulling out her best southern drawl.

"Good night my handsome knight."

Rennet smiled brightly as he walked away. He shook his head and sighed heavily, trying to gather his thoughts and composure.

"One more week Rennet," he said to himself as the cart sped out of Aurelie's driveway.

Chapter 25

The following week passed quickly with busyness while the entire community prepared for Aurelie and Rennet's wedding. Today was the day and the wedding was to take place that very evening.

Reesa had made the simple adjustments to Aurelie's dress days before and had finished up the suit for Rennet yesterday.

Claire, Emilie, and Jess had taken it upon themselves to decorate the pavilion and prepare Rennet's cottage for the honeymoon, kicking him out and sending him to Sophanes' and Jess's place to get ready.

Jess was happy to help, remembering her own wedding night as she helped to prepare Rennet's cottage.

She said to Emilie and Claire, "I was so delighted to find my place decorated for my honeymoon. The candles, flowers, music, wine, and strawberries were all perfect. You two did an amazing job. I was so thankful for that gesture."

Emilie laughed. "It was so much fun!"

Claire agreed. "Yes, it was. And now we get to do it all over again."

"Wherever did you two get that bottle of wine? It was wonderful."

Claire answered, "As far as the wine goes, Eloi dabbles in more than moonshine. The man has a veritable cellar that he's created over at his place. It even has some very old bottles of wine he collected for years before the collapse. I bartered with him for a few bottles for myself a while back. I just gave you one of mine."

"Claire, thank you, that was so sweet; literally."

They all laughed at the reference to the taste of the wine.

"I have another bottle for Rennet and Aurelie, plus, I hear that Archie makes a wonderful tasting, creamy, flavored, moonshine. I got a jar of that from him too just in case they don't like the wine."

Jess said, "I didn't know Archie made that."

Claire said, "Apparently there is a lot we don't know about Archie. Rennet said the man has all sorts of secrets."

"Yeah, like that suit he let Sophanes wear for our wedding. That was a very expensive suit at one time."

Emilie said, "Yeah, and Sophanes looked great wearing it. I wonder if Archie will wear it to Aurelie's wedding? I'm curious to see him dressed up."

"Me too," Claire and Jess said in unison.

The women laughed and chatted as they worked for the next hour before heading home to get ready for the wedding that was to take place in just a few hours.

Aurelie stood in front of Sandra's full-length mirror admiring her mother's beautiful antique dress. The bodice was V-shaped at the neck, but modestly so, was sleeveless, and had wide lace straps that went over the shoulders to a lower squared off back. The bodice was solid white with an embroidered floral design that covered it to the waist. The slim, but full skirt, had a solid silk white front panel with the same floral, embroidered pattern near the bottom third of the dress, and lace panels that went off either side all the way around to the back that had the same floral pattern design. The ribbon at the waist was solid white silk that tied at the back and hung down the skirt of the dress. The train was short and had a wrist tie tucked underneath the edge of the skirt that allowed for dancing. Her headpiece was a simple wreath of flowers and ribbon lying on piles of curls on top of her head, spilling out and down the back. Thin, wispy, white, silk ribbons intertwined in her curls.

Sandra nearly cried. "Oh, Aurelie, you look absolutely stunning. I can't believe you've had that dress tucked away in a closet for years."

"Yes, and it never even crossed my mind that one day I would actually wear it. I'm so glad Reesa was able to alter it."

"She did an amazing job."

Kei stuck her head in the bedroom. "Are you ready? It's time."

Aurelie turned to the people waiting for her in the other room.

"Absolutely." She smiled happily as Sandra grabbed her bouquet and handed it to her. The party of five left the house and headed toward the pavilion.

Rennet stood at the front of the pavilion with Procne waiting for the bride to make an appearance.

He fingered the rings in his pocket that also once belonged to Aurelie's father and mother. Her father's hands were a little larger than his own, but Archie told him that one of the men in the community was a metal worker and he could get it resized later.

Everyone's attention for the first five minutes had been on Archie in his tailor-made suit. It did fit him like a glove. Sophanes had worn it well, but not as well as Archie; and since this was the first time anyone had seen him in anything other than leather, cotton t-shirts, or denim, it was a big deal. The entire community was once again dressed in their best attire, everyone excited to get another opportunity to wear something out of the ordinary.

Rennet looked around at the crowd now seated and waiting when his gaze landed on Arjit. The man happened to look at him at that moment and Arjit smiled and nodded, throwing an arm around Jen Grayson. Rennet grinned and nodded back.

Just at that moment, Jess ran forward and excitedly said, "The bride's coming."

The musicians began the wedding march as everyone in the pavilion stood up to receive her. Kim Yamada drove up in Sandra's golf-cart, and escorted Aurelie to the pavilion.

Katie, the flower girl, beamed happily as she tossed flower petals to the ground in front of Aurelie.

The Barter

The crowd gasped when they saw Aurelie approach.

Rennet's breath got caught in his throat at her appearance. He had never seen anyone look more beautiful. His chest constricted, and he had to take a deep breath as he felt lightheaded; which was probably from the shot of moonshine Archie insisted he take before the service to steady his nerves.

Aurelie soon stood by his side in front of everyone as Procne began the service, which again, was short but sweet.

When they turned back toward the crowd, Procne introduced them as Mr. and Mrs. Aurelie and Rennet McCabe.

The crowd cheered loudly as flower petals flew through the air as they walked back down the aisle, greeting friends and loved ones along the way. Soon the chairs were cleared away, the music started, and the revelry began with dancing, bouquet tossing, cake, moonshine, and wine, and finally a late night send off in Anytos' decorated golf-cart.

Eloi and Archie stood together, each with their own moonshine in hand, several glasses into it by now.

"Well," Eloi stated, "there goes another one."

Archie looked sideways at him. "Another one what?"

"Another anti-bachelor fella'. What's wrong with these boys all wantin' ta go off an' get married?" Eloi's words were slurred and he hiccupped.

"Can't say as I blame them. Besides, no man likes being alone all the time." Archie defended.

"I do! I don't need no woman tellin' me what to do or how to live!"

"Eloi, you're just an ornery old coot. I don't reckon there's a woman here that would have you anyway."

Eloi scrunched up his nose and turned to face Archie, peering up at him menacingly.

"What's that supposed ta mean? You trying to say I ain't good enough to get a woman?"

Aurelie and Rennet, who heard the argument start, stopped the cart and turned to watch with everyone else who was still at the party.

She looked at Rennet with a questioning gaze and a wide smile. "You want to go break them up?"

"Nope. I learned my lesson last time."

Rennet and Aurelie watched as Archie turned to Eloi, his hands flying to his hips in a defensive posture. "I'm just saying that she'd have to either be a saint or more ornery than you to put up with you. Besides, you just said yourself that you didn't want a woman."

"Well maybe I changed my mind just ta prove that you're wrong; Archimedes Galileo Bourgeois!" Eloi accented his name as he shoved his pointer finger in Archie's chest.

"Now, why do you gotta go and start all that?"

Eloi cackled loudly at Archie's discomfort.

"Eloi, I'm dressed up tonight, and I'm not getting into any fights with you."

"Chicken!"

Eloi stood looking at Archie out of one eye to balance his current double vision.

The Barter

Archie shook his head and said, "Just remember, you asked for it."

He punched Eloi in the nose, making sure not to hit him too hard. The force knocked the man over backwards into the sand as Archie walked away to enjoy the festivities.

Eloi laid there cackling loudly until he soon passed out cold, once again, from too much moonshine.

Rennet and Aurelie took off again, laughing at the scene they just left behind.

"Never a dull moment around this place," Rennet stated as the cart soon came to a stop at the bottom of his cottage.

He stepped around to Aurelie's side of the cart and held out his hand, bowing slightly.

"My fair maiden," he said playfully as he pulled her up from the cart.

"Why thank you my handsome knight." She pretended to be bashful, batting her lashes at him.

Rennet turned to her and planted a kiss on her lips that took her breath away.

He then pulled away, looked at her, and asked, "Okay, so do I attempt to carry you up all the steps, or do we wait until we are at the top?"

Aurelie looked at him like his question was crazy. "We wait, or else our honeymoon may be cut short by one, or both, of us ending up with injuries."

"Okay, we'll wait."

Rennet grabbed her hand and pulled her up the steps as fast as they could go.

Aurelie was laughing so hard at his haste that by the time they reached the top she had to catch her breath.

Rennet scooped her up into his arms and she grasped the doorknob and flung open the door as he carried her through. Once inside, they both were stunned by what they saw. They had not expected all the decorations, or candles to be lit when they arrived. They breathed deeply of the wonderful scent wafting through the air.

As Rennet set her feet on the ground, Aurelie said, "I'll bet Emilie, Claire, and Jess came and did this during the reception."

Rennet said appreciatively, "Look, they even have wine and Archie's flavored moonshine chilling on ice."

He turned to Aurelie and said with a bright smile, "Let's hope it's still cold later."

Aurelie laughed as he pulled her to him, both content and excited for what lay ahead.

Aurelie woke early, the coolness of fall in the air. She crawled out of bed and pulled the overly-large tunic sweater over her head that she had traded Rennet for some fruits and vegetables the very first day he walked into her life. She smoothed her hand over the soft weave and beautiful ocean colored fabric. It was so long it hit her mid-thigh.

Rennet stirred in the bed, waking, and searching the still dark room for her.

"Aurelie?"

"Right here," she said, coming over to sit on the bedside. "It's morning. Would you like some coffee?"

The Barter

"Sure." He yawned and stretched. "I'll throw on some pants and join you in the kitchen."

Aurelie padded barefoot through the house and started the coffee. She then walked over to the large picture windows in Rennet's living room that looked out toward the water. The sun was just beginning its ascent toward the horizon, streaking glorious shades of yellows, oranges, and purples in an arch above it.

She felt Rennet slip his arms around her waist and pull her to him.

"I sure like that sweater on you."

She smiled and turned to face him. "I like it myself. It's warm and comfortable, and the perfect shade of blue."

"I'd have to say that in all my years of travels, this sweater was the best barter I've ever made because it led me to you."

"Well, I certainly have to agree with you on that."

They embraced and kissed each other; their future together as bright as the rising sun.

The End.

About The Author

SG Boudreaux is a stay-at-home mom who has home-schooled her children for over twenty years. Two have graduated, and her youngest is a nineteen-year-old, special-needs child. She and her husband of twenty-seven years live in the country, in a small rural area, just outside of Lake Charles, Louisiana. She was born in West Virginia, lived in Florida for many years before moving to Louisiana with her mother and youngest sister. She married a local boy and has lived there ever since. She loves the culture, the people, the sense of community, and definitely the wonderful Cajun food. She is currently working on several new titles. One is fiction, fantasy, time-travel, and the other is a Bestiary to go along with the Peregrination Series and the Zanchier Series. You can find out more about her and her books on her Facebook, Instagram, Twitter, or her website at www.sgboudreaux.com

Her previous series of books are clean-reading, fiction, fantasy, and time-travel.

Other Books

Peregrination Series

Bestiary

Zanchier Series

Non-Fiction Titles

www.ingramcontent.com/pod-product-compliance
Lightning Source LLC
Chambersburg PA
CBHW072052190726
48294CB00005B/1480